DR. INCREASE

Mathews Family Saga Book 2

TRANA MATHEWS

While this is a work of historical fiction, it is based upon known facts of my ancestor's lives, and transcripts of actual letters between family members are included. In 1932, a limited publication of Increase's 1798 journal along with a Mathews Family Record was distributed to family members. A transcript of his journal is appended within this novel, and the family record is contained within *The Mathews Family: Mathews Family Saga Book 1*.

ISBN: 9798585300127

MATHEWS FAMILY SAGA:

The Mathews Family

Dr. Increase

Life in Ohio *(upcoming)*

DEDICATION

To my children,
Tessa and Jase
and to
future Mathews generations

PREFACE

At some point the family surname changed from Matthews to Mathews, and this spelling has remained in effect for over 200 years. I have used Mathews throughout this novel for consistency, except for the names of actual roads.

Some dialect may be considered politically incorrect or offensive by today's standards but is accurate for this time.

FAMILY LISTS

Dr. Increase Mathews Family
Daniel Mathews Jr. (father)
Huldah Putnam Mathews (mother)
Susannah Mathews Stone (eldest sister)
Elisha Mathews (eldest brother)
Sarah Mathews Willson (older sister)
John Mathews (older brother)
Abigail "Nabby" Willis Mathews (wife)

Elisha Mathews Family
Hannah Snow Mathews (wife)
Elisha Putnam Mathews (son)
Daniel Mathews (son)
Frederick Mathews (son)
Oramel Mathews (son)
Charles Cotterworth Pinkney Mathews (son)

The Snow Family
Hannah Mathews Snow (Daniel's sister)
Hannah Snow Mathews (Hannah's daughter and Elisha's wife)

The Stone Family
Captain Jonathan Stone (Susannah's husband)
Francis Stone (Jonathan's brother)
Grace Stone Dana (daughter)
Benjamin Franklin Stone (son)
Samuel Stone (son)
Rufus Putnam Stone (son)

John Stone (son)
Melissa Stone (daughter)

The Willson Family
Lieutenant Joseph Willson (Sarah's husband)
Luther Willson (son)
Melissa Willson (daughter)

Abigail "Nabby" Willis Family
Nathan Willis Sr. (father)
Sarah White Willis (stepmother)
Martha Willis Howard (sister)
Jonathan Howard (Martha's husband)
Nathan "Nate" Willis Jr. (brother)
Sophia Tupper Willis (Nate's 1st wife)
Lucy Fearing Willis (Nate's 2nd wife)
Betty Willis Hayward (sister)
Luther Hayward (Betty's husband)
Molly Willis Howard (sister)
Gideon Howard (Molly's husband)
Chloe Willis Packard (sister)
Silas Packard (Chloe's husband)
Vashti Willis Howard (sister)
Martin Howard (Vashti's husband)
Judge Howard (Martin's older brother)
Elijah Willis (brother)
Lucy Willis (sister)

The Rufus Putnam Family
Brigadier-General Rufus Putnam (Huldah's brother)
Persis Rice Putnam (Rufus's 2nd wife)

Elizabeth "Betsey" Putnam (daughter)
Persis Putnam Howe (daughter)
Perly Howe Jr. (Persis's husband)
Susanna Putnam Burlingame (daughter)
Christopher Burlingame (Susanna's husband)
Abigail Putnam Browning (daughter)
William Browning (Abigail's husband)
William Rufus Putnam (son)
Edwin Putnam (son)
Martha "Patty" Putnam (daughter)
Catherine "Caty" Putnam (daughter)

It is to be much regretted that Government did not take the measures they are now pursuing at an earlier period. Besides saving vast sums, it would have given a weight and dignity to the Federal Government that would have tended greatly to check the licentiousness and opposition to Government unfeverable in this country, and I really believe that the present insurrection in the back counties of Pennsylvania would never have existed, had not the slow and ineffectual prosecution of the Indians have given them a contemptible opinion of the strength of the Government.

The idea that the Atlantic states, particularly the Eastern, are unfriendly to the population and prosperity of this Country is prevalent and has an unfavorable operation on the minds of these people, and the extreme reluctance Government have observed to enter into the Indian war, but too well supports the opinion. However, I hope the result of this campaign will convince the western inhabitants that the protection of Government will be equally & impartially extended to all.

I hope too Government will take prompt & effectual measures to suppress the insurrection in the western parts of Pennsylvania. They are a factious and ungovernable set, principally Irish, or Scotch-Irish as they are called here, or their immediate descendants. I feel a little flash of national pride in observing that the American-born inhabitants of this Country whose father or grandfather never felt, nor hardly heard of, oppression are much more governable and have more confidence in Government than the Europeans, who cannot divest themselves the idea that Government & the people have separate interests.

John Mathews
1794 letter written at Fort Washington

TABLE OF CONTENTS

ONE

I turned twenty-five last December. I'm old enough that my path through life should be certain. Yet, my situation remains unsettled because two physicians had already established their practices in New Braintree, Massachusetts when I finished my apprenticeship and returned to my father's house. So, while my name is Dr. Increase Mathews, I've been unable to put my medical knowledge to much use. My relatives have written of many opportunities available in the frontier and have urged me to come there. With so little to do here, I decided to take their advice and explore its possibilities. My request for leave from the commonwealth's militia has been approved. After months of planning and anticipation, I'm now ready to depart.

My brother John, my brother-in-law Jonathan Stone, and my uncle Rufus Putnam settled in Ohio ten years ago. Jonathan returned here to sell their Brookfield farm and to bring my eldest sister Susannah and their children to Belpre in 1789. My uncle's family also joined him in Marietta about the same time. They lived through a period of great difficulty.

Britain had ceded the Northwest Territory in the Treaty of Paris, but the British had not given up their forts. They had also provided support to Indians who opposed American settlement of the frontier. Many massacres and battles had taken place before Indian tribes signed the Greenville Treaty in 1795.

Now that there's peace, men are traveling to the west, hoping to find wealth and success. The land here has been parceled out through the generations and used up. Its forests cut down for firewood. Many central Massachusetts farmers have switched to only growing grazing crops. The land in Ohio is fertile. My relatives have grown abundant wheat and corn crops.

The price of frontier land remains expensive because of the 640-acre purchase requirement. Uncle Rufus has written that Ohio now has 5,000 male residents and the process to elect the territorial legislature is underway. If William Henry Harrison is elected as Ohio's first delegate to the United States House of Representatives, he will introduce a bill to implement credit terms and reduce the purchase-size requirement for land in the territory.

I've spent months corresponding with friends and acquaintances, seeking others willing to travel there by boat with me. Nathan Willis Jr. was the first one to agree. Like me, he has relatives who live in the Northwest Territory. His first wife was General Benjamin Tupper's daughter, Sophia, who had died during childbirth. Their child had died eight months later. The general and his family had settled in Ohio.

Through his law practice, Nate had met, then married the widow Lucy Fearing Dogget. Her father and many of her brothers had also settled near Marietta in the 1780s. Paul Fearing had written urging Nate to visit.

Nate's already a stalwart friend though I've only known him for a few years. When he introduced me to his younger sister, I fell in love with Abigail. Because of my financial circumstances, I'd been hesitant to declare my feelings. Nate had organized matters last month so I could spend a few minutes alone with her.

Abigail said she'd be willing to live in Ohio and asked me to tell her father my intentions before I left, so Nate arranged a meeting. The elder Mr. Willis did not like the possibility that his daughter might move to live so far away from home, so he proposed a condition contrary to my beliefs. I'll have plenty of time to reflect upon this matter during my journey.

∞ ∞ ∞

Nate and his family now resided in Rochester. Living close to the coast, he started investing in ship building. He'd suggested New Bedford's harbor would be the best place to buy a boat. Since many of my correspondents live in this vicinity, I agreed to meet them in Rochester on June 6th.

TWO

I attended services at New Braintree's Congregational Church. During his sermon, Reverend Fiske lectured about the dangers and temptations I might encounter. Every member's eyes were upon me before he finished. Though embarrassed, I was pleased when many of our neighbors stopped to wish me Godspeed on my journey.

It was a pleasant surprise to find my older sister Sarah and her family had come from Leicester. Matters had been strained between us since my niece Melissa died from smallpox three years ago. Though I'd still been a medical apprentice, Sarah blamed me for not arriving quick enough to save her daughter, though I'd ridden there as soon as I received her summons. Hopeful that she'd forgiven me at last, I rode in the Willson's wagon as we returned to my father's house.

My nephew Luther asked, "Are you all set to go?"

"Yes. My gear is already packed. I plan to go to Oakham after we eat."

Joe turned and spoke over his shoulder. "We can give you a ride there if you'd like. It's not out of our way."

"That would be wonderful. Thank you."

My sister still hadn't said a word to me. Now she picked up a basket and rushed inside the house. At my glance, both my brother-in-law and nephew shrugged their shoulders.

My oldest brother Elisha drove his wagon into the yard behind us. My cousin Hannah also picked up a basket and went inside, leaving her husband to help their children down from the wagon. I took three-year-old Oramel from Lish's arms as he helped Fred disembark. He said, "Junior and Dan keep an eye on Fred. I'll call you to wash up when dinner's ready."

He took his son from me as we headed indoors. Before we left for church, Aunt Hannah had started a ham and sweet potatoes roasting. The aroma made my mouth water. Sarah was making a salad. I tried to reach past her to grab a tomato slice, but she turned and waved her knife at me. "You know better. Get out of here. We'll call you in a few minutes."

I followed Joe, Lish, and my nephew into the living room. Father was seated in his favorite rocker reading his Bible. My brother put his son down. Luther sat down next to the child, pulled out the basket of wooden blocks, and helped Oramel build a tower.

My brother sat down on our settee and motioned for me to sit next to him. I noticed several strands of silver in Lish's dark hair as I joined him. He said, "Remember the trick I taught you about only carrying a little pocket change in your money belt."

"Yes, I do, and plan to do so."

His face showed some distress. Lish cleared his throat, then murmured, "Uhm, I'm not sure how to say this." His smile revealed his embarrassment. "Be careful of the women you meet." He blushed. "The Reverend was right. You may encounter a temptation that'll be hard to resist. You don't want to end up in a mess like I did."

Lish mentioning his encounter with a barmaid surprised me. My eldest brother was a stickler about his privacy. This was the first time he'd confided anything of a personal nature. I hoped that my answering smile showed my appreciation. "I'll be careful. Thank you for your concern. It means a lot to me."

My sister called from the kitchen. "Time to wash up. Hannah is setting the table."

Along with the others, I followed my father into the kitchen. Lish went out to call his sons inside. I washed up, then helped my youngest nephew wipe his face and hands. We gathered around the table. My sister-in-law's girth was swelled with child, so I eased past her to take a seat. Sarah coaxed Oramel onto her lap though he'd wanted to sit with his mother. Cousin Hannah gave my sister a thankful grin. We held hands as Father led our prayer.

I'd loaded my plate with food when my sister turned and gave me an impish grin. "You might want to save room for dessert. I made your favorite."

I smiled at her. "Cherry pie. Thank you, Sarah."

4

Cousin Hannah said, "I made cherry pie for you too."

"Thanks. Guess I'll have to force myself to have a slice of each." I paused long enough to put a suffering look on my face. "Such torture!"

Everyone laughed. And, I did have a slice of both. After I finished, I went upstairs to retrieve my things.

I didn't plan to take my medical kit. It would be an obstruction since I'd be carrying my knapsack and musket on my walk to Rochester. My earlier conversation with Lish reminded me to retrieve John's letter. I wanted to confront my older brother about the horrible things he'd written to our eldest brother. I buried the missive in my Bible and placed it inside my sack, then I took my musket and bag downstairs. The women were just finishing washing dishes when I returned to the kitchen. I put my items outside the back door.

I shook hands with my father and Lish. Aunt Hannah wiped her hands dry, then enveloped me in a huge embrace. She said, "Don't forget to come back home."

As I hugged my cousin, I whispered, "I hope you have a girl. I know you've been praying for one."

Hannah grinned. "I surely hope so!"

I tousled the hair on the heads of my brother's four sons. "Be good boys for your mother and father. I'll see you in a few months."

I followed my brother-in-law out to the Willson's wagon. He held Sarah's hand while she boarded. I stowed my things in the rear and climbed up to sit next to Luther. My family stood on the back porch and waved goodbye as Joe drove us out of the yard.

THREE

It was a short trip of about five miles to the home of Dr. Spencer Field where I would spend the night. My sister chatted the entire way. It was as if a floodgate had opened. After months of being ostracized by her, it was a relief to know she forgave me.

When we reached my destination, Sarah climbed down from their wagon. She cried as she embraced me. "Please be careful around any Indians you meet. I expect you to come home safe."

I returned her hug. "I'll be sure to visit you as soon as I return."

My brother-in-law and nephew shook my hand. Luther said, "Have a good trip."

Joe said, "May the Lord watch over you."

I watched and waved as they boarded their wagon then drove away. I saw Mrs. Field standing inside the front door, waiting for me, when I turned toward the house. "Welcome home. Come on in."

I'd lived with the Field family for almost four years while I completed my medical apprenticeship. Indeed, this place seemed more of a home to me than my father's house had ever been. I crossed the threshold and asked, "Where's Spencer and Jack?"

"Just finishing up the chores. They'll be here in another minute or two. Would you like something to drink?"

Before I could answer, she turned and headed into her kitchen. I followed and watched as she filled a beaker with hard cider. I sat down at the table and took a sip from the tankard she handed me. "Delicious. Thank you."

I heard footsteps on the rear porch and stood up as the men entered. I crossed the room and returned the doctor's hug. I smiled at Jack and shook his hand. After we were seated, Spencer asked, "What are your travel plans?"

"We're going to New Bedford to purchase a boat. We plan to hug the coastline to reach Chesapeake Bay. Our first stop on land will be Alexandria, Virginia. After this, we'll follow the Potomac River to reach Redstone Old Fort. We'll then take the Monongahela River to Pittsburgh where it becomes the Ohio and float down this river to arrive in Marietta."

Jack asked, "What kind of boat?"

"Not sure. We hope to purchase a keelboat if we can afford one, but Nate's said these are more expensive than flatboats."

Spencer said, "If you have any time to go to Fairhaven, please give my best regards to my friend, Dr. Stephen Foster."

I grinned. "Be glad to do so."

Mrs. Field had left the table to prepare supper. She now placed plates and utensils in front of us. I washed up at her dry sink, then rejoined the family. Spencer led our prayers and finished by saying, "Lord, guide this young man's footsteps and keep him safe."

I grinned at him and nodded my thanks while I spooned a small amount from each dish to my plate. I wasn't very hungry because of the feast my family had made.

Mrs. Field frowned. "Is that all you're going to eat? I made plenty. You know better than to be shy. Help yourself but save room for some cherry pie."

I wanted to grimace but managed to smile. "Yes ma'am. Thank you for making my favorite pie." I added a drumstick, tomatoes, and mashed potatoes. I stifled a groan when she added a second slice to my empty plate. Instead, I said, "Your cherry pie is delicious. Thank you."

When I finished, Spencer said, "Come into the study with me. I'll share my latest correspondence."

I followed him down the hallway and sat down across the desk from him as I had done so many times over the years of my apprenticeship. He handed me three letters. While I read these, he retrieved the brandy bottle and poured us a small tot. He watched me until I finished reading. "What's the matter? I can tell something is troubling you, Ink. Since you didn't return here after your meeting with the Willis family, I gather he didn't accept your proposal."

I sighed. "You know me too well." I paused and drank the tot so I could organize my thoughts. "Mr. Willis said we couldn't marry until I proved to him that I would treat Abigail as an equal. I would never treat her as my servant. How could he possibly think I would do that?"

Dr. Field smiled. "I think you misconstrued his meaning. He meant you should seek her advice before making decisions on her behalf."

"You know I've been taught to believe women are not equal to men."

"Hmm." Spencer paused to drink his tot, then poured another for both of us. "I learned early in my marriage that our life was better when I consulted my wife. When I didn't, there was discord between us which spilled over into our daily life. Did you ever notice anything but harmony between us?"

I shook my head.

"Think about what I've said. I know you love her. I'm sure you'll figure out what's best for both of you."

"Thanks for your advice," I said. Spencer put our brandy things away, and I headed upstairs to the room I'd share with Jack. After I changed into my nightshirt, I took out my Bible and prayed for guidance.

FOUR

Monday, June 4, 1798

I missed riding my horse as I walked from Oakham to Rochester. I'd forgotten how much longer it took to travel by foot. I hoped my father would put my mare to good use by purchasing a chaise.

It was a pleasant day, and I reached Mendon by late afternoon where I decided to spend the night at Miller's Pub. Mr. Saul and his daughter joined me at my table. A stringed trio, who softly played their instruments while we ate our food, and our agreeable conversation made the evening enjoyable. Expenses: $0.21.

Tuesday, June 5th

The skies looked stormy when I rose at dawn. I decided to eat a hearty breakfast before I left the pub. By the time I finished, a hard rain was falling. I'd planned to buy supplies after our boat was purchased. Now, I asked the innkeeper where the chandlery was located. Splashing my way through puddles, I hurried to the shop. Its owner recommended a large oilcloth. I knew it would provide many uses, so I made a purchase, flung it over my head, and resumed my journey at 8 o'clock. It was late afternoon before the skies cleared. I reached the town of Raynham after dusk. Expenses: $1.04.

Wednesday, June 6th

I'd asked the innkeeper to provide bran muffins so I could leave at dawn. Munching my food, I walked at a brisk pace and arrived at the Chaddock's home before dinner.

I was happy to meet the man with whom I'd corresponded for months, yet he was nothing like what I'd imagined him to be. I had pictured him as tall and muscular, somewhat like Nate. Instead he was a bit stout and an inch shorter than me. I enjoyed our meal. He was an educated man, and our conversation covered many topics. I left their company late afternoon and walked five miles to the Willis house.

Nate, and his wife Lucy, warmly welcomed me into their home. They introduced their three children: Sophia age seven, Noah age five, and Charles age one. As we ate supper, Nate and I made plans to visit the boatyards the next day. Lucy said she would not accompany us. Expenses: $0.62.

Thursday, June 7th

Nate and I, along with the Chaddocks, headed to New Bedford where we met Mr. and Mrs. Levi Tomlinson. Levi suggested we look at Anchor Shipyard to examine flatboats. The smallest one measured 14-by-40 feet. The cost at $1 per foot would equal $560. An additional $20 would provide us with four divided rooms, including tarred cloth coverings, a pump, cable, and a sand-filled firebox for cooking our meals. We asked what the price would be for a 15-by-40 with five divided rooms and were told $625.

Nate said, "Keelboats are sold at the New Bedford Marine Dockyard."

When we arrived, we spoke with the yard foreman and found out the only one available had a broken rudder. The boat, as is, could be purchased for the sum of $550. The man gave us directions to the Thomas Smithy and said he was the best smith in the area.

We went into Murphy's Inn, located next door, and ordered dinner. Nate invested in ocean-going vessels and was not well versed on smaller boats. I asked the innkeeper, "Do you know anyone knowledgeable about keelboats and flatboats?"

He turned and pointed at a sailor seated nearby. "Captain Jack is your man."

We invited Jack to join us. Once he was seated at our table, Nate said, "Captain, we're planning to travel to Ohio and back by boat. Which would be a better purchase: a keelboat or a flatboat?"

The sailor laughed, then took a sip of his ale. "And back you say? Then my answer is easy. A flatboat won't work because they can't make the return journey. Many men break those apart and use its lumber once they reach their destination."

I remembered my eldest sister Susannah writing that her husband had used their flatboat's lumber for the floor and doors of their blockhouse. I nodded. "What can you tell us about keelboats?"

"You can use one to make your return trip, but you'll need manpower to do it."

Levi asked, "What do you mean?"

Jack hawked chaw into a spittoon. "There are three processes." He lifted a stained index finger. "One, poling the boat." He raised his middle finger. "Two, having one of you, or a mule, on the riverbank pull the boat forward using a rope." His ring finger went up and joined the other two in the air. "Three, bushwhacking."

"What's that?"

He drained his draught of ale before he answered my question. "You grab plants on-shore and pull your boat forward."

The innkeeper came over and refilled his empty trencher. Jack took another sip. "Of course, the keelboat is more expensive because of its rudder and sail."

We thanked the captain for sharing his knowledge and repaid him by paying for his dinner and ales.

Outside the inn, I said, "We need to find out how much the blacksmith will charge to fix the rudder or create a new one. I'll go to the smithy tomorrow."

Levi nodded. "Have you ever gone sailing? A rocking boat makes some people ill. We should know if it will bother anyone before we make a purchase. We can rent a sailboat at the yard one street over."

We spent the afternoon sailing. None of us got sick. Expenses: $0.25.

Friday, June 8th

I located the Thomas Smithy in New Bedford early in the morning. "Sir, I need to know how much you'll charge to fix a keelboat rudder."

He rubbed his chin. "Others have already made enquiries about the one at the marine dockyard. Is that the boat you're asking about?"

I nodded. He said, "Its rudder cannot be repaired."

I sighed. "How much would you charge to make a new one and how soon would it be ready?"

"I have other commitments. I think it'll take about three weeks to complete and cost $350."

"I need to discuss this with my companions. Thank you for your time."

∞ ∞ ∞

Remembering Spencer's request, I went to see his friend in Fairhaven. While we chatted, Doc Foster said, "I plan to see a family ill with smallpox tomorrow. One caught it in the natural way, and I inoculated the other members as described in Dr. Jenner's article. Why don't you come along on my house calls?"

"I'd love to accompany you. I'll be here in the morning."

I returned to the Willis home. Nate gave me a note from the colonel inviting me to supper on Sunday. I told them what I'd found out from the blacksmith. While sailing, Mr. Chaddock had told us he couldn't take a journey at this time. If Colonel Sturtevant decided not to go, it was unlikely we would buy a keelboat.

Saturday, June 9th

Nate gave me a ride to Fairhaven. Dr. Foster had his one-horse shay ready, waiting for my arrival. In between house calls, he told me that leeches worked best in the inflammatory stage of this disease. He agreed to loan me the recent medical article if I would return it the following day. It was almost mid-morning when we reached the home of the family sick with smallpox.

They had been treated a week earlier and were in good spirits. The naturally infected member was almost fully recovered, and the other members had only suffered a very slight fever. As the doctor showed me the scabbing, he told the family, "I won't visit again but—send a messenger to me if anyone's health worsens."

I thanked the family for allowing me to observe. When we returned to his house, Mrs. Foster had dinner ready and invited me to stay. After we ate, I spent some time chatting with the doctor and remembered to borrow his medical journal.

The afternoon was pleasant. I enjoyed my walk back to Nate's home as I thought about this exciting medical knowledge which should reduce the death rate from smallpox.

DR. INCREASE

Sunday, June 10th

Early in the morning, Nate said, "A Methodist church has been constructed, but an ordained minister hasn't yet answered the call. The traveling minister who serves this area doesn't come until next week. I'm sorry, but the only church service available today is Quakers."

"If you don't mind, I'll stay here and read." After breakfast, I immersed myself in Dr. Jenner's smallpox article. I joined Nate's family for dinner, then finished reading the medical periodical. I stopped by the doctor's house to return his journal on my way to the Sturtevant home.

The elderly man suffers from gout, and he was very querulous during our meal. I could tell his father's behavior embarrassed the colonel, but I could understand his father's travel concerns. It would be a difficult trip by boat, even for healthy young men. It would be unwise for his father to make the journey. The colonel cannot go without him.

Arrived at the Willis home after dark. They had left a welcoming candle burning in the window. I blew out the candle, retired for the night, and fell into a troubled sleep, upset that our travel plans had gone awry.

FIVE

As we ate breakfast, I said, "Colonel Sturtevant decided to remain home with his father."

"I thought this would be his answer." Nate paused. "It's now you, me, and Levi to cover the boat cost."

"Yes." I calculated. "Each man must now come up with $300, not including our food supplies. It's much more than I want to spend."

"So—it's now unfeasible to purchase that keelboat."

I nodded. "Are you still interested in making the trip if I purchase a horse?"

"I promised I would go with you." Nate briefly chuckled. "Besides, Lucy's father and brother have commanded me to come there. I dare not disappoint either of them."

Lucy laughed. "That's a wise decision." She reflected for a moment. "Will traveling by horse take longer?"

"Yes, dear."

She smiled at her husband. "Then I'd prefer to stay with Aunt Martha in Hingham while you're away. The weather on the east coast will be cooler than here. Our children will enjoy time spent at the beach."

He considered her suggestion. "You're willing to drive our buggy? It'll be a tight squeeze."

Lucy smiled at him and nodded. "I'll put Charles in a basket. He'll probably sleep most of the way. There's enough room on the seat for our other two children. I promise I'll only pack what's absolutely necessary to take."

Nate turned to me. "It'll take time for me to escort Lucy then return.

I'll also stop in Boston to file several motions to delay since we'll be gone longer than I thought. How about I meet you in Oakham, say Saturday or Sunday?"

When I nodded, he said, "You need to find a horse, and one of my sisters lives near a breeder. If you go with us to Bridgewater, I'll introduce you to my sister Vashti and her husband Martin Howard. I'll ask him to take you to Silas Packard's place. My sister Chloe is married to Silas, and both families live near each other."

It didn't take Lucy long to pack, and we departed by mid-morning. When we started out, Nate rode his mare next to their buggy, ready to provide advice to his wife. She proved she was an adept driver, and he dropped back to ride near me. We stopped by Levi Tomlinson's home and informed him of our changed plans. He agreed to meet me at Martin's home in Bridgewater on Wednesday afternoon.

With spirited conversation, our trip was quite pleasant. Always a gentleman, Nate insisted we share his horse by walking a mile, then riding a mile. Following this formula, we reached the Howard residence by late afternoon.

I was surprised by Nate's introduction. "Vashti and Martin, this is Dr. Increase Mathews. Treat him well. He's already asked for Abigail's hand, so he's a future brother-in-law. Please provide hospitality for a few days while he waits for Levi Tomlinson to arrive. I told him you'd introduce him to Silas, because Ink needs to buy a horse to travel to Ohio."

I looked at my hosts. Vashti had a fair complexion with dark hair and was as tall as me. Martin was an inch taller with black hair. I said, "Your father hasn't given his consent yet."

She laughed. "If Nabby wants you as her husband, she'll get her way."

We wished Nate and Lucy safe travels when they continued to Hingham. After they departed, Martin said, "Silas and Chloe live in East Bridgewater. We'll go there in the morning. I'll ask him to take us to see his breeder friend. Then, I must discuss some business with my older brother Judge Daniel Howard. After that we'll visit my cousin Jonathan who is married to Vashti's and Nabby's sister Martha and we'll spend the night at their home in West Bridgewater."

The couple made me feel welcome. Our supper was enjoyable and filled with laughter. By the time I went to bed, I knew they accepted me into their family.

Tuesday June 12th

Traveling in his chaise, Martin and I went to visit the Packards. After introductions, Silas asked about my travel plans. His older brother had recently returned from Ohio, so he gave me some tips. "Salt is always needed. Burr coffee mills are in demand. Most families decide not to take the mills because of their bulk."

"Thank you for the great advice. I'll bring one of the mills; two if there's enough room on our packhorses."

Martin said, "Speaking of horses, the doctor needs to buy one to make his journey to Ohio."

"Please call me Ink. All my friends do."

Both men grinned. Silas said, "My friend breeds and raises Morgans. One of those would be great for traveling long distances. He lives about five miles from here. Let me tell Chloe we're going there and will be back in time for dinner."

Silas went indoors. Martin turned to me. "Let me warn you before we go. These horses are selectively bred, so they're more expensive than most. I think they're worth it."

I nodded my understanding. When Silas joined us, we went to James Hawkins's stables. Their glowing description of this breed wasn't erroneous. A pinto caught my attention. Her eyes showed intelligence, her lines sleek and sturdy. I viewed several other horses before I returned to the pinto. After some haggling and insisting that a saddle, saddlebags, and blanket be included, I purchased this four-year-old Morgan for $65. Though expensive, I knew my money was well spent. More importantly, both Mr. Hawkins and I were pleased with our bargain.

We left the stud farm and returned to the Packard home. When Silas introduced me to his wife Chloe, I was stunned because she could have been Abigail's identical twin. Their similarity was striking. Chloe's hair was a shade darker, a bit more brunette than auburn.

During our dinner, her green eyes twinkled as she laughed. "I hope Father will allow you to marry Nabby. Then, I'll no longer be the misfit!"

I quizzically raised my eyebrows. She said, "All of my sisters are married to men whose surname begins with an H. Our oldest sister Martha married Jonathan Howard, then Betty married Luther Hayward, followed by Molly marrying Gideon Howard."

Martin said, "And then Vashti married me."

I joined the family's laughter. "I do hope your father allows me to marry Abigail."

After we finished eating, Martin and I said our goodbyes. Riding my mare, I followed him to West Bridgewater where Judge Daniel Howard lived in an imposing, two-story stone, manor house. While the brothers discussed business, Daniel's wife Abigail gave me a tour. I was impressed. I hoped to own such a fine residence someday.

We passed an amicable hour in conversation on many topics. A Masonry member, the judge loaned me pamphlets about this esoteric group and urged me to consider joining. Aware that many of our Founding Fathers were members of this illustrious organization, I was intrigued.

We left them and within a few miles arrived at Jonathan and Martha Howard's place. After stabling our horses, we ate supper with them then spent the night.

Wednesday, June 13th

After breakfast, I saddled the Morgan while Martin readied his chaise, then followed him back to his home. While riding, I admired my purchase. Fine sturdy lines with quick response; her ride smooth with an ambling gait. When we reached their home, we were greeted by Vashti who exclaimed over the pinto as Martin showed me where I could stable the filly.

∞ ∞ ∞

While I waited for Levi Tomlinson to appear, I read the Masonry pamphlets to pass the time. These inferred the organization existed from the time of Solomon, but the supplied materials failed to prove its existence prior to 126 A.D. I remained unconvinced that Masonry was a path I wanted to pursue. Finished reading, I returned the pamphlets to Martin.

At two o'clock a Mr. Nye came to inform me that Levi was sick and would arrive tomorrow. I had hoped to leave this evening. Now, I needed to spend another day biding my time. Vashti and Martin were graciously understanding and extended their hospitality for another day.

Thursday, June 14th

A wonderful host, Martin suggested taking a morning ride, so we ventured into the countryside. He admired the pinto as I paced her, working her up to a gallop. Because of her spotted coloring, I decided to name her "Beanie".

A short time later, the day became humid. We returned to their house, and I stabled Beanie. Martin left for his store, so I wandered their property until Vashti called me for dinner.

While we ate, hazel-eyed Vashti asked, "Are you willing to help me collect dandelions? I want to make some wine before the blossoms disappear."

Thankful for their hospitality, I agreed. Enamored with baskets, we went to a nearby field filled with dandelions. We filled two baskets with blossoms while her toddler followed us and chased butterflies. While we worked, we shared stories about our families.

"Why didn't you warn me that Chloe and Abigail look like twins?"

She laughed and a slight flush came up her pale cheeks. "To be honest, I hadn't given it any thought. By the way, we call her 'Nabby'."

I told Vashti about my brothers and sisters. She said, "Your family was more boys than girls. Ours was the opposite. With one older and four younger sisters, Nate felt overwhelmed by females. Can you imagine his relief when Elijah was born?"

I laughed and nodded. A short time later, we returned to the house. Vashti took her son inside for his afternoon nap, then returned for the baskets. I asked, "Do you mind if I stay on the porch while I wait for Levi to arrive?"

Vashti nodded. "That's fine. I'm going to start the wine while little Fred sleeps. Then, I'll fix an early supper so you can leave after he gets here."

I sat in the porch rocker and bided my time. Listening to the drone of bees on nearby lavender, I dozed. Levi looked ill when he arrived in the afternoon. We ate the early supper, bid Vashti and Martin farewell, and departed at 5 o'clock.

While we rode, Levi complained of difficulty breathing and rubbed his breastbone. Due to his pneumonic inflammation, we failed to arrive at our planned destination. The ride to Mansfield had taken so long that we spent the night at Clapp's Inn when we reached there at 9 o'clock.

Friday, June 15th

We left at dawn and traveled to Foxborough where Mr. Everett provided a hearty breakfast. Feeling indisposed, Levi didn't eat much. I asked him if he wanted to remain here with his friend, but he insisted on coming with me. We made frequent stops so he could rest. By early afternoon, Levi was feverish. I wished I had brought my medical kit because I felt at a loss to help him. We arrived at Barnes's Pub in Grafton after dusk. Expenses: $0.63.

Saturday, June 16th

I went to the town's chandler in the morning and purchased chamomile tea. With Silas's tip in mind, I asked the owner, "Do you carry burr coffee mills?"

"No. If anyone wants one, I order from Boston."

"Is there a widow nearby who sells herbal remedies?"

Following the man's directions, I found her home where I purchased dried willow bark and contents for a mustard plaster. I made and applied the poultice to Levi's chest as soon as I returned to the pub. I combined willow bark and chamomile tea then added some whiskey from my flask. I handed him this concoction. "Levi, drink all of this."

A few hours later, his fever broke. "Levi, you shouldn't travel to Ohio in this condition. You need several days of bed rest before you make any trip and need to keep the compress applied for at least three days."

He frowned. "I don't want to remain here for several days. I promise to rest once I reach my brother's place. I feel well enough to make it to Oakham."

I nodded. Reverend Daniel Tomlinson was pastor of the Congregational Church there. It made sense for Levi to remain with family while he mends. We parted company when we reached his brother's house. Expenses: $1.00.

SIX

The Fields were surprised when I arrived. It was 6 o'clock, and they were eating supper. Mrs. Field got up and added another plate and utensils to the table. "Sit down and eat with us. There's plenty of food."

Famished, I sat down and filled my plate. While we ate, I told them about our changed traveling plans and my horse purchase. Spencer and his son followed me outside to look over the Morgan when I went to put her in their barn. Jack said, "She's a beauty. May I take her for a quick ride?"

I nodded. While he was gone, I asked, "Did Nate Willis stop by here?"

Spencer said, "I haven't seen your friend."

"He's supposed to meet me here today or tomorrow."

∞ ∞ ∞

Nate failed to arrive on Sunday. On Monday morning, Mr. Parkman arrived with a note from Nate which said, "Sorry, but I've been delayed. I need to remain in Boston for several days. I promise to be there by June 23rd at the latest."

I asked this man if he would be willing to carry a return message. He agreed.

"Please buy a coffee burr mill. If there's enough room in your saddlebags, purchase two. Levi Tomlinson has pneumonia. He's going to remain at his brother's home to mend. I'll buy two packhorses for our journey. We can settle any difference once you arrive. Godspeed to you on your journey."

Finished with my missive, I asked Mrs. Field to make some sandwiches and gave these to Mr. Parkman along with my note.

∞ ∞ ∞

While I helped Jack hoe weeds on Tuesday, I said, "I need to buy a couple of horses for packing our gear. Do you know anyone willing to sell?"

"Maybe Widow Wallace's son Bill. She's moving to his farm in Rutland."

Early in the afternoon, I rode Beanie to her place. The late Mr. Wallace had a keen eye for horses. Two of them were eight-years old and sturdily built. After a bit of dickering with Bill, I bought these two for $20.

"May I return to pick them up on Friday?"

Bill agreed. We shook hands before I left.

Riding into the doctor's yard, I noticed the previous night's thunderstorm had torn some shingles off the roof. As we ate supper, I said, "Saw some roof damage when I came back today. How about I earn my keep and make repairs?"

Spencer said, "There's no need for you to do that. My house is your home."

"I know, but I need to do something while I wait for Nate."

∞ ∞ ∞

I started the repairs Wednesday morning and found that it would be best to replace all shingles on the western side. I wasn't daunted by this prospect because it would keep my hands and mind occupied. I dreamed about what I might find in the Ohio Country while I worked.

∞ ∞ ∞

On Friday morning, Abigail sent a servant with a note asking if I could call upon her on Saturday before noon. I retrieved my packhorses from the Wallace's farm early in the afternoon, then continued repairing the roof. Thoughts of Abigail filled my mind. I missed hitting the nail on the head and caught my thumb or forefinger several times. I decided it would be best if I stopped thinking about her and focused my thoughts on Ohio. I finished the repairs by suppertime.

Saturday morning dawned bright and clear. By 11 o'clock it was already hot. Glad to ride Beanie and not walk in the heat, I headed to the Willis home. Abigail and Lucy were already seated upon their horses when I arrived. With her stepmother's permission, Abigail had arranged for us to take a ride through the countryside. After a short time, her sister's mare set off at a brisk trot.

I turned to Abigail. Her green-eyed gaze held mine as a serene, yet somehow encouraging, smile flitted across her lips. "Would you like to walk our horses?"

My answering smile was enormous. The only time I'd been alone with Abigail was when Nate arranged for me to speak to her of my intentions. Amazed at my good fortune to have her company without a chaperone, I dismounted Beanie, helped her dismount, then retrieved our reins.

"Won't this upset your father?"

"Increase, may I speak frankly with you?"

I nodded, relieved that she would be candid.

"Father won't know about today. Lucy and Sarah are sworn to secrecy. I know why my father refused your pledge. He said it was because you were taught that men are superior to females."

I flushed and pushed a strand of sandy hair out of my eyes. "Abigail, I've been thinking—"

"Please call me Nabby."

I paused to smile. "Nabby, living with me may prove difficult, especially if we live in Ohio. There, land must be cleared before I can even build us a home. It will be rough. We'll probably have to sleep under a wagon. You're used to better—"

"May I call you Ink?"

I nodded.

She smiled. "Ink, we didn't always have indentured servants to do our bidding. Life with my mother was very different than our life since Father's remarriage and our move to Oakham.

"My mother taught all of her daughters how to scrimp and make do, because my father was miserly back then. From her, I learned to churn butter, to sew and darn socks, to cook and clean, and to use the loom to weave cloth. I was fourteen when Father met Sarah. She insisted that he convert to Unitarianism before they married. Since their wedding, he's been a changed man.

"You're already doing what he's asked of you. You've asked my opinion about an important matter. Yes, I'm willing to go where you go and to do whatever it takes." She took my hand in hers.

We walked for another mile in companionable silence. Neither of us spoke about our feelings, instead we talked of inconsequential things. Nabby seemed to trip. My hands spanned her waist to steady her. "Are you all right?"

"I'm fine now." She leaned forward and gave me a chaste kiss upon the lips.

My heart pounded; I flushed. Flustered, I said the first thing that came to mind. "I enjoyed meeting your sisters and their families. Chloe could be your twin!"

"Do you think I'm prettier?"

"I love your auburn hair." I wanted to touch her tresses but didn't.

"That's not what I asked!"

I saw her mischievous smile. I grinned. We continued walking and soon came upon Lucy, who had laid out the food on a blanket next to a stream. Our horses grazed as we enjoyed our picnic lunch in the shade of a red maple tree.

Riding back, Nabby said, "We've heard from Nate. That's how I knew you were nearby. He plans to be in Oakham before suppertime tomorrow, and he'll spend the night with you so that you can get an early morning start. Have you gotten supplies yet?"

"I plan to stock up at the military store in Springfield."

When we reached their home, Lucy said, "Our stepmother would like to give Nate some travel bread before he leaves."

"I'll make sure he stops by. Please thank her for our delicious picnic."

With a sweet smile, Nabby gave me a hug after I helped her dismount. "I'll wait for you. I'm sure you and I will convince my father."

Glad Beanie was a steady ride, I didn't concentrate on the road heading back. I put the pinto in the barn, then spent the afternoon chopping firewood. After supper, I retrieved enough water from the well so the entire family could have a hot bath. Refreshed, I retired to bed and dreamt of Nabby.

∞ ∞ ∞

I attended church with the Field family. I spoke with Reverend Tomlinson after the service ended. "I thought I'd see Levi here today. Is he better?"

"Yes. He left for Rochester on Friday morning. Thanks for the care you gave him. I'm surprised you're still here. When do you leave?"

"Hope to be on our way later today."

He nodded and turned away to speak with another parishioner.

∞ ∞ ∞

When Nate arrived Sunday afternoon, we went to the barn so he could view the horses. "I've heard about the Morgan breed. She's a fine filly. I wouldn't mind having one for myself. The packhorses look sturdy. How much did you pay?"

"Twenty for both. Did you get any coffee mills?"

"I got two for $10 each. I could barely fit those in my saddlebags."

I said, "Then we're even on the amount spent."

Nate glanced at me. "How is Levi? Any chance he'll come with us?"

"I spoke with his brother this morning. The Reverend said Levi was better and returned to Rochester on Friday."

"Uhm. Robert Parkman wants to come with us as far as Wheeling, Virginia. I hope you don't mind…" Nate's expression turned contrite. "I told him to meet us at your father's house. He can't get here from Boston until early Tuesday."

I thought a moment before I answered. "I'm not happy about another delay, but I suppose it's all right. You'll be able to spend time with your family. It will help to have another share our expenses, especially since Levi isn't coming with us."

Mrs. Field called us for supper. After we ate, we wrote a list of supplies to be bought when we reached Springfield. Before Nate left, we agreed to meet at my father's home.

Monday, June 25th, 1798

Riding Beanie and leading both packhorses, I stopped at our sawmill early in the morning. I waved my arms to get my eldest brother's attention, then waited as he slowed the mill blade. His face showed surprise, and he shouted to be heard above the buzzing blade. "What are you doing here?"

"Our plan to purchase a boat failed. We're now going to make our journey on horseback. Nate will be here later today. Come see the Morgan I bought."

When we were outside and away from the mill noise, Lish said, "Hannah delivered another boy on June 12th. They're both doing fine. We've named him Charles Cotterworth Pinkney Mathews."

I shook his hand. "Congratulations! I'll go visit them."

Beanie whickered as Lish ran his hands over her withers. "Oh, she's a fine filly."

"Where's Father?"

"He went into Worcester and won't be home until tonight."

I nodded. "I need to let Aunt Hannah know Nate and I will be here for supper. I'll see you for dinner."

He headed back inside.

I found my aunt at Lish's house where she was helping her daughter fix the meal. I hugged her and my cousin, then answered their questions about why I was back as I admired baby Charles. "Nate plans to be here before supper and will spend the night. We'll leave in the morning. Since I have some time, I thought I'd go gather some medicinals now."

Both Hannahs nodded. My cousin grinned. "You'll be back in time for dinner?"

"Of course."

I stabled the horses in father's barn, then retrieved baskets from my apothecary shed. I picked chamomile then calendula flowers and spread these herbs to dry on separate racks in my shed.

After dinner, I returned to father's house. I carried my mattock to the barn, saddled Beanie, then put my tool inside her saddlebags. I rode to a field near our mill where I dug up dandelion roots. When I returned to the farm, I spent the afternoon grinding dried herbs and making potions. I retrieved my medical kit from indoors and made sure it was generously stocked.

Because our journey would take much longer than I'd originally anticipated, I decided to sell some of my wares to the chandler and purchased two 25-pound sacks of salt to give as gifts. Nate arrived shortly after I returned from town.

SEVEN

Tuesday, June 26th

In the morning, we dallied over breakfast. When Mr. Robert Parkman arrived, Nate introduced us. I shook his hand. "Since we'll be together for weeks, feel free to call me Ink."

He smiled. "I will if you'll call me Bob."

I said goodbye to my family while we gave Bob time to let his horse cool down and be watered. Before we mounted, I turned to Bob. "Do you need to purchase anything in town?"

He shook his head. "I have everything I need."

Leaving New Braintree, we took the road leading to Palmer. Curious, I asked, "Bob, where do you live? What's your occupation?"

"After the war ended, I moved with my family from Westboro, Massachusetts to Westmoreland, New York. Six years ago, I moved to Cayuga County to study law. I taught school and dealt in real estate to pay my way, but…" His pale countenance turned red. "I became sick and had to return to my father's place in Oneida County."

Bob noticed my concern. "I assure you that I'm well enough to make this trip."

I gave him a searching look, then nodded for him to continue.

"Last year my uncle, Samuel Parkman, purchased about 17,000 acres in the Western Reserve from the Connecticut Land Company. His lands are located near Lake Erie, and my uncle wants me to view his acreage, then provide advice. Uncle Sam also suggested the trip would be good for my health. So here I am."

∞ ∞ ∞

At Western, we reached the new turnpike road and paid the toll. It was a joy to travel on the turnpike with its well-maintained, smooth surface, and we quickened our pace. We would remain on this road until we reached Springfield.

We stopped for dinner at Bates's Pub in Palmer and discussed what supplies we needed. With Bob's input, we added a few more items to our list. We pushed on to reach Springfield and arrived at Captain Ames's home at dusk. Expenses $0.30.

Wednesday, June 27th

Captain Ames and his wife provided breakfast in the morning. Then he escorted us to the military store where we purchased supplies: canteens, a hatchet, a small handsaw, mosquito netting, and cakes of lye soap. We also purchased a cast-iron skillet and a corn mill in case we ever had to prepare our own meal.

Before we parted company, Captain Ames mentioned that we would pass close to Newgate because we anticipated stopping near Barkhamsted in Connecticut. I had never been more than a hundred miles from my father's house, so I said, "I propose that we stop along our way to visit worthwhile sights."

Nate and Bob agreed, so we stopped to tour the cavern. Formerly the Simsbury copper mine, the Newgate prison was becoming famous for the harsh treatment of its inhabitants. One obstinate prisoner, who refused to make nails, had severed three of his own fingers from his left hand. After being isolated, this man finally began making nails.

I was appalled at the conditions and health of the prisoners. This was a breeding ground for infection because they had to endure the underground conditions of dampness, vermin, and darkness. Most animals were better treated than these poor men.

After we left the prison, we crossed the Barkhamsted Reservoir at its narrowest point. Bob said, "I have friends who live nearby. I suggest we stay at the Merrill's home."

This family was amenable to our remaining with them overnight. After we ate supper with the family, we took our bedrolls and bedded down for the night in their barn. Traveled 32 miles. Expenses: $0.87.

Thursday, June 28th

Rising early, we traveled eight miles into Colebrook where we breakfasted at Shepard's Tavern. Because of his blacksmithing background, Nate said, "I'd like to visit the Forbes rolling and slitting mill in East Canaan."

This was located on the banks of the Blackberry River. We stopped and toured the manufacture workings and the variety of products made of the best quality iron. I found it informative to compare the inner workings of a rolling mill to our sawmill. The heat inside was intense, so I was glad to exit the mill.

We stopped at the chandler to buy food supplies and more feed for our horses. We sat on a bench in the town square, under the shade of an oak tree, while we ate sandwiches made from our stores.

With the time spent at the iron works, we only traveled 30 miles; instead of the 50 miles we'd hoped to make. We shared a room at Farnum's Inn in Salisbury. After we ate supper, I started a letter to Nabby before I wrote in my diary. I plan to add my thoughts each day to my letter, then post it at the beginning of the week. Expenses: $0.66.

Both men snored by the time I went to bed. I tried to join their slumber but my concern over what we might find once we crossed the mountains kept me awake. My brother had written about the anti-government sentiment which existed in western Pennsylvania. *Does this area still breed malcontents? Did the deployment of Federal troops and state militias during the Whiskey Rebellion end their dissatisfaction?*

I glanced at my sleeping friends. Nate's large build and broad shoulders should make any man think twice about starting an argument with us. Bob was only a little shorter but had a muscular frame. Reassured I was in good company for whatever we may encounter, I closed my eyes and slept.

Friday, June 29th

Rising at 6 o'clock, we made sure our canteens were full, left Connecticut behind, and started our climb through the Appalachians. We breakfasted in Armenia, which is nestled in a valley between mountains just after entering New York. Bob said, "My family lives in Cayuga County which is in the northwestern part of the state near Lake Ontario, but I know my way around here too."

His knowledge of this area proved beneficial. We followed the mountain trail towards Millbrook where we stopped for dinner. Purchasing a newspaper, I read out loud an interesting article about a local farmer who was using a plaster of Paris manure to increase his hay yields. Many of his neighbors, seeing his results, had adopted this practice. We asked the pub owner about the gypsum usage, and he confirmed that many farmers had increased their crop yields.

Continuing to Hopewell, we stopped at a farm along the road. The farmer explained how gypsum was ground, then added to manure and spread on the fields prior to planting. "This reduced the acidic nature of the soil. The following year, I planted the fields with clover following the rotation ideas of Thomas Mann Randolph. I've almost doubled my crop yields by doing this."

We thanked him for his explanation, then continued our trip. We put up for the night at Tomkin's Inn. Traveled 41 miles today. Expenses: $1.10.

Saturday, June 30th

At 8 o'clock, we reached the Fishkill Ferry and ferried across the Hudson River. We breakfasted in Newburgh and topped off our canteens. We made sure the horses were thoroughly watered before we continued.

Traveling southwest we had dinner at Ruder in Blooming Grove where we passed a Liberty pole with a "no stamp act" sign affixed to it. We knew there was political discord west of the Appalachians, but we hadn't thought our travel would take us into a hotbed of discontent before we reached Pennsylvania. Had the pole been recently erected in response to President Adams's urging Congress to support an expanded Federal military? Or had the pole been erected during the Whiskey Rebellion?

I had been rather reticent on our trip because my thoughts were filled with the question of gender equality. When we passed this pole, Bob said, "I don't believe there is any need for a standing army or navy. Our distance from Europe is great enough to protect our country."

I believed differently. "Without a navy, how do we protect American ships from being confiscated by the French or British?"

Nate said, "The President only wants us to be prepared in case we go to war with France."

Our discussion continued and became heated, so we agreed to disagree on political matters. Bob's voice was sonorous, while Nate's had a more melodious quality. It was pleasurable to listen to both men speak, even when they were arguing. I could easily picture them orating in a courtroom.

We spent the night at Drake's Tavern. All of us felt uncomfortable here. We couldn't understand how such a petulant innkeeper remained in business. Traveled 32 miles. Expenses: $1.15.

EIGHT

Sunday, July 1, 1798

S et out extremely early, wanting to get away from our nasty innkeeper. We traveled nine miles to Warwick and stopped for breakfast at Pasts' Pub. Entering New Jersey, we stopped at Cole's for sandwiches in Vernon Township, filled our canteens, and made sure our horses were watered. We continued southwest to reach Hamburg where we stopped for an early night at Dariah's because it was the Sabbath. In one week, we've traveled 194 miles from my father's house.

We spent the night talking about religion, and we again had different opinions. Their beliefs were more liberal than those I'd been taught. Bob said, "I'm an evangelical Methodist. I believe salvation is for everyone."

Nate said, "After my father converted, I also became a Unitarian. I now believe in free human will and the loving benevolence of God."

Since Bob was unmarried, I directed my question to my friend. "Nate, I noticed how you deferred to Lucy when we discussed changing our traveling plans." I felt the flush on my cheeks. "Do you feel she's your equal?"

Nate stood up and stretched. "Yes, I do." He paused and thought for a moment. "Let me ask you a question. What did your mother and sisters do when your father and eldest brother joined the army?"

"They pitched in and did the farm work. Without their efforts, we wouldn't have survived the war years."

Nate smiled. "There, you see?"

While I pondered, I brushed my sandy hair away from my eyes. "But none of them could do as much work as a man."

"That's only because women are built differently than men, and I'm thankful for that!" He chuckled. "My point is…" He raised his index finger. "None of them said they couldn't do it because it was a man's work."

Bob spoke up. "He's right, and you know it, Ink."

Nate cleared his throat. "Based on my two marriages, I'll give you some advice. Make your wife happy, and you'll be happy too."

A quirky grin appeared on my face as I remembered the few occasions when Mother had been angered by Father. The frigid atmosphere inside our home had been unbearable. Nate had made a valid point.

I reflected upon gender equality as I read my Bible. Even with what Nate had said and Nabby's assurance of our future betrothal, I was still concerned their father would find some way to deny my marriage pledge.

After I changed into my nightshirt, I finished my letter to Nabby, so I could mail it before we left in the morning. I spent several minutes trying to determine the best closing line because I knew her father would read my missive. I finally decided upon "With warm regard" and hoped he wouldn't find this offensive.

Monday, July 2nd

Headed north from Hamburg and reached Sussex early in the morning. We ate breakfast near its courthouse. I mailed my letter before we left town. We then headed southwest and reached Hardwick where we hoped to eat, but this town didn't have any pub or tavern. Our offer to buy dinner at a nearby home was refused, so we stopped by the roadside where I fixed some flapjacks for us. It wasn't much of a dinner, but at least it was filling. Continuing southwest, we came to Amy's Inn in Hope. We only managed to travel 30 miles today.

After we entered the common room, we were greeted by some of the local militia who asked, "What is your political persuasion?"

"Federalists."

They joined our table, and we chatted amicably with them for about an hour. When other members of their party became boisterous and started dancing, it upset our landlord. Our new friends went to assist their brethren in calming the innkeeper. When this failed, they asked that we join them in leaving the premises. We declined.

Tuesday, July 3rd

Heading southwest from Hope, Bob's horse stumbled against the cliff wall of Pohatcong Mountain. Both Nate and I simultaneously asked, "Are you all right?"

"I'm fine, but I don't think my horse is." Bob dismounted and examined his mare's foreleg. "Her bruise looks nasty. I don't think I should ride her."

We walked our mounts until we reached Fair's Pub in Phillipsburg. After we ate breakfast, we asked the pub's stableman to examine Bob's mare. As he applied a poultice, he said, "She shouldn't be ridden for several days."

Bob sighed. "Would walking the animal without a rider suffice?"

The man nodded. "Aye. That would keep the joints limber while her leg heals."

As we ferried across the Delaware River into Easton, Pennsylvania, we discussed how to proceed. Bob said, "You two should go on without me. I can walk until her leg is healed."

Nate said, "We can take turns riding our mounts."

Bob said, "No, that would still delay your journey."

I started to argue that we should stay together but was interrupted by a nearby teamster. He said, "Sorry, I couldn't help overhearing your conversation. I have a suggestion." He waited until we nodded for him to continue. "Would it help if your friend here rides with me to Reading?"

I said, "Sounds like an excellent solution."

Bob and Nate agreed. Bob removed his saddlebags, then tied his unburdened mare with our packhorses. As he boarded the teamster's wagon, he said, "See you in Reading in a few days."

NINE

Worried about the injured animal, Nate and I traveled at a slow pace. When we reached Old Orchard, we decided to stay at a Dutch tavern, so we only traveled 28 miles. By stopping early in the evening, we could do our laundry and allow the mare's leg to rest.

From the tavern's furnishings and the large farm fields surrounding it, we could tell the owner, named Henry, was rich—but it wasn't by his own industry. He was heavily jowled and very lazy. Sitting on his haunches, he made his family do the work while he treated them like servants. I was dismayed by his behavior. I expected better from a Pennsylvania Dutchman. When I made a comment to this effect, Henry uttered curses about our New England women.

Nate pulled me aside. "You better curb your words. If you don't, he may oust us from his inn."

When Henry wasn't within hearing, his wife and daughters asked us how New England women were treated. Their questions revealed their uneasiness about their situation.

Wednesday, July 4th

In the morning, we rode southwest to reach Bethlehem. We had originally planned to tarry here to see the famous sights, but with the injured horse slowing our pace, we didn't stop. From there, we took the more westerly trail and ferried across the Lehigh River into Allentown. Once across the river, we headed southwest through fields full of grain just waiting to be harvested. When we arrived in Maxatawny, the town's square was filled with people celebrating Independence Day, so even though we'd traveled only 28 miles, we decided to put up at Kemp's Inn. We joined the celebrations and found the people very polite.

Thursday, July 5th

As we left Maxatawny at dawn, we encountered some residents involved in a drunken argument. It looked like it would turn into a brawl, so we took a side street, then hurried out of town.

Heading southwest, we reached Barr's Inn in Reading. Bob stood outside the building, watching for us. "Well it's about time you slow pokes arrived."

Nate and I laughed at his teasing. We entered the stable and waited while the poultice was removed. Bob asked, "Is it safe to ride her now?"

The stable owner nodded. "She's fit to travel."

After we left Reading, we forded our horses across the Schuylkill River and headed due west from Reading to reach Lebanon which lies in a fertile valley. We didn't want to push Bob's mare too hard with more mountains to cross, but we did manage to travel 46 miles today. We stayed overnight in Lebanon.

Friday, July 6th

Determined to make good mileage before we reached the Allegheny Mountains, we left at dawn and breakfasted at an Irishman's tavern in Londonderry. We paid a man to use his flatboat to take us across the Susquehanna River at Harrisburg. Bob's horse was faring well, but we decided it would be wise not to push her too hard, so we only traveled 31 miles. In New Cumberland, we spent the night at Brigg's Inn.

Saturday, July 7th

Just after sunrise, we passed through Carlisle and stopped for breakfast three miles outside this town. This tavern was dirty. We quickly finished what we could eat of our greasy meal.

After filling our canteens and watering the horses, we headed southwest to reach Shippensburg. Unlike our breakfast, we had an excellent dinner at Porters. Leaving town, we headed west to reach Upper Strasburg. We spent the night at the Davis Inn. We managed to travel 40 miles today, but we will reach the mountains tomorrow and our travel will slow.

Sunday, July 8th

Because we wanted to get through the Blue Mountain range today, we left at dawn. We headed over North Mountain, then proceeded 3 miles to Skiner's. Here we took the trail over Middle Mountain to Fannettsburg where we stopped for breakfast. We made sure our canteens were full, got onto the trail, and climbed over the Tuscarora Mountain then into the valley where we dined at Dansdill's Tavern.

Next, we traveled over Sideling Hill. This was a tedious route, treacherous to cross in winter. Reaching the western side of the hill, we put up for the night at May's Tavern. There were six families also traveling to the Northwest Territory. We spent an agreeable evening discussing what we knew of the Ohio Country.

We began our journey two weeks ago and have traveled a total of 430 miles. Before I went to bed, I finished writing another letter to Nabby.

Monday, July 9th

We forded the Juniata River shortly after leaving our lodgings and stopped for breakfast at a family's home. Following the trail, we passed through Bedford. This area had been the center of the Whiskey Rebellion of 1794, and President Washington had called out state militias to Bedford County to suppress the whiskey-tax revolt. The town was laid out with a grid pattern that was pleasing to the eye. It was unlike the haphazard layouts of many other towns we'd passed through. We stopped by the chandlery so I could mail my letter.

About 4 miles past Bedford, we decided to eat at Ward's Tavern where we refilled our canteens and watered the horses. When we reached the top of Dry Ridge, we stopped for the night at Wright's Inn. Traveled 30 miles today.

Tuesday, July 10th

Continuing across the top of the Allegheny Mountains, we came upon Hallar's Pub where we breakfasted. We then headed to Somerset. Shortly after we passed through this town, we ate dinner at The Old Irish Woman. The owner named Reed sold us some oat cakes for our horses.

We traveled another 12 miles to Donegal and spent the night in a log hut. Its owner said, "I'm already at full capacity. You'll need to sleep three to a bed. I'll arrange for the others to shift over and do likewise."

Managed to travel 40 miles.

Wednesday, July 11th

It was a very rainy morning, so we didn't depart until noon. Just outside of New Stanton the road divided: the right heading north to Pittsburgh; the left went south to Wheeling. We followed the Wheeling trail. About nine miles further, we ate an excellent meal at Neil's.

Traveling on, we encountered a teamster who was ill and going to sleep in his wagon. Knocking at the door of a nearby farmhouse, I persuaded this lady to allow us and the teamster to spend the night. With our late start, we only traveled 23 miles today. I spent a fitful, restless night because of a lumpy mattress and scratchy pillow casings. It didn't help that I was upset over the landlady's lack of charity to the poor teamster.

Thursday, July 12th

We ventured out through light rain and roads slippery with mud. A little over three miles farther, we waded across the Youghiogheny River near Budd's where the river was shallower. In another eight miles we reached the Monongahela River which we also forded. We stopped for dinner at Parkinson's tavern then continued northwest to reach Washington where we spent the night at Scott's Inn. Because of rain and hilly terrain, we only traveled 32 miles.

The land from the river to here consists of many large and steep hills, and we passed many fields sown with wheat. Washington is a flourishing town and, like most of western Pennsylvania, had participated in the Whiskey Rebellion. Passing through the town, we noticed several Wanted Posters. One of the prominent lawyers, with a $500 warrant on his head, had escaped President Washington's army and fled by boat to the Spanish territory.

Friday, July 13th

Nearing the Ohio Country, we stopped at a chandlery to replenish our supplies, hoping prices would be cheaper here than Wheeling, which is still considered a frontier town. Nate said, "I don't like how some of these men are looking at our horses. I'll stay outside to watch our stuff."

Bob and I nodded and entered the shop. When we left Washington, we traveled ten miles. We hadn't found any inn or tavern, so we stopped by the side of the road near a small brook. I again fixed flapjacks, then the other men washed our things in the water.

Continuing another 12 miles, we reached the head of Wheeling Creek and followed this into town. We cheered when we spotted the Ohio River at 4 o'clock. We spent the night at Gooding's Tavern. We've traveled 585 miles from New Braintree, Massachusetts, and it's been 19 days since we left my father's house. The next leg of our journey will be a shorter trip by boat.

TEN

Saturday, July 14th

After breakfast, we said farewell to Bob who will begin his solo journey, going north to reach his uncle's lands on the Grand River which lies several miles below Lake Erie. I wasn't worried about his leaving us. He now looked healthier than when he joined our expedition. After he departed, Nate and I walked to the wharf to speak with the dockmaster. "Sir, will any boats arrive today?"

"The post one should be here by late afternoon." He glanced at us. "It's a small canoe. There'll only be room for one of you."

"Are any packet boats coming soon?"

The man nodded. "Expect one by Thursday afternoon."

We stepped outside. Nate said, "I know you want to see your relatives, so I'll stay here with our horses and take the packet. We'll meet in Marietta on Friday."

"Now that I'm so close, I'm anxious to see my family. You're a wonderful friend."

Back inside the office, I purchased a post ticket and paid the fare for my horses on the packet. We then headed to Denny's Stable to speak to the owner. For a small fee, the stableman agreed to pasture our horses until Thursday.

After eating dinner, I finished my current letter to Nabby so I could post it on the next boat heading east. Late in the afternoon, we took our horses to the stable. We reached the wharf about 4 o'clock, and the canoe had arrived. The crew had unloaded the mail and were eating supper nearby. We supped with the men at the same tavern. After eating, I said farewell to Nate, embarked at 6 o'clock, and expected to arrive in Marietta by morning.

Sunday, July 15th

Though it's cooler and not as humid as previous days, I'm not enjoying the weather because I'm upset over another delay so close to reaching my destination. Last night, our boat had to pull into shore to wait until the fog lifted. There are five of us crowded into the small canoe so there wasn't much room to sleep, and I'm feeling the effects of not enough rest.

We have endeavored to quickly reach Marietta, so we can return to Massachusetts by early autumn. From the start, this trip has been plagued with delays. Though I'm miserable and disgruntled today, I should get to Marietta by early morning.

ELEVEN

Monday, July 16th

I finally reached Marietta at 7 o'clock this morning. My brother John and his friends were awaiting my arrival. We spent several minutes backslapping each other and exchanging introductions. I was surprised by my brother's appearance. He wore buckskins; his face bearded and sun burned. The hair on his chin whiter than his flaxen head of hair.

It's been eleven years since I've seen my brother. I'd still been a teen when he last visited our home. I'm shocked to see I'm now four inches taller than he is, though I'm still shorter than our oldest brother Lish. John had always been small in stature, and his adult height is only two inches over five feet.

Though I had written him of our changed travel plans, he expected me to arrive a week ago and had been pestering the dockmaster for any news. We stopped at a nearby pub where I told some of our adventures while we breakfasted. When I finished eating, I turned to John. "What's this you're wearing?"

John said, "Buckskin doesn't tear easily. When I wore breeches through the brush, they always became tattered. Cloth is too expensive to constantly replace them."

My brother said goodbye to his friends and led the way to the Putnam house. I'd been expecting to see my uncle's home inside a fort, instead I saw a home like the one he'd left behind in Rutland, Massachusetts.

When we arrived, Uncle Rufus was away from Marietta on business, but Aunt Persis warmly welcomed me. She re-introduced me to my cousins, Catherine, who everyone called "Caty," and Martha, who preferred to be called "Patty". I remembered them as children. Now both were fine young ladies. Patty was age 21 and Caty was age 18.

The years have been kind to my cousin Elizabeth, who we call Betsey. She looked much the same as I remembered her when she asked me to read her letter to John. Betsey hugged me. "It's so good to have you here!"

Caty showed me where I would sleep, and I took a much-needed nap.

Just before dinnertime, my brother woke me. "Going to sleep the rest of the day, lazy bones? Don't you want to view the settlement?"

I staggered out of bed and got dressed. As I put the money belt around my waist, I remembered my mother's letter and pulled it out. "Oh yes, Mother asked I share this with you."

I saw John's astonishment and the tears in his blue eyes as he read her words. "I can't take half, Ink. I'm doing all right. You need the money more than I do. How about…" He reflected for a moment. "I take $200 and you keep $300. Let's call it a delivery fee."

"That's not right. It's not what she wanted done!"

My brother was stubborn. His mind made up, there was no persuading him otherwise. We argued for several minutes before I gave up.

After dinner, we went outside. Since John's arrival as part of the original 48 settlers in 1788, Marietta had grown. No longer necessary, the fort had been dismantled as people used its lumber to build their homes. I asked my brother to describe what Campus Martius had been like.

John gestured as he explained. "The fort was erected in a large square shape. All buildings were adjoined and surrounded by a wooden palisade. At each corner there was a strong blockhouse which was 20-feet square at the main level and 24-feet at the second level which was constructed six feet above, and projected over, the palisade.

"On the center side, which faced the Muskingum River, another building with similar construction provided protection for the fort's gate when it was under assault. Dwelling houses, located between the corner blockhouses and gate, had accommodated forty or fifty families. In the center of the fort there'd been a parade ground with a well located in one corner. A combined church and meeting hall, located on the main level with a ballroom on the upper floor, had been inside one of the corner blockhouses. Officers lived in the other corner ones."

As we walked, John said, "After the war ended, Uncle Rufus purchased another blockhouse, dismantled it, and used its lumber to add four additional rooms to his home. It's the only remaining structure from the fort."

I turned and looked back. My uncle's residence was situated on high ground overlooking the Muskingum. The town had been laid out adhering to the tenets of the original Northwest Ordinance which required land be set aside for education and religious purposes. John stopped walking. "This is where the Congregational Church will be built. It's already been chartered."

As we continued north, I could see a large two-story structure with a gabled roof and a massive central chimney. "What's this?"

"It's the Muskingum Academy. They completed it last year. Come along, I want to show you something at our courthouse."

Though construction was incomplete, part of the building was open. My brother led me to a display of leaden plates found earlier in the year. "They say French explorers buried these to claim the land for France."

Many Indian burial mounds had been found near this area. Venturing outside of the settlement, we climbed Great Mound which offered a fine view of the town with its broad streets lined with mulberry trees. Next, we visited Carpenter's Station, a fortified house built at the juncture of Short Creek and the Ohio River.

∞ ∞ ∞

As we ate supper I turned to my brother. "I'd like to visit Susannah tomorrow. Will you come with me?"

John agreed. With this settled and still feeling exhausted, I went to bed.

TWELVE

After breakfast, John contacted a friend and asked him to take us to Belpre in his canoe. The journey by boat was less than five miles, and we quickly reached Belpre. John said, "I need to take care of some business. I'll be along in a bit."

Jonathan and Susannah Stone owned about two thousand acres, located in the upper portion of this settlement. These were bottom lands northwest of the juncture of Virginia's Little Kanawha and the Ohio Rivers. During the Indian war, they had built a garrison with a stockade on their land, about three miles above the one called Farmers Castle. My sister had written that their fort had contained four blockhouses, a schoolhouse, and several log cabins. Like Campus Martius, most of these buildings had been dismantled, but the Stones still lived in their blockhouse. Constructed with logs, it was approximately 16-by-16 feet at the lower level with an upper story that projected another two feet. The only door was located at the rear of this building.

My sister rushed outside when I knocked. With a delighted squeal, she pulled me into a firm embrace. "You finally made it! I feared this day would never come. I've missed you so much." She kissed my forehead and cheeks, then pushed me slightly away. "It's been ten years since the last time I saw you. Let me get a good look at you."

Tears of joy dripped down my cheeks as she inspected me. "I've missed you too, and I've often dreamt of this day." I examined my sister. Her blue eyes glistened, and she wiped moisture away from her cheeks with her apron. Susannah's hair remained a honey-gold color. The sunlight played with it, bringing out glints of red and highlighting a few strands of silver.

Her smile was tremulous. "You're a fine young man now. No longer the boy I remember. I wish Jonathan was here to see you. I'm sorry, but he's out surveying."

Some of her children had gathered around us. I became reacquainted with my niece Grace who was now age 20 and engaged to be married. Since moving to Ohio, Susannah had given birth to three more children. After she introduced John who was three and baby Melissa who was one, she said, "My other two boys are at school right now. Sam is age 13 and Rufus is 8."

"Where's Frankling?"

She laughed. "He hasn't been called that in years. He prefers Ben. He's 18 and farms his own portion of our land. He'll be here later. Let me show you around. I can't wait for you to see my dairy herd."

My sister had ridden on horseback and driven two cows on their journey to Ohio. She now had eight heifers, and two calves stood next to their mothers. "Jonathan went into Virginia and bought two. We've also used Colonel Barker's bull as stud."

The day was becoming hot and humid though it wasn't mid-morning yet. When we finished viewing her pastured animals, I followed Susannah and her children inside their home. "Come sit at the kitchen table. I've got something to show you. Grace, please take Missy into the other room. I don't want her drooling over her father's handiwork."

My sister left the room and returned with a large sheet of paper in her hands. Her voice bubbled with excitement. "Look at this plan Jonathan drew up for our new house. Actual construction will begin next year, but he's already started crafting the wallboards. I can't wait until it's finished, and we live in a real home."

Susannah showed me his drawing. I was surprised by the size of their planned two-story residence—much larger than my father's farmhouse in Massachusetts. It measured 30-by-40 feet. This home would contain eight large rooms and two spacious halls.

I said, "Goodness! It'll be quite an undertaking for Jonathan and your sons without a sawmill in the area. Will he dismantle this house?"

She said, "He's not going to take this one apart until all walls and the roof are completed on the new one."

I smiled at her. "It'll be impressive. I'm sure they'll craft every detail with love."

I played with her youngest children while Susannah and Grace fixed dinner. As they worked, I shared family news. "Hannah prayed for a girl but gave birth to another son. They've named their boy Charles Cotterworth Pinkney Mathews."

Susannah said, "Oh my! Who came up with that?"

I shrugged my shoulders. "I think Lish intended to name him after Minister to France, Charles Cotesworth Pinckney, but botched his name." I laughed and shared a grin with my sister. "I've been meaning to ask, why is this area called Belpre?"

"The French explorers called it Belle's Prairie which means beautiful meadow." She grinned. "We Americans shortened the name to Belpre."

"With your view overlooking the river, it is a beautiful area." I cleared my throat, a bit embarrassed to bring up my failed marriage proposal. "Before I left, I asked Nabby if she would be willing to live here. She said yes but requested I meet with her father. He doesn't want her moving this far from home, so he came up with a reason to deny my pledge. I plan to ask for her hand again when I return."

Susannah hugged me. "I hope you'll be successful next time." Then she chased me outside. "If you want dinner soon, go pick some peas, tomatoes, and lettuce."

Their vegetable patch lay a few feet outside their door and contained a wide variety of produce, including melons, squash, and potatoes. I was still picking vegetables when my brother arrived. He came into the garden and helped me. Inside, Susannah gave me a clean pot. "Go shuck those peas!"

I laughed and complied. After John and I were seated on their porch, I asked him if he had a girlfriend. Because of what he'd written to me the previous year, I thought John might tell me that he was engaged. Instead, he'd made no mention of anyone of the fairer sex and seemed annoyed by my question. We gave the peas to our sister when we finished.

A short time later, Susannah came out and told us to wash up before dinner. Though it wasn't a Sunday, her table was set with her best dishes. She and Grace had made chicken and dumplings, peas, salad, and hasty pudding. Thankful, I said, "This is the best meal I've had since leaving home."

My sister flushed with embarrassment.

"I'd forgotten how easily you blush."

After we ate, John went to visit Ben. Still exhausted, I dozed in a rocking chair in the shade on the back porch. I woke when I heard voices on the path. Sam and Rufus appeared around the corner of the house and stopped. The older one said, "You must be our Uncle Increase! I confess I don't remember you."

"And you must be Sam and Rufus." I smiled at them. "You both have your father's dark hair, but you have your mother's blue eyes and smile."

∞ ∞ ∞

When John returned, Ben was with him. My brother and I helped the boys with their afternoon chores. Ben said, "Want to know the best thing about living here?" He grinned, then took off running with Sam and Rufus close behind him. When they reached the Ohio riverbank, they took off their shirts and breeches. As they waded into the river, I glanced at my brother who grinned. We removed our clothes and joined them. I couldn't swim and stayed close to the shoreline. My nephews glided through the water like fishes. When they came close, they splashed us. We laughed at their antics until I heard my sister ringing the bell.

We ate a cold supper of watermelon, cheese, and cornbread, which my sister called pone, outside under the shade of a buckeye tree. "Did you make the cheese? It's wonderful."

My sister nodded, then fed Missy another bite. I wiped a drop of sweat from my brow. "What has the winter weather been like?"

"We've experienced only one blizzard with snow piled up higher than eighteen inches. Most winters here have been milder than those in Massachusetts."

Ben said, "Sliding on the river ice was fun, but Mother worried it would crack. She made us come inside."

I remembered my sister had written of a food shortage several years ago. "Why did the famine occur in 1790?"

"Because they had to fence their acreage, remove tree stumps, and otherwise prepare their fields, many planted their crops late. People were caught by surprise by an early frost. A Virginian, who'd planted early, sold his corn to us at the normal price and saved the day. He'd been asked by speculators to sell his crop for more than triple the normal price, but he refused.

"The Indians had purposely hunted the wildlife in the area, so any type of game was scarce. The price of salt was $8 per bushel during this time. Not many people could afford this expense, so they didn't cure meat for winter storage."

Susannah cleared her throat. "Even with more river traffic in recent years, the price for a bushel of salt has only dropped to $6 per bushel. Luckily, salt was found at Salt Lick Creek, and a factory is being built."

"Oh yes. I brought salt for you, but it's on my packhorse. My friend Nate Willis will bring our horses on Friday's packet boat. Speaking of creeks, why didn't anyone fish since the rivers and streams are filled with an abundance?"

John said, "Do you remember the first time I took you fishing near our mill?"

When I nodded, he asked, "How long did it take to catch a fish?"

I didn't answer, and he didn't say how long it had taken. Instead, he just grinned. "Not many of the settlers were fishermen, and it wasn't safe to journey to the river to fish without a military escort."

I knew my embarrassment showed. John deftly changed the topic of our conversation. A few minutes later, the baby began fussing. Susannah stood up. "Time for bed, Missy."

We helped Grace carry the leftover food and dishes indoors. Ben said, "I'd better be heading back. It's already dark." He shook our hands before he left.

Indoors, our sister showed us to Sam's room, and my brother and I shared what had once been Ben's bed. The night was hot and very humid. After a few minutes, I rose and went out on the porch where I gazed at the stars and pondered what I had seen of the land thus far and what life might be like if I decided to move here. I eventually returned to my quilt and managed to slumber.

THIRTEEN

L ittle John decided the best way to wake me was to jump on my stomach. "Wakey, Unky Inky!" He then did the same to my brother. We helped our nephews with their morning chores, then went inside for breakfast. While we ate fried mush, John said, "I need to write reports today, so I'm going to work at the library. If I don't turn these over to Uncle Rufus soon, he'll fire me. I'll return later and go with you tomorrow to meet the packet boat."

Sam and Rufus finished eating, picked up their things, and headed to school. A few moments later John left. Susannah turned to me. "Today is dairy day. Grace churns butter, and I make our cheese."

I nodded. "May I help? Do you have many customers?"

She grinned and handed me a bib apron to wear. "The single men. I have many repeat visitors."

Inside the barn, I picked up two wooden buckets filled with milk, then followed her down a well-worn path. Near a log cabin stood a two-room, stone springhouse. A small rill ran through one side of this building. Missy and little John played outside.

Susannah and Grace used a piece of cloth to strain any debris out of the fresh milk from our buckets, then set these aside to wait for the cream to separate. I saw a butter churn in the next room, and wooden shelves lined one wall. These held rounds of cheese and small blocks of butter. Both rooms had stone flooring. The walls had been whitewashed with lime and looked immaculate.

My sister pointed at several buckets which had been kept chilled by flowing water. "Ink, please help me carry this older milk to the cabin."

Carrying two buckets, I followed her to the one-room log house. I helped my sister start a fire, then Susannah strained this milk into a large cauldron which hung on a tripod over the hearth. We returned to the springhouse for more buckets and added these to the kettle. "Leave three buckets here. Please rinse out the rest and put those in the barn."

When I returned, she swung the pot away from the fire using a hook, then used her index finger to test the heat of the milk. "Almost but not quite hot enough. It only needs another minute." She smiled at me as she returned the cauldron to the fire, then stepped outside to check on her children. When Susannah returned, she picked up a large wooden paddle and handed it to me. "Please stir while I add the rennet."

A few minutes later, she said, "Now it needs to simmer for about an hour and a half, but I stir it from time to time to make sure it doesn't get too hot. I'm going to check on the butter. Please stir this while I'm gone." I nodded, and Susannah headed to the springhouse.

I glanced outside a few minutes later. It was almost mid-morning. I saw my sister pick up Missy, take little John by the hand, and head down the path. A short time later, Grace came out. My niece carried some butter on a covered platter as she headed to their house.

I stirred the pot, then turned back to the worktable and examined the two wooden presses. I admired the fine craftsmanship of each one. I knew my sister had brought a cheese press to Ohio. Jonathan must have made the second one. Underneath each press was a small wooden basin.

I was again stirring the cauldron when my sister returned. I grinned at her. "Jonathan is a fine carpenter."

Susannah kissed my cheek. "Yes, he is." She smiled. "We'll have peace and quiet for a bit. I nursed Missy and put her down for her morning nap. Grace will watch John while she fixes dinner."

I shared her smile. "If I return, will I be able to purchase cows from you?"

"Probably. It depends upon how many heifers we have when you return." She hooked the cauldron away from the fire then picked up a long wooden knife from the table. Her utensil reminded me of a ruler. She used this to cut the curds into small chunks. "Hand me a bucket please." She used her ladle to skim whey, poured this into the bucket, then returned the kettle near the fire. "It'll be awhile yet."

Susannah snipped pieces from a bolt of cloth and laid these on her worktable beside several long lengths of string. As she worked, she pointed to a barrel in the corner. "Please get out two cups of salt and place it inside that bowl."

I carried the bowl, then set it on the floor while I lifted the barrel's top. Inside was a large metal cup. I used it to measure out two scoops of salt, then bunged the lid back into place and carried her dish back to the worktable. While I was doing this task, Susannah said, "Any type of cloth is very dear, and I use a lot of it making cheese. We tried growing cotton, but an early frost destroyed our crop. Guess our climate isn't right for it." She sighed. "Turning flax into cloth is time consuming. I miss the ease of obtaining cloth back east."

"Wish I'd thought to bring some with me. I'll be sure to bring it if I return."

She used her elbow to brush an errant strand of golden hair away from her eyes. "I wish we'd brought a few sheep along with our cows. I've asked Jonathan to go to Kentucky and buy a small flock, but I guess it'll have to wait until our new house is built. He's always so busy with one thing or another."

My sister was quiet for several minutes. "How is Sarah? I mean how is she truly?"

I saw the serious expression on my sister's face. *How much does she know?* "To be honest, I can't say. She spoke to me for the first time in almost three years before I left Massachusetts. She's done her best to avoid me since Melissa died."

Susannah frowned. "That's not what I meant to ask. Does Sarah still experience quick mood changes?"

I shrugged. "I'm not sure. I noticed those for a time after Melissa was born. As I said, she hadn't spoken to me in ages until recently. Joe won't talk about it."

Susannah sighed. "I worry and pray for her daily."

I nodded. "I do too."

A short time later, she turned to the fire, removed the kettle, then placed it on a small bench. Next, she plunged her hands into the curdled milk. I watched her movements, then helped her break the curds into small pieces.

She grabbed a piece of cut cloth from the worktable. Susannah scooped small curds into its center several times. She used her fingers to mix salt into it, then twisted the cloth. She pressed the sides of her makeshift sack to drain more whey into the bucket. Her nimble fingers tied string around the top. "Move the bucket over here." She reached up and hung her sack from a hook on the far side of the table.

With another cloth in her hand, she returned to the pot. Susannah again skimmed whey from the cauldron. With deft movements, she scooped up the remaining curds, added salt, twisted the cloth into a sack, and hung it on another hook. This time I moved a bucket underneath before she asked.

"Mother never let us boys enter her dairy. What's next?"

Susannah laughed. "You know how she felt about dirt. No woman wants it in her dairy! You're more fastidious than most men. That's why I allowed you inside." She smiled, then pointed at the hanging sacks. "While those drip, I strain the cauldron." She placed another cloth over the remaining bucket. "There's always curds left, and I don't want it to spoil the whey."

I tilted the pot, careful not to splash its contents onto her puncheon floor. By the time I finished, Susannah had removed the follower from one mold. She reached up, took down a sack, and opened it. "Brush the curds from that cloth into this one please."

While I did this, my sister mixed the curds with her fingers, then added more salt. Within moments, she placed the cloth inside the form, then the follower on top. She nodded to me. I turned the handle, and more whey gushed out, pouring into the wooden catch basin. By the time I finished tightening the handle, Susannah had worked more salt into the other batch. We then repeated this process with the other press. Susannah wore a satisfied smile as she wiped her hands on her apron. "Done for now. I'll come back later to flip these over, then wash everything."

I combined whey from the two drip buckets into one, then picked up the other bucket. "You want these stored in your cellar, right?"

"No. I need one in the house, so I'll take one of those. Could you please wash the other, fill it with water, then bring it inside?"

We exchanged buckets then headed up the path. I set the empty one outside and carried the other into her cellar. Grace had dinner on the table when I returned with the water. I handed my apron to Susannah and sat down to eat.

After I ate, I said, "Going to take a ride over to Ben's place and see if I can give him a hand."

My sister smiled at me before I left.

DR. INCREASE

∞ ∞ ∞

John returned as I helped Ben, Sam, and Rufus with afternoon chores. We again ate a cold supper outside in the shade of a buckeye tree. Before we left for Marietta the following morning, I promised my sister that I would be back soon.

FOURTEEN

Leaving Belpre, my brother and I took the easterly trail which followed the circuitous path of the Ohio. The trail was now wide enough that it could easily accommodate two oxen carts. By the number of wagon ruts, it received a lot of traffic. Sometimes the river was in sight; in other spots forested areas blocked our view. John said, "This route was traveled by President Washington when he surveyed here."

While we walked, I contemplated broaching the subject of his letter to our oldest brother. I was unsure when I'd get another opportunity to discuss this matter. I decided now was the time to confront him, because when I didn't respond to his comment, John turned to me. "Is something wrong?"

"Ah." I was still hesitant to broach this subject. *Now is the time. What are you waiting for?* "Yes, there is." I reached into my money belt and took out his letter to Lish. "I want to ask you about this. I never realized you could be so mean and hurtful."

John looked startled. "What are you talking about?"

"This—" I handed him the missive. "Were you drunk when you wrote it?"

He stopped walking and unfolded the letter.

My honest friend Lish,

I received a letter dated sometime last winter. I have forgot the exact date—but that's no matter—I remember it contained your good wishes for my health and happiness and a confirmation of the steady friendship you have ever manifested. How different your conduct from some who

54

grudgingly see a little assistance lent to younger brothers. Your generous exertions to prevail on the old gentleman to help me along a little shall always be remembered though they were unsuccessful.

I hope finally no such assistance will be necessary. I shall surmount by degrees my ill luck—indeed I don't know that I may call it ill luck. I think the experience I have gained is worth much more than my losses. This is a kind of property of the best nature when well managed.

I continue still in public business at this place and shall, at all events, until next spring. I am able to clear thirty dollars per month and live well. But I hope to do better still next spring.

Anyway, I shall run some more risks. I am always prepared for events for I have steeled myself against misfortune. I don't care a fig for her.

Never to act meanly or dishonorably is the ground I hope I shall ever stand on. And then I think there is little to hear. Pray I ask is the Devil in you? Are you never a going to get married? Do you intend to grow old without having the pleasing name of Father?

No by heavens—what have you not heard? Oho, oho, yes. Yes, Phineas told us all about it. Well then don't you think he'll learn to talk—good God you never mean to call him your—.

Lish, Lish, you grow old and wicked both together. Well then, my honest fellow, to satisfy you on this score, know that I intend to strike a bargain with the first female that is not older than myself who pleases me and is ready to take me on.

John[1]

After he read a few words, he recoiled as if I'd slapped him. "How did you get your hands on this?"

"I stole it from Lish. How else would I have it?"

"Oh, Lord, no! I thought it was lost. I don't know how it got posted." Tears filled John's eyes. He wiped these away with the back of his hand. "I

---

[1] Transcript of actual letter from John Mathews to Elisha Mathews: Samuel P. Hildreth Collection, Volume 3, No. 69. Minor changes for spelling, grammar, punctuation, and clarity.

swear to you, I never mailed this."

He took several shaky steps forward, then returned to me. Tears still beaded his cheeks. "No wonder I haven't received any letters from him!"

I glared at him. "What tale did Phineas tell you?"

John's shoulders were slumped as he explained what our cousin had said. When he finished, he sighed. "I'm so sorry. You're right." His sunburned cheeks became redder, and he paced back and forth. "I was drunk when I wrote this. After I read it the next morning, I knew I shouldn't send it. If only I'd torn it up instead of putting it in my pocket. Now I must find some way to make amends with Lish."

He stopped pacing and shook the papers in his hand. "With your permission, I want to keep this. It will remind me to be more careful with my words."

I nodded.

John removed a cloth from his pocket, wiped his face, and blew his nose. "Can you tell me what really happened?"

I was the one who sighed, then paced this time. Our eldest brother was a stickler about his privacy. He had made me promise not to share this. *If I don't tell John, will he continue to believe the malicious rumor our cousin Phineas has spread?* Reaching a decision, I stopped pacing. *I'm sorry to break my pledge, Lish, but John deserves to know the truth.*

I sat down in the shade of a red maple tree which stood a few feet back from the trail. I patted the ground next to me. "Come sit." Once he was seated, I said, "Promise me that you'll never let Lish know I told you because I'm breaking my word of honor."

"I swear I'll never tell anyone."

The look in his dark sapphire-blue eyes convinced me this was true. "Lish never told me, but he knows I overheard the argument with Father. A hussy seduced him while he was with the militia during Shays's Rebellion."

"Oh, dear Lord!"

"Hush let me finish. Lish said the tavern wench flirted with him and kept his tankard full while he ate supper. He locked his door when he went to bed. She used her father's key to unlock his door, stripped naked, then climbed into bed with him. Her actions were skillful, so Lish thought she had done this before."

"How did Father get Lish out of this?"

I shook my head. "I can't say for sure. Neither of them wanted me to know. This is only hearsay—" I paused to clear my throat. "I heard a rumor that she married another soldier. I imagine she also seduced this man."

FIFTEEN

J ohn and I reached Marietta by late morning. When we neared the wharf, we could see the boat approaching. Within a few minutes, it was tied at the dock. Beanie whickered when she saw me. I introduced the men, then we helped Nate unload our horses and led them to the stable.

John said, "That's a fine-looking mare. I'd like to own one soon, but for now I just walk." His next words came out in a rush. "I need to turn in my reports at the land office, then take a canoe up the Muskingum River to continue surveying military lands. I've dallied too long. I must get back to work. I should be back here by the end of August."

I gave my brother a searching look. *Have I upset him so much that he needs to get away?*

As we exchanged hugs, John said, "This is a dangerous place with plenty of wild animals. Always take your musket if you go out exploring! Oh yes, if you perchance visit Gallipolis, please give my warmest regards to Monsieur Bureau."

My brother departed. Nate and I curried our horses, then burdened with saddlebags and sacks left the stable. We stopped at the chandlery, sold the coffee mills, then split the profit. I led the way to the Putnam home.

Uncle Rufus had returned from his business trip, and we found him seated in his study. Though he was less than six feet tall, his commanding presence and brawny frame overwhelmed me as he stood up and pulled me into a bear hug. Before I had a chance to introduce the two men, my uncle had his hand extended. "You must be Nathan Willis. General Tupper always spoke highly of you, and so do the Fearings."

A look of consternation on his face, my friend shook the proffered hand. "I'm honored to make your acquaintance, General. The Tuppers and

Fearings have always held you in the highest esteem."

After several more minutes of conversation, my uncle led the way to the Tupper home, then excused himself. Nate introduced me to his former mother-in-law Martha Tupper, who lived with her oldest son Anslem and youngest son Benjamin. Before I returned to my uncle's home, Nate and I made plans to meet on Tuesday at the Fearing's home in Harmar.

Back at the Putnam house, I went through my pack and retrieved 25 pounds of salt. Aunt Persis was thrilled with my gift. During my absence, she arranged a family gathering for Saturday, July 28th. She then gave me invitations from my cousins for dinners and suppers throughout the week culminating in a Friday night dinner with Territorial Governor Arthur St. Clair and the other local dignitaries.

I tried to demure the invitation to the governor's dinner because I had only packed travel clothes. Aunt Persis wouldn't accept my refusal and insisted that she and her daughters would make a homespun suit for me.

It was much easier to accept than continue to decline. My week was filled with activities as I became reacquainted with my Putnam cousins. Persis had married Perley Howe in May and now lived in Belpre. Susanna, her husband Christopher Burlingame, and their four children lived across the river in Harmar. William Rufus was an apprenticed surveyor and unmarried. Edwin, also unmarried, was acting Register for the Ohio Company's Land Office. Abigail had married William Browning. They were expecting a child, had a four-year-old son, and lived in Belpre.

∞ ∞ ∞

On Tuesday afternoon, I ferried over and met Nate at the Fearing home in Harmar. Its fort had been built at the confluence of the Muskingum and Ohio Rivers in 1785, and its location had influenced the Ohio Company's decision to settle here. Like Campus Martius, the fort had been dismantled and its lumber used to build homes. Coming back across the river to Marietta, we stopped and viewed the area where the Picketed Point Stockade had been built in 1791.

∞ ∞ ∞

I attended an afternoon picnic held at the Browning's home on Thursday. After we had eaten our fill, the gentlemen gathered into a group. A jug of hard cider was passed between us. Since I was only a visitor to

59

Ohio, I kept my mouth closed and listened intently to what my relatives said.

Some were in favor of Ohio gaining statehood as soon as possible; others agreed with St. Clair's delaying tactics. The men discussed the merits of electing William Henry Harrison and his likely change to the existing land laws. They also discussed the territory's current anti-slavery laws. I agreed with their anti-slavery sentiment, but some feared that this law would change because of the influx of men from the southern states. As I listened to these men discuss Ohio politics, I realized that Ohio would not become a state for several more years.

∞ ∞ ∞

Before Friday's dinner with the Governor, my uncle asked me to accompany him. We ferried over to Harmar and visited the Fearing home. Worried that Nate or I might commit a faux pas, Rufus said, "Please be closed mouth in your conversations with St. Clair. When he served as Major General and Commander of Fort Harmar, his tactics led to the most crushing defeat in the history of the United States! You both know President Washington requested and received his military resignation. However, he continues to hold the position of Governor. He does *not* want immediate statehood for Ohio, while many inhabitants want statehood as quickly as possible. St. Clair continues to exercise a tyrannical supervision over his subordinates in the legislative process and is opposed to the election of William Henry Harrison as the territory's first delegate to Congress."

Rufus sighed. "I believe his sole purpose in coming here is to determine who is likely to be a candidate for the territorial legislature. He'll try to use his persuasion to sway the voting populace. Please don't tell him that I plan to be a candidate."

We thanked him for sharing these insights and assured him we would be careful in our speech.

∞ ∞ ∞

Thus forewarned, the ballroom dinner went smoothly as Nate and I managed to steer clear of any touchy subjects when we met Governor St. Clair. We were introduced to many dignitaries, such as Andrew Craigie who was here on a brief visit. We also met many war veterans, such as

DR. INCREASE

Colonel Ebenezer Sproat, Major Hatfield White and Captain Jonathan Devol. I enjoyed hearing their descriptions of the lands they had traversed during the Indian wars.

Shortly after we had eaten, the Governor and his entourage departed to return to Chillicothe. The remaining gentlemen gathered into a group, and a barrel of whiskey was tapped. Uncle Rufus raised his drink high into the air. "To the *USS Delaware!*"

Newspapers from the east had arrived on the packet boat. All reported that the *La Croyable* had been taken captive by the *USS Delaware* because of a recent attack on a merchant ship by a French privateer. Congress had recently authorized the capture of any French vessel which preyed upon one of our merchant ships. This was the first time the new United States Navy had been successful.

My uncle's toast was greeted by a chorus of "Delaware!" followed by a loud cry of "Down with the French!" made by several men. Our relations with both Britain and France were strained due to their continued war in Europe. Both countries had taken to attacking our merchant vessels and to impressing men into service on their ships.

I turned to Nate. "Do you think France will declare war on us?"

He said, "No. I think they have their hands full fighting the British." Nate turned, grinned at an approaching man, then slapped him on the back. "Ink, this gentleman is my brother-in-law, Paul Fearing. Paul, this is my friend, Dr. Increase Mathews."

I shook Paul's hand, and he pointed to his companion. "He's Will Skinner. We plan to explore the countryside to the west, but we can't leave for several days. Would you like to come with us?"

Nate and I arranged to go with them.

SIXTEEN

Wednesday, August 1, 1798

I forded my mare across the Muskingum early in the morning to meet Nate, Paul, and Will at Harmar, then we headed west on a new road. Its trees still showed the trail-blazing marks made by surveyors.

I thought both men appeared closer to Nate's age than mine. Paul had moved his horse to ride beside me as we left the settlement. "I must say you look like you're barely twenty. Isn't that awful young to be a doctor?"

"I'm twenty-five, Sir. I finished my medical apprenticeship three years ago."

He nodded. "No need to be so formal. You make me feel old by calling me Sir." He rode in silence for several moments. "So, Doc, Nate told me you may return to settle here. Do you have any idea where you want to look?"

"Please call me Ink. I'm not sure. I've dreamed of becoming a farmer who owns a lot of land, so I'd like to find acreage near a river. This would allow me to transport my goods to market."

Will raised his voice so I could hear him over the clopping hooves. "New people are arriving almost daily. The land along waterways is always first to be sold. When will you return to buy?"

"I need to wait for the price to be lowered or credit terms to be implemented, because I can't afford to purchase any acreage now."

Both men nodded, then we continued riding in silence. When we came upon a rock which had been excavated and was large enough to shelter a regiment, we marveled at it and wondered whether it was French or American soldiers who had used it as a temporary fort. We continued westward through a forest of birch, cottonwood, sugar maple, and buckeye trees. When we reached a small clearing in the woods late in the afternoon, we made camp.

I pulled Nate aside. "I confess I've never had to set up a tent."

Nate looked surprised. "Didn't you learn while with the militia?"

"No. We only bivouacked."

He nodded, then helped me cut the oilcloth and set up my tent. We draped mosquito netting over the entrance. Once this was finished, we gathered kindling and started a cookfire.

Nate and I tried fishing in a nearby stream but didn't catch anything. Luckily, Will was a capable shot, and we soon had a rabbit stew cooking over our fire. After we ate, Paul kept us amused by sharing events that happened during the Indian War. When it grew dark, we settled into our tents for the night.

Thursday, August 2nd

In the morning, we continued our westward course. We traversed hills and valleys. The land appears good for grain and pasturing. We reached a branch of Federal Creek, called Big Run, where we stopped and refilled our canteens with its cold, clear water. Will said, "They named it Federal Creek because of its 13 branches. We'll cross it several times."

Following Big Run, we encountered another branch. We followed this one south until we reached the falls where the creek empties into a river. Paul said, "The Indians call this one the Hockhocking because of its bottle shape." He pointed north. "It's narrower up there, then widens here at the falls."

We stayed on its east side and went up this river. The bottoms seem excellent land for growing grain. Shortly after the falls, the Hockhocking flowed southward. We followed it and camped by a small run.

Nate and I caught fish upstream in a narrow shoal. We enjoyed the catfish along with vegetables supplied by Will. After we ate, Paul asked, "Where else do you plan to explore?"

"I'd like to join Captain Stone and see the lands he's currently surveying for the university."

"Please stop by and tell me about it when you return."

I nodded. Worn out from my exertions, I headed to my tent. It wasn't long before I snored.

Friday, August 3rd

We'd left the horses free to graze last night. While we slept, our mares had wandered away. It took us several hours before we found them three miles from our camp. Once again riding, we followed the Hockhocking south then turned east when we came across a blazed trail heading toward Marietta. We followed the trail for several miles until we heard the rapids. We then turned south and came across Plum Run, a section of Wolf Creek.

The day had turned stormy in the afternoon, so we made an early camp. The night was miserable because the ground and bushes were soaked, and we were much fatigued from our travel in the rain. By morning, our tents were drenched.

Saturday August 4th

Traveling today was miserable. The rain continued and increased in intensity. The countryside was full of underbrush. With this much pouring rain, the oilcloth couldn't shield it all, and I, like my companions, became soaked. Paul and Will were not familiar with this area, so we often had to traverse precipices and cross Wolf Creek several times in order to proceed.

We arrived at Ford's farm late in the afternoon then followed the road to Major Hatfield White's homestead where we slept on his floor. It was a relief to be out of the rain, and the major was kind enough to start a fire so we could dry our things.

Sunday, August 5th

The morning was drizzly. Before leaving, we toured the mill built by Major White, Colonel Robert Oliver, and Captain John Dodge. This was the first stationary, instead of floating, gristmill to be built in the Ohio Territory and supplied much of its grain to Marietta.

Setting out, we followed Wolf Creek generally north until we reached the Muskingum River. We followed this south to reach Wiseman's Bottom which lies a few miles above Marietta. My brother-in-law and Captain Jonathan Devol had built a floating mill in Belpre and, when Captain Devol moved to Wiseman's Bottom in 1797, he constructed another floating grain mill.

DR. INCREASE

We stopped at the captain's home to eat dinner and dry out. It was pouring when we left his house. When we arrived in Marietta, Nate and I said farewell to the other men who forded across the river to Harmar. We stabled our horses then hurried through the rain to the Putnam home.

SEVENTEEN

We were thoroughly drenched when we arrived. I led the way into my uncle's study and started a fire in his hearth. My aunt appeared with steaming cups of cider, then retreated to her kitchen. Though it remained inclement, it had been a warm day, so it wasn't long before our clothes were dry.

Nate had been rather reticent during our trip. I thought this had been due to the miserable weather. Now, he sat in front of my uncle's desk with a brooding look on his face while he stroked his square chin. After several minutes of silence, I became worried that I'd done something wrong. "Nate, what's the matter? Have I—?"

"What? Oh sorry, Ink. No, it's not you."

"There's something wrong. Would it help to talk about it?"

His strong brow wrinkled. Several moments passed and the brooding look remained on his face. Finally, he started speaking. "Didn't you think it was odd that the Tuppers requested that I travel with you?"

I nodded. He cleared his throat before he continued. "It was a delicate matter that Mrs. Tupper didn't want to address in a letter. She wanted to meet me face-to-face."

Puzzled, I waited.

"This is so difficult to discuss." He let out a small gasp. "She wants me to exhume Sophia." Another larger gasp escaped his lips. "She'd like to have her daughter buried here. Her sons agree but have left the decision in my hands."

"Oh my! It is a tough situation, indeed. Have you reached a decision?"

He shook his head. Tears stood in his eyes, and misery cloaked his face. Silence descended as I tried to think of words to help my friend. "I'm sure

Lucy and your three children keep you very busy. How often do you have time to visit Sophia's grave?"

"I make it a point to go every spring and fall, tend her site, and trim the weeds."

My thoughts would be difficult to convey without further upsetting him, but I thought the words must be said. "There's no easy way for her mother to visit Sophia's grave. Wouldn't her mother and brothers tend it more often than you can?"

He nodded. I pondered for a few moments before I continued, hoping he would understand my position. "She was your wife for only a short time, but Sophia will always be her daughter."

"Yes." He stood up then strode back and forth across the room. After a few minutes, he said, "I see your point."

His pace slowed. When he reached the window, he stopped and gazed at the rain outside while he continued to contemplate my words. "I don't like it, but you're right. Her final resting place should be here with her family, where they can visit her grave often. Thanks for sharing your thoughts."

While I saw some relief on his face, his misery was still apparent. However, with his decision made, he was now anxious to see his family. "As soon as there's an open passage on the packet boat, I'll begin my return journey to Rochester. Don't worry about repaying me for my packhorse."

I nodded. "I plan to go to my sister's home tomorrow, and I'm unsure how long I'll be away because I'd like to join my brother-in-law's survey."

"That's fine. Let me know when you return to Massachusetts. Thanks again for your advice. It clarified my thinking."

"Are you willing to wait a few minutes while I write a short letter to Nabby?"

When he nodded, I sat down at my uncle's desk and composed a short two-page letter in which I told her of my resolve to marry her and described what I'd seen since reaching Marietta.

I hugged Nate as I handed him my letter. "Godspeed your journey home and keep you safe."

EIGHTEEN

Hoping to explore more of the area, I rearranged my items, fitting as much as I could into Beanie's saddlebags. I left the packhorses in the stable and took the trail to Susannah's home.

She answered my knock. After we exchanged hugs, I handed her my gift. "Here's the salt I brought for you."

"This will help a lot with making cheese and curing meat! Thank you so much."

By now, her family had surrounded us, but I didn't see my brother-in-law. "Where's Jonathan? I hoped to join him on a survey."

"He was home for two days last week so he could file his paperwork. Sorry you missed him." Susannah paused to think for a few moments. "I think he may be surveying near Gallipolis. I suggest you talk to the surveyors. One of them is usually inside their office in Belpre. Whoever is there should be able to give you directions to his camp."

I hugged her, then rode Beanie to the survey office. Inside I introduced myself. The gentleman said, "Oh, you must be John's brother. He's talked about your arrival for weeks now."

"I'd like to know where my brother-in-law is surveying. Susannah said you'd be able to tell me."

"Hmm, let me look it up." He shuffled some papers. "Yes, Jonathan is out near Raccoon Creek, southwest of the Gallipolis settlement. You'll need to take a packet to reach Gallipolis. Once there, ask for directions to Mr. Safford's place. He cares for Captain Stone's provisions, and he'll be able to give you better directions than I can." He extended his hand which I shook. I thanked him, then headed to the wharf.

The dockmaster said, "Packet boat won't arrive until next Monday and should be here about 1 o'clock."

I nodded my thanks. As I turned to leave, I took a step back and trampled on the feet of the gentleman behind me. "Oh, excuse me. I'm sorry I bumped you." From my glance, I could see he was close to my age. Dark hair and eyes with prominent cheekbones, he was dressed in frontier-style clothing and wore a coon skin cap.

"No harm done." He smiled then extended his hand. "I'm Edward Tupper and I plan on taking that boat too."

I shook his hand. "I'm Dr. Increase Mathews."

He said, "Do you mind if I ask why you're going to Gallipolis?"

"My brother-in-law, Jonathan Stone, is surveying near there."

"I thought so! You're Susannah's and John's youngest brother. You must be Nate's friend."

When I nodded, he grinned. "I'm another son of General Tupper."

"Oh! I've met your mother and your brothers Anslem and Benjamin. Well I guess I'll see you next Monday."

Edward nodded. "You can count on it."

As I rode back to my sister's home, I noticed the Putnam Family/Farmers Library which had been established in 1795 by my uncle's second cousin, Colonel Israel Putnam Jr. This was where John had gone to work on his reports. When I returned to the Stone's home, I told Susannah that the packet would not arrive until next Monday. "Are you and Jonathan library shareholders?"

"Of course we are."

"Please accompany me to the library. I'd like some books to pass the time."

"Always the bookworm." She smiled. "Give me a few minutes to put on better clothes. Grace please watch the little ones while we're gone."

Susannah went to change. Since it was a pleasant morning for a walk, I put Beanie out to pasture. When we reached the library, I was amazed to see such a large collection of books in the frontier. With my sister's assistance I borrowed two books: Edmund Burke's *Reflections on the Revolution in France* and *Observations on Respiration and the Use of the Blood* written by Joseph Priestly.

Grace had dinner ready when we returned. After eating, I started reading about respiration. Priestly's work had been mentioned in several medical periodicals I'd borrowed from Dr. Field. While these articles had included brief quotations, I was happy to read his work in its entirety. Absorbed in this book, the afternoon passed quickly, so I was surprised when Sam and Rufus arrived home from school. While we ate supper, my sister said, "Since the packet won't arrive until next week, how do you plan to spend your time here?"

"I thought I'd take morning trips to explore this area, then read in the evenings." I paused. "Is there anything you need me to do?"

She smiled. "Could you make a batch of dye? I have cloth for a new dress for Grace but would like the material dyed." Susannah turned to her daughter and laughed. "He has a knack for making the perfect colors!"

My niece squealed. "Oh, yes please. It would be lovely to have a new dress to wear to the next ball."

"I'll look for something in the morning."

∞ ∞ ∞

Once again, little John decided to jump on my stomach to wake me. This time I managed to grab him before he ran away and proceeded to tickle him until he cried, "Uncle!".

After breakfast, I filled my canteen then saddled Beanie. I took the more northerly one of the two trails which headed toward Marietta. This trail headed due north for several miles and had not yet been widened into a road. Once I passed Crooked Creek, I kept a lookout for a trail which headed west. When I reached the Mill Branch of the Hockhocking, I noticed some wild mulberry trees. I hurried back to my sister's home because I needed something to hold the fruit.

Susannah and Grace were in the springhouse. "You're back much sooner than we expected."

I smiled. "I found some mulberries, so I came back to let you know and to get buckets."

My sister returned my smile. "Wonderful! Grace is done churning the butter. She can go with you in our wagon while I finish making cheese."

Beanie had never been hitched to a wagon. My niece brought buckets, then climbed on board. The pinto snorted her displeasure and shook her head several times, but she settled down once we were on our way. I let

70

my mare graze on the grasses near the stream as we filled buckets with mulberries.

After we ate dinner and the littlest children were napping, we sorted the berries. While my sister and niece made jam and syrup in their kitchen, I went outside and mashed up damaged berries to make the dye. When this was bubbling, I heated salt water in another pot, added the cloth then allowed it to simmer. It was over an hour later when I strained the berries from the liquid, then added the cloth to soak. When Grace said the material was dyed the perfect purple, I rinsed it in vinegar water to set the dye. My niece then pegged it on the line to dry.

∞ ∞ ∞

I turned to Susannah after all her children were in bed. "Why do you have a son named Rufus, but not a son named Daniel?"

She hesitated. I thought she wasn't going to answer, but then she spoke. "Did Mother ever mention that Uncle Rufus was apprenticed to Father?"

I shook my head and settled in a chair near the hearth to listen.

"Instead of treating Rufus like a member of the family, Father refused to allow him to attend school. Our uncle didn't like working in the mill, and he began studying in the loft every night. He would take a candle upstairs so he could study books about mathematics, geography, and surveying. Father constantly harassed him saying Rufus would burn the house down. Mother told me that she and Father argued constantly while Rufus lived there.

"I was just a toddler when Uncle Rufus left. He'd finished his apprenticeship and decided to follow his father's cousin Israel into military service. He was placed in Captain Learned's company, and they left Brookfield in 1757 to fight in the French and Indian War.

"I missed him because he'd always taken time to play with me." Susannah stared at me. "You know what Father is like. The only person who ever mattered has been his golden boy, Elisha."

I nodded. "I'm sad to say that's true."

"Even back then, Jonathan and Francis Stone didn't get along. My husband fled his apprenticeship with his brother and boarded a whaler. When he returned, we were at war, so he joined the Continental Army. Did you know that Uncle Rufus introduced us?"

Susannah did not wait for me to respond. "I was lucky because he was assigned to our uncle's command. When Rufus learned of Jonathan's interest in surveying, he took him under his wing. He always has our best interest in mind, so we honored him."

I hugged her and thanked her for explaining then went to bed in Sam's room.

∞ ∞ ∞

I spent the next several days exploring in the mornings, helping Ben in the afternoons, and reading in the evenings. I went to help Ben pull tree stumps on Friday morning because it looked like rain.

It was storming by mid-morning, so I hurried to my sister's house. I was barely inside when lightning struck nearby. Little John cried out. I picked him up and tickled him. "Your grandmother always said the boom was caused by angels kicking over the potato wagon up in heaven." He thought this was funny and smiled. When I put him down, he scampered away from me.

NINETEEN

A few hours later, Ben arrived. From the doorway he called for Susannah to come outside. Curious, I followed my sister. He was thoroughly drenched and looked upset. Ben wiped water from his face and spoke in a low voice. "There's a runaway slave. He's in the back of my wagon. I didn't know where to put him, so I drove it inside the barn. The man's in bad shape."

"Move him to the cabin." Susannah stepped inside to pick up the tinderbox and a candle. She grabbed her cape from its peg by the door. "Grace, watch the children and finish fixing supper."

We headed into the pouring rain. I retrieved my medical kit and cloak from Beanie's saddlebags, then hurried after Ben. I glanced at the slave when Susannah lit her candle. Before I could start my examination, she said, "Wait."

My nephew pushed the table which held the cheese presses, and it moved back several inches. Underneath it, I could now see a trap door. "Here, let me help you."

Susannah held the candle high when we opened the door. I assisted Ben with getting the runaway down a ladder to the area below. My sister followed us and lit another candle on a nearby table. My nephew left.

With the light from the candles, I could see the hidden area was a hole in the dirt, much smaller than the room above, but large enough to contain a table, chair, and straw mattress on the floor. Susannah helped me seat the poor man sideways on the chair.

I had just removed my cloak when Ben returned with rags and a bucket of water. After he set these down, my nephew pushed a wet strand of hair away from his forehead. "I think there's a catcher near. I'm going to close the cabin's door. I'll keep watch from inside the house."

I nodded then turned to examine my patient. His shirt was firmly stuck to several pus-filled scars on his back. I took scissors from my kit and cut as much cloth as I dared to remove. I took a rag, dipped it in water, and set it to soak on his back. My patient was delirious, his skin extremely hot to my touch. I removed a small pouch of ground willow bark from my kit and handed it to Susannah. "Please make a pot of tea with this. Do you have honey?"

My sister nodded. "Do you want some in the tea?"

"No. I want to apply it to his infected wounds."

She nodded and left. Several minutes later, I removed the wet rag and plucked the remaining bits of cloth away from his skin using tweezers. Once this was accomplished, I could see the extent of damage to his back. He bore numerous scars; some were quite old. However, two scars below his left shoulder blade were close together and heavily infected. I would need to lance both to drain the pus. To do this, I decided it would be best to wait until I could lay the man down on his belly on the straw mattress.

Susannah arrived. She carried her teapot, beaker, spoon, and a container of honey. I poured some whiskey from my hip flask, added tea, and a pinch of ginseng, then stirred it. Rubbing his throat, I managed to get the poor man to swallow some of this liquid concoction.

"He'll need to be kept still while I work. I'm afraid he'll thrash too much for you. Please ask Ben or Sam to come help me."

"It'll have to be Ben. Rufus is still too young to understand or to keep quiet about this. He follows Sam everywhere, just as you always followed John."

She returned with my nephew a few minutes later. I said, "Ben, sit on the ground by the man's head. Do your best to hold his arms outstretched."

I seated myself on the slave's lower back before I picked up my surgical knife. As I lanced the larger carbuncle, the man writhed beneath me. Susannah whispered to him in a soothing voice. "Hush now. You're safe. Everything will be all right. Please lay still while the doctor tends your wounds."

The runaway's squirming eased. I drew my knife down the length of the second one. Susannah handed a rag to me. I kneaded the boils and wiped away pus until only blood flowed from the wounds. "Susannah, burn these rags and the man's shirt."

She nodded. I wiped the area with a clean, wet rag to remove any remaining residue from his skin then stitched his wounds closed. Ben helped me move my patient to the chair, then returned to the house. Next, I applied honey to the slave's wounds, then covered it with walnut salve from my kit. Taking a long length of rag, I firmly wound it around the slave's back and chest.

While I worked, I told Susannah, "Get that pouch of ginseng and add two pinches to another beaker of tea."

I added a splash of whiskey to this concoction, stirred it, and held it for the man to drink. The runaway was terrified. His eyes bulged and shifted around the room looking for a way to escape. Susannah kept addressing him in her calm voice. Her soothing manner soon convinced him we meant no harm. At last, he drank the tea and grimaced when he finished.

We eased the man from the chair and once again laid him on his stomach on the straw mattress. "You shouldn't move too much or rollover. You could tear your stitches out if you do. You need to rest and heal."

I turned to my sister. "Go eat supper. I'll keep watch."

It wasn't long before Ben returned. A cold rain was still falling when I ran back to the house. I dried my hair with an old towel. Someone had added another log to the fire. I was grateful for its warmth. Susannah sat at their table and spoke in a quiet voice while I ate. "Once my little ones are asleep, I'll return to the cabin and send Ben home, because everything *must* appear normal in the morning. Someone could be watching our movements. Would you take care of the poor man later so I can get some sleep?"

I nodded, changed into my nightshirt, draped my wet things near the hearth, then went to bed. I awoke several hours later and dressed. I made some chamomile tea in a hollowed gourd, then poured a dram of peach brandy from the jug on their mantlepiece into another one. It was still raining, so I pulled on my hooded cloak, slipped Burke's book into its pocket, cradled the trenchers under it, and headed to the cabin.

Down in the room, Susannah donned her cape. "He's slept the entire time."

I nodded and she left. I put the trenchers on the table. I shook water from my cloak before I draped it over the chair. I added two pinches of willow bark and ginseng into the beaker which held hot tea. I added whiskey from my flask, stirred it, then set it on the table. I roused the runaway and helped him to the chair.

He remained very feverish. I held the beaker to his lips and managed to get him to drink it. Then I gave him the trencher of peach brandy. After he drank about half, I helped him back to the mattress, once again placing him to sleep on his belly.

Susannah had covered him with an old sheet, and I gently pulled this up over his back. I removed the book from my cloak, settled into the chair, and stretched out my legs. It wasn't long before I heard snores as my patient fell into a deep sleep. I read for a bit, then dozed off to the sounds of snoring and the patter of raindrops.

TWENTY

Before dawn on Saturday, Grace came to watch over the patient. I helped Sam and Rufus with the farm's chores. After we ate breakfast and the boys went out to hoe weeds in their fields, I prepared more healing tea. My sister walked beside me as we headed to the cabin. She said, "I'm afraid Ben's right, and there may be slave catchers nearby. We must close the trap door today and move the table back over it. Will you mind being left down there?"

I shook my head. "I'll use a candle and spend my time reading."

"If you hear voices, blow it out. I'm afraid light may show through the chinks."

I nodded. "Does this happen often? Why do you help?"

"Several times a year. Why shouldn't we help when they are so desperate to get away?" Susannah exhaled a deep breath. "Every one of them has been abused in some way. One woman's child was as white as you and me. She told me her master raped her almost daily. She was still a child when he started doing this to her. He had done the same to her mother. She wanted to get away before he raped her daughter." She glanced at me. "Don't you think that's evil incarnate?"

My words came out in a rush. "Of course I do. Where do they go from here?"

"As soon as they're able to travel, we send them north. I don't know where they go."

Susannah remained upstairs as I went down the ladder. After Grace climbed up, they shut the trap door. I heard the table moving across the floor above me. When I touched the man's shoulder, he was awake, more aware of his surroundings, and extremely scared. In a quiet voice, I said,

"I'm a doctor and performed surgery on your back. You need to drink this." I handed him a beaker filled with willow bark tea, ginseng, and whiskey. When he finished, I gave him the brandy trencher. When it was empty, he stumbled back to the mattress. I again settled into the chair, picked up Burke's novel, but didn't read many pages before I dozed.

I was startled awake by the distant sound of voices outside. I glanced at the man and saw he was sound asleep. I blew out the candle and did my best to remain calm. My heartbeat raced.

The cabin door thumped. Someone entered the room. Sam's voice floated down. "See, I told you my mother uses this building to make her cheese. If you follow me to the springhouse, I'll give you some. She makes the best in this area."

No one answered my nephew. The puncheon floor reverberated with the heavy tread of boots overhead. I held my breath. After several moments, the trudging steps retreated. The door closed, then there was silence.

Spots flared in my eyes. My breath escaped in a rush. I was afraid to light the candle and sat there, shaking in the darkness. I'm unsure how long it was before I again heard voices on the outside path. I waited several minutes before I used the tinderbox to relight the candle.

I saw my patient was awake. His eyes were wide, and he trembled. To ease his fear, I whispered, "You should be fine now. The catcher has gone." I helped him move to the chair, then removed his binding and examined his back. There wasn't any sign of recurring infection. While I worked, I asked him questions in a subdued voice. "What's your name? Where did you come from?"

His voice was deep, and he spoke in the southern manner with long, drawn-out vowels. "Johari, but Masta called me Tom Two." He gasped as I applied more honey, then walnut salve to his wounds. "Born in Caroleenah. Masta sold wife and daughter to man in Vageenny. Tried to find 'em but almost got catched. Knowed I had to keep moving cause I been catched before."

I rewound the rag around his back and chest. "You're on the mend, Johari, but you must rest. I'm afraid if you move around too much, you'll rip the stitches."

He nodded and returned to the mattress. He soon drifted off to sleep. I sat in the chair and thought about this poor man's plight.

DR. INCREASE

I remembered the 1781 Worcester County court case which awarded freedom to Quock Walker because his previous master had promised him manumission when he died. Instead, Walker had been sold to another slave owner. Our judicial system had ruled perpetual servitude was contrary to the Commonwealth's constitution and to the Bible. While Massachusetts hadn't abolished slavery, no slaves remained by the 1790 Federal Census.

This had been an eye-opening experience for me. No one I knew kept slaves. Father said some of our ancestors had come to America as indentured servants. *What if our family members had been perpetual servants? Would I have even been born?*

I had never thought about this matter. Now, I became convinced any form of slavery was an abomination.

∞ ∞ ∞

It was dinnertime when I heard Grace overhead. "Oh, fiddlesticks. What a mess." Sam shifted the table, and my niece opened the trap door. "I know Momma will have me cleaning this floor today." Disgruntled, she groaned. "She'll want it spotless!" She leaned over the ladder. "Here take these, Uncle Ink."

I took a bowl of chicken broth from her, then a trencher from him, and placed both on the table. Grace climbed down the ladder. She pulled a new candle from her pocket and put it near the candlestick. "Momma said you should go eat. I'm to stay here until you get back."

I added pinches of ginseng then whiskey to the beaker before I headed upstairs. My nephew was waiting for me. We closed the trap and moved the table. "I'm surprised to see you Sam. Where's your shadow?"

He grinned. "I told Rufus to muck out the barn. I'm going to help Ben this afternoon."

I nodded as we headed outdoors. The sun had broken through the clouds and the fields steamed. My nephew turned and took the path to his brother's place.

The kitchen was empty when I entered the house. A plate of food was being kept warm next to the hearth. Before I finished eating, my sister entered the room. Susannah smiled. "Melissa and little John are napping." She picked up dirty dishes from her table. After she washed these, she sat down near me. "Did you get enough to eat?" I grinned and nodded. She stood, then took my dirty plate and utensils. Before she turned back to the sink, she asked, "How's our patient doing?"

"Johari's fever has broken. He's on the mend though his stitches should stay in for a few more days."

"So, Tuesday?"

I thought for a moment. "At least until Tuesday. Wednesday would be better."

My sister nodded. "'Bout what I expected." She wiped her wet hands on her apron. "Wait for me. I'll go with you."

We walked down the path together. "Aren't you afraid of being found out?"

Susannah said, "Yes, I do worry, but both Jonathan and I feel it's worth the risk." She smiled. "When he builds our new home, there'll be a small, hidden room upstairs, above the kitchen. Then there'll be less chance of our being found out."

When we reached the cabin, my sister got angry. "Oh my! We can't have this mess near my cheese!"

I shifted the table, and she opened the trap door. Grace grinned up at us as we climbed down. "Yes, Momma. I'll get started cleaning right away."

The slave was still seated at the table. My sister turned toward him. "My brother told me your name is Johari. Is this correct?"

"Yes ma'am."

She smiled to reassure him. "Here's what we're going to do. I'm sure in a little while men will come here to buy my cheeses. Several always show up on Saturday afternoons." She paused for a moment and patted his right shoulder. "We need to shut you inside here for now, but we'll be back to bring food and drink. You must remain down here alone for several days while your wounds heal. Can you do this?"

Though his eyes displayed his fear, Johari nodded. Susannah turned to me. "It would be best if you weren't around either. The less questions asked, the better. Why don't you go help Ben and Sam?"

Upstairs, we closed the trap. Grace left to fetch a bucket of water and soap. Susannah got her broom and swept the dirt toward the doorway, then I helped her move the table back. "Should I take Beanie with me?"

"Yes, that's a good idea. Some men might poke their head inside our barn to look at the heifers."

DR. INCREASE

On Sunday, we went to the meeting hall where church services were held. Usually one of the settlement's members served as deacon, but Reverend Daniel Story was here today to preach the Sunday service. He had been employed by the Ohio Company and continued to provide traveling ministerial services to the settlements at Marietta, Belpre, and Waterford. My sister introduced me to the congregation and told them I'd be joining her husband on his survey.

While Grace and Susannah finished dinner preparations, I returned to the cabin to check on Johari. As I applied more salve to his injuries, I said, "I'll be leaving tomorrow morning. There's no sign of infection, but you need to keep drinking willow bark tea if you don't want your fever to return. Susannah will remove your stitches in a few days. After these are removed, try to keep your back dry so the infection doesn't return. Someone will bring you some food in a little bit. May you have safe travels." I shook his hand, picked up my medical kit, and returned to the house.

When Rufus went out to do his chores, I said, "It would be best to let Johari recover until Wednesday. Here's a pouch of willow bark. He should be given tea for two more days."

Ben said, "I'll assist Johari and show him which way to go."

TWENTY-ONE

Monday, August 13th

I put Beanie out to pasture after breakfast then got ready to depart. As Susannah helped me bind my bedroll across my shoulders, she whispered that I shouldn't mention Johari to Jonathan because she didn't want him to worry. I murmured my agreement and gave her a kiss. I hugged Grace, tousled the children's hair, then slung my saddlebags over my shoulder along with a full canteen and my musket. When I reached the settlement, I stopped by its library to return the borrowed books.

Edward Tupper was there when I reached the wharf. "I've been hoping you'd be here early. Have you heard about the mansion that's being built on the river island?"

I shook my head.

With a mischievous grin, he said, "I thought you might like to see it, so I've borrowed a canoe."

We rowed across to the island. The Harman Blennerhassett family already resided in the large, two-story, central wing of their home. They made us welcome, and we toured the remaining construction. Two other smaller wings would be adjoined to the main home by a covered gallery when it was completed within the next few weeks. It rivaled any mansion I'd seen in Cambridge, Massachusetts.

We were introduced to Miss London who was visiting. She seemed an unaffected, amiable young woman. We chatted with her and Mrs. Blennerhassett for a while then rowed back to Belpre.

The packet to Gallipolis left the pier at 1 o'clock. It was a cooler, pleasant afternoon. I dozed, lulled by the gliding rhythm of the water as we floated downriver. Early in the evening the boat made its scheduled stop in Belleville, Virginia. We decided to go ashore for supper.

Edward took a swallow of ale then grinned. "So, what did you think of their mansion?"

"I thought it was an excessive display of extravagance. Is the man trying to recreate some Irish castle?"

My companion shrugged then took a bite of food. "So, did you attend the Governor's dinner?"

"Yes, and I had the pleasure of meeting the celebrated Andrew Craigie."

"Pfft!" Food spewed from his mouth. Startled, I looked to see if he was choking. Face red with anger, he said, "He's a scoundrel of the worst sort! A mountebank!"

"What makes you say that?"

Edward took a swallow to clear his throat before he replied. "Do you know Craigie was a close crony to the infamous William Duer?"

"No. I only knew he was appointed as Apothecary General during the war."

Edward continued before I finished speaking. "Well, he was one of the principal land speculators in the Scioto Company debacle." He pointed at me. "You know his company swindled the French who settled in Gallipolis?"

I nodded. I was aware of the difficulties the French encountered, but I hadn't realized Craigie had been involved in the Scioto Company. "My Uncle Rufus wrote us about that travesty." I thought for a moment. "This must be how Craigie had the means to build a mansion in Cambridge. Why would such an honored man be so greedy?"

Edward shrugged. "Some men will use any means to make money." He cleared his throat. "So, my purpose in traveling to Gallipolis is to inform four French families that Congress has made an additional land grant to them. This law was enacted at the end of June and we just received word."

"How did Andrew Craigie survive the financial panic of 1792 when so many other Scioto speculators, like Royal Flint and Richard Platt, were bankrupted?"

He said, "I have no idea, but I truly wish Craigie had joined Duer, Flint, and Platt in debtor's prison."

Edward and I had been so engrossed in conversation that we'd failed to keep track of time. When we reached the wharf, we found our boat had left. We went inside the dockmaster's office to check the schedule. The man said, "Next stop will be Pond Creek. If you hire a canoe, you should be able to beat it there."

We followed his advice, reached Pond Creek ahead of the packet, and requested shelter in a nearby cabin because it was now drizzling. Its owners gave us blankets to use, but these were infested. Troubled by fleas and afraid that we would miss the packet, we could not sleep and went out into a light rain to await the boat.

Tuesday, August 14th

The rain stopped before we boarded about half past midnight. Fearful of snags, our downriver progress was slow until daylight. About noon we reached the rapids called Letart Falls which is about 65 miles from Marietta. Navigation through this area was tricky, especially with the river's level as low as today.

The day remained overcast, and we were still about eighteen miles from Gallipolis at dusk. Our boatmen continued rowing until 9 o'clock, then decided to sleep and let the boat float along the current. Concerned we might encounter a deadhead in the dark, I didn't sleep well.

We were still about three miles from our destination at dawn and arrived in Gallipolis just after sunrise. Edward gave me a brief tour of the settlement, then we parted company.

TWENTY-TWO

Wednesday, August 15th

I followed directions I'd received from the Belpre surveyor and found Mr. Safford's place. I told him I was Captain Stone's brother-in-law, and he provided a hearty breakfast. While I ate, he said "Contact Mr. Bufford. He'll take you out there for a fee." When I finished eating, he gave me some supplies to take to the surveyors.

I located Mr. Bufford, engaged his services, and we left Gallipolis by 7 o'clock. I'm unsure how many miles we rowed until we reached the mouth of Raccoon Creek, but it had taken us several hours to arrive there. It headed due west from the Ohio then changed to a more northern route. While the creek generally headed north and west, it would sometimes switch back and flow to the northeast. While we could easily row the canoe without much bushwhacking, I thought it would be difficult to transport any type of product to Gallipolis due to the creek's meandering path.

I was glad that Mr. Safford had provided me with such a filling breakfast because we did not arrive at the surveying camp until 5 o'clock. When Jonathan returned to camp at dusk, he didn't recognize me, because he was not expecting me to just appear in his camp and he hadn't seen me in almost ten years.

Thursday, August 16th

Jonathan departed at dawn, but he had left word for me to head west. I left camp at 9 o'clock and found his note nailed to the first mile post. It said the packer should pitch camp at the first waterway he found south of this post. Shortly afterward I found what I assumed to be the correct place and waited for the packer. When the packer hadn't arrived within two hours, I returned to the mile post which contained Jonathan's note and stayed there waiting for the packer's arrival.

Mr. Carr, Jonathan's hunter, appeared. He told me the packer had missed this post with its note and gone a mile further west. He'd found the packer and told him to return to last night's camp and start over.

When the packer finally arrived, we headed south. I assisted the man in setting up our camp. Mr. Carr arrived with a deer and turkey which we roasted on the fire. Our Sandy camp is three miles west of the Ohio and six miles south southwest from Gallipolis. Jonathan returned before sunset then we feasted on an excellent supper prepared by the hunter.

Unlike other areas of Ohio, the soil here does not appear good for grain crops. However, there are many types of hardwood trees, such as oak, beech, sugar maple, as well as a few hickory trees.

Friday, August 17th

I noticed some snake root in the woods yesterday, so I decided to remain near camp to harvest these herbs. I'm sure I'll find somewhere I can dry the roots. Maybe I can sell some before I return to New England.

Jonathan returned to our camp about noon. "I felt ill after running just one mile which is unusual. I thought it best to return and rest."

I checked him and he wasn't running a fever, so I wasn't worried. After my saddlebags were packed to the brim with snake roots, I borrowed the packer's fishing rod. We roasted trout for supper.

Saturday, August 18th

Stayed in camp again. Jonathan was better than the previous day but did not feel well enough to resume work. I thought my change in diet or sleeping on the ground affected me because I was also ill. I made willow tea. It tasted horrible without any sweetener.

Rain in the afternoon, continued through evening. We put a tent over our campfire to protect it. Numerous swarms of large flies annoyed the packhorse, but I found its antics amusing. Trying to avoid flies, the mare stationed itself almost on top of our fire. This animal doesn't graze much during the day, but at twilight goes out to feed until sunrise. As soon as flies stir after dawn, it returns to camp.

"Your packhorse always returns. During my trip with Fearing and Skinner, our mares wandered away from camp overnight. It took us hours to find them."

Mr. Carr snorted. "Don't you know how to hobble a horse?"

When I shook my head, he said, "You're not the only one to lose your mount. Many military men lost their horses during the Indian wars because they hadn't learned how to hobble them. I can show you how it's done if you'd like."

When I nodded, he took a rope from his sack and demonstrated the process. "This is a sideline." He doubled rope into a simple figure eight pattern and placed it with a twist. "This form is a pastern." For this one, he used a longer length of rope, then placed it around the horse's hind and foreleg on the same side of its body.

While I practiced, the hunter kept an eye on my movements and corrected me when necessary. I grew proficient with both hobbles but thought the pastern one was more restrictive.

Sunday, August 19th

I'm sicker today than yesterday and unsure what caused the illness. Maybe we didn't roast our turkey long enough, or it might have been the brackish tasting creek water. Near noon, we moved camp about one mile west and one mile south. Mr. Carr later brought in a deer and broiled the venison on a stick. I ate a small piece. It tasted good, but my stomach was still unsettled.

Monday, August 20th

About an hour and a half after he left, our hunter returned with another deer. Camp was moved one mile south before noon. Not as sick today, I explored but didn't go far. There was too much underbrush. If I had been able to ride Beanie, I would have ventured farther.

My brother-in-law returned near dusk. "Jonathan, how much longer will you be surveying this area?"

"Another week or so. Why?"

"If I head back to Gallipolis tomorrow, I'll be able to catch the packet on Wednesday."

He nodded. "We could use more supplies. I'll have the packer show you the way."

Tuesday, August 21st

After breakfast, the packer and I traveled overland. Our destination was nearly ten miles northeast. We reached Gallipolis at noon which surprised me, because going out to their camp by canoe had been an arduous trip. Mr. Safford agreed to let me stay at his house instead of paying for lodging at the pub.

Later, I explored the settlement. I wanted to speak to my cousin Phineas, who was employed as a county tax collector, but he wasn't there. A note on his office door said he would return next week.

I found the chandlery where my brother John had supplied provisions during the Indian war. A dark-haired gentleman stood behind the counter. "Hello. Are you Monsieur Bureau?"

"Oui." When I didn't respond, he again said, "Oui?"

My brother had become fluent speaking French when he lived here. I was not at all conversant. I hoped this man would understand my English. "I'm Dr. Increase Mathews. My brother John asked me to give you his warmest regards."

He grasped my extended hand and shook it. "Ah, John. Yes, Johnny is good. I think of him often. We miss him here."

When I continued my walk, I encountered an old Frenchman who was selling peaches from his cart. It was wonderful to eat something other than venison and turkey. To repay Mr. Safford's kindness, I bought a bushel. I gave him these when I returned to his home.

Wanting to send a letter on the boat, I spent the evening writing.

Dear Nabby,

I sent a note for you with Nate when he left here about two weeks ago. I know you haven't yet received it. I confess I've been remiss in writing since then. I assure you, you have been foremost in my thoughts, but I lacked the opportunity.

After your brother departed, I took a packet downriver to Gallipolis, so I could view more of the frontier lands. I joined my brother-in-law's survey party, and I'm now on my way back to Belpre.

The settlements are growing, and many fine residences have been constructed. These are equivalent to any house back east. Susannah showed me plans for their future home, and it will be impressive and as large as your father's place in Oakham. Would you believe there's a mansion being built on an island in the Ohio River? If I hadn't seen it with my own eyes, I would have doubted it.

I've had the opportunity to observe the abundance of crops grown here and know people have not exaggerated the fertility of the soil. It will take hard work to clear the land of shrubs and trees, but the end result will be worth any effort.

Time has passed too quickly, and there is still much I'd like to see. I've only explored to the west of Marietta so far but would love to view the lands to the north, yet my time here grows short. I plan to begin my return journey by the beginning of September.

I have missed seeing your sparkling green eyes, beautiful auburn tresses, and impish smile. I look forward to being together again and hope to persuade your father of my steadfast resolve to marry you. Please know that I remain,

Deeply devoted,
Ink

Wednesday, August 22nd

The packet left the dock at 9 o'clock. Traveling upstream required a combination of rowing and bushwhacking, so it was a slow process. We stopped for the night on the Virginia side of the river. I lodged at Rowse's Dutchman's Tavern. The owners were hospitable people. They made sure my stay was comfortable. Wonderful to have a bath, change into clean clothes, and sleep in a bed again, especially after the day's sweaty exertions.

Thursday, August 23rd

I purchased breakfast from Rowse's tavern before boarding the boat. Because we were able to row more than bushwhack today, we traveled 40 miles upriver and reached Pond Creek just after dusk. I chose to sleep in the boat, rather than on shore, because this was where Edward and I had been annoyed by fleas. My sleep was quite restless; I kept waking with leg cramps.

Friday, August 24th

After leaving Pond Creek, our boat passed near the town of Belleville where a large boat from Illinois laden with furs and bound for Pittsburgh was tied at the wharf. I recalled seeing this same boat on my way downriver about ten days ago. With the low water level and the craft's heavy load, it had not made much progress going up the Ohio.

When we neared the Hockhocking, I asked the boatman to stop because I was very hungry. Since I hadn't had breakfast, I went into Mr. Guthrie's Tavern and bought us some refreshments. I reached Susannah's home by early afternoon.

TWENTY-THREE

My sister greeted me with a hug and whispered that Ben had assisted Johari on his way. I gave her news of her husband, then excused myself for a nap because I was fatigued from my trip. After supper, I rode Beanie for a few miles. The pinto seemed glad to stretch her legs even though Sam had assured me that he'd ridden her every afternoon. I think my nephew had enjoyed having a mare to ride for a change because the Stones only had a pair of oxen. Their only horse had died during the Indian War.

I slept later than usual then spread my snake roots on the porch to dry in the sunshine. In the afternoon, I did my laundry with some help from Grace after the women finished their washing. "Will you be here for church tomorrow, Uncle Ink?"

"Yes, I can stay one more day."

∞ ∞ ∞

When I finished carving the roast pheasant, Susannah passed a dish of mashed potatoes to me. "You haven't said much about your trip. I take it you didn't see anything you liked."

I heaped a small mound on my plate then took the bowl of gravy from Grace. "Not as much as what I've seen here and at Marietta. You have easy access to the river. It would be a nightmare to send goods down something as circuitous as Raccoon Creek."

Ben handed me the dish of creamed corn. "Are you going to settle here?"

"I haven't decided on it yet." I frowned. "The price of acreage here is

91

unaffordable, even with assistance from Uncle Rufus. I do like what I've seen, but my future is too uncertain. Right now, all I see are a lot of ifs."

I took the platter of tomatoes and cucumbers from Sam. He said, "What do you mean, Uncle Ink?"

"If Harrison is elected; if he can get Congress to implement credit terms; and if I can earn more money." I frowned. "My biggest one is if I can convince Mr. Willis to allow me to marry Nabby."

"Mother would tell you that you've forgotten to put your trust in our Lord." Susannah smiled to remove the sting from her words. "Who's ready for some peach cobbler?"

Monday, August 27th

I packed up my herbs and departed from my sister's home after dinner. As promised, I stopped at Paul Fearing's place in Harmar because he was curious about the land near Gallipolis. While we chatted, he shared peaches which were delicious. After fording the Muskingum, I sold some of my snake roots to the chandler. I walked to the Putnam home after stabling Beanie. Aunt Persis re-introduced me to her nephew Levi. He is the son of her sister Priscilla and Francis Whipple Jr.

I barely remembered him. His family had moved from New Braintree to Westboro while I was still young. I shook his hand. "It's been years since I last saw you. What are you doing here?"

"There wasn't much for me to do back east. I arrived on foot this past spring, looking for work. I was hired as a surveyor in June and came today to turn in my reports."

I nodded. "Where did you get sent?"

"I've been surveying up the Muskingum near the trail called Zane's Trace. It has excellent soil for agriculture. I really like what I've seen there. When I earn enough money, I'd like to purchase some land by the confluence of Muskingum and Licking Rivers. I know you helped in your father's sawmill." He paused and smiled. "This area would be an excellent place to build mills to attract settlers. Sandstone has been found there too."

I smiled. "Sounds perfect, and what I'd like to own. Wish I had time to see it, but I'm planning to leave on Sunday."

"Too bad, but I'll show you the area when you return."

∞ ∞ ∞

Captain Jonathan Devol had invited the Putnam family for supper. After my cousin William arrived, we traveled about five miles north of Marietta up the Muskingum to reach the captain's home in Wiseman's Bottom. I enjoyed the watermelons he gave us as dessert.

Tuesday, August 28th

Riding Beanie, I went with my cousin William to view his farm and mill. Because Levi was heading back to survey, he walked with us. We took the north trail from Marietta which followed the meandering Muskingum. When we reached Wiseman's Bottom, Levi continued north.

William and I turned our horses and rode along Rainbow Creek, which is a branch that heads generally north and west from the Muskingum. After several miles we reached his floating gristmill. He said, "Captain Devol gave me this one when he built his stationary one. I'm working on building one of those."

He showed me around his farm. "Over here will be my peach and apple orchard. I hope to have enough land cleared to plant more of those before winter. I harvested my wheat crop last week, so now I have time. My cabin isn't much, but I plan to have Joe Barker build me a house next spring. I should have enough cured wood by then."

As I rode back to Marietta, I was envious of my cousin. Only a year older than me, his path in life is already determined and he owns a lovely place. So far, I much preferred the rich land along the Muskingum over the acreage I had seen near Gallipolis.

My cousins greeted me as soon as I arrived. Voices filled with excitement all three spoke at once. Patty said, "There's going to be a ball this Friday!"

Caty said, "You're invited too!"

Betsey said, "Father persuaded his cousin to hold it before you leave." She smiled. "The colonel usually holds it in mid-September, but it's been a good year, and many have already harvested their fields."

Caty said, "I bet Betsey's wishing your brother will get here in time."

With a frown and a twitch to her skirts, my cousin left the room. Patty said, "Why do you tease her so?" She frowned at her sister then hurried after Betsey.

Wednesday, August 29th

John arrived before dinnertime because he wanted to finish his paperwork then turn in his survey reports to Uncle Rufus. After we ate, he said, "It won't take me long. If you'd like, we can visit Susannah after I turn these into the land office."

I nodded, and he headed into our uncle's study. While he was occupied, I chatted with our cousins who were busy sewing new dresses for the ball. When Caty once again began teasing her sister about my brother, I went to repack my saddlebags. I slung these over my shoulder and joined John in the study. He said, "I'll just be another minute or two."

"I'll go saddle Beanie. We can ride double."

∞ ∞ ∞

We were close to Belpre when I coughed, then cleared my throat. John said, "Whenever you do that, I know you have something to discuss. What's wrong now?"

"Uhm. You do realize that Betsey is fixated on you. Why don't you—?

He gasped with exasperation. "I have! Tried to tell her in a nice way, but it did no good. Ignoring her hasn't worked either. If we weren't related, I could tell her she isn't attractive. Besides, I have no desire to marry a first cousin like Lish did."

We rode into the Stone's barn, and John helped me pasture Beanie. Susannah had anticipated our arrival and fixed plenty of food. While we ate, Susannah said, "I won't attend because Jonathan hasn't returned yet. Grace is thrilled and can't wait to dance with Luther."

My niece blushed. "May I please be excused?"

Susannah nodded. After her daughter was gone, my sister laughed. "Please excuse her. She's a bit frantic. She thinks she doesn't have enough time to turn that purple cloth into a suitable dress before the ball. Betsey

Leavens showed her how to tat lace. She plans to make some to embellish it. I'm sure I'll have to help her."

∞ ∞ ∞

While we helped the boys with chores on Thursday morning, John said, "Probably be a good idea to go explore today."

I saddled Beanie after breakfast. As we rode along the north trail, John spoke in my ear. "You know if we'd stayed, the women might have put us to work sewing." He chuckled. "So, are you going to settle here? Got your eye on any land?"

"I'm still unsure. I prefer the lands here and along the Muskingum over what I saw near Gallipolis. What about you?"

"There's two areas I'm considering. Eb Buckingham wants to be partners for land along the Tuscarawas River. The other place is by Moxahala Creek, a tributary of the Muskingum." He grinned. "Still saving my money, like you."

"Is this near the area where Levi Whipple is surveying?"

John said, "Close. It's a bit further to the south and west."

Friday, August 31st

Spent an agreeable evening attending the ball held at Colonel Israel Putnam Jr.'s home. Young ladies, dressed in their finest, had arrived from Marietta, Harmar, and Wiseman's Bottom. Even Miss London and the Blennerhassetts had a servant row them across the river from the island. While Mrs. Blennerhassett was attired in brilliant scarlet, I thought my niece was lovelier in her purple dress edged with white lace and told her so when she returned to the refreshment table. Grace introduced me to her beau, Luther. I learned he was the oldest son of Captain William Dana and he was only a year younger than me. I was impressed by his character as he talked about building their future home at Newport, which is a newer settlement on the Ohio to the east of Marietta.

A little later, I overheard Grace chatting with Caty. "I think Zerviah Cooley has set her cap for my brother Ben. That's the third time I've seen them dancing together."

Caty said, "Oh I wish I could get Eb Buckingham to dance with me that often!"

John seemed to enjoy dancing with Sarah Woodbridge. I had seen them together multiple times. After overhearing my cousin's comment, I wondered if Sarah had also set her cap.

While I had enjoyed this evening, my thoughts had often turned to Abigail, and I was anxious to return home where I hoped she was waiting for me.

TWENTY-FOUR

Sunday, September 2, 1798

I attended church services with my sister's family then stayed for dinner. With tear-covered cheeks, I said farewell and set out at 2 o'clock.

Because I didn't want the burden of feeding packhorses during my trip, I decided to sell them. I also wanted to be certain I make it through the mountains before any snow falls. Since I won't be leading these animals, I anticipate reaching New England within three weeks.

Horses are a rarity here because many settlers only brought oxen. At the ball, Chris Burlingame said he wanted to buy mine, so I rode Beanie to Marietta and retrieved the packhorses from the stable. I reached my cousin Susanna's house at dusk. Their homestead in Harmar lies about one mile below the Muskingum River. I spent the night with my cousin's family.

Monday, September 3rd

It was raining when I left the Burlingame's home and forded the Muskingum. I stopped in Marietta to say goodbye and gratefully accepted my aunt's offer of breakfast. I didn't leave their home until the skies began to clear in the afternoon.

Duck Creek was swollen with runoff, deep, and muddy. I had to almost cross the Ohio to reach the other side, and Beanie lost a shoe during this ordeal. I hope this will be the only unfortunate thing to occur on my trip.

After getting my horse reshod, I hired a flatboat to cross the Little Muskingum. I stopped at the Courtney homestead for the night. With the rain delay and lost shoe, I only managed to travel 13 miles from Marietta.

Tuesday, September 4th

Left early in the morning but, after only traveling four miles, stopped at Denny's homestead because I was hungry. He said that I could probably get some refreshment at the Dutchman's place and gave me directions to ride another seven miles. Mrs. Sheets gave milk to me then some cornstalks and ears for Beanie. As I chatted with the Dutchman, he told me to cross the Ohio about two miles upriver. I located the area he'd recommended. Here I found excellent fording with the water not more than knee deep on my mare. Once I reached the Virginia side of the riverbank, the road was well-cut and easy to travel.

A violent storm engulfed me a short time later, but I managed to take shelter in an old deserted cabin. Waiting for the worst of this to pass, I'm writing in my diary. From the appearance of this building, I speculate it was abandoned during the Indian War.

I spent the night at Peden's homestead after traveling another 18 miles. They are a Quaker family. From what I'd heard about this religious sect as a child, I almost expected any I met to have some mark of the devil, but this was not the case. They were very hospitable to a stranger. Mr. Peden, a humorous man, told many comical stories.

They keep a still and turn their excess grain into whiskey. The husband and wife both denounced the whiskey tax. He said, "Much easier to send whiskey casks over the mountains, rather than heavier grain. Can't understand why it hasn't been repealed."

She said, "'Tain't right. Unfair to us who live in western lands."

Wednesday, September 5th

I ate breakfast with them, then Mr. Peden was kind enough to use his flatboat to help me cross Fishing Creek which lay about five miles from their homestead.

At noon, I noticed a house near the riverbank and stopped to ask for some food. Unfortunately, the owner was drunk and argumentative. He followed me and shouted, "You get off my property! Ain't got no business stopping here."

At length I was able to get away from him. There has been steady drizzle today. My path slick with mud. These woods are filled with blade and grey squirrels and, to pass the time, I counted 32 of them this afternoon.

With evening approaching and continuing rain, I stopped for the night about four miles below Grave Creek. Henry Baker allowed me to bed down in front of his hearth.

Thursday, September 6th

Mr. Baker accompanied me 18 miles into Wheeling and pointed out the homes of its famous people. "In 1769, Ebenezer Zane had claimed this land by tomahawk rights."

Puzzled, I interrupted him. "What does that mean?"

"Marking the bark of trees with your initials. This area had originally been named Zanesburg. Fort Henry was established here and played a pivotal role during the Revolutionary War." Barker led me to the edge of a bluff. "This is where Major McColloch made his famous leap. Surrounded by Indians, he rode his horse over the edge." He shook his head. "What an incredible feat. Still can't believe he survived!"

My brother John had become friends with Colonel Zane while surveying the Seven Ranges for our Confederated Congress. He had often mentioned the Zane family in his letters.

Rain had continued falling, so I stopped at Neilson's Inn for refreshment. The innkeeper allowed me to stable Beanie while I ate, and I also bought grain for my pinto before I left.

Eight miles outside of Wheeling, James Craige hailed me. "Come in out of the rain. Rest a spell." Once I was indoors, he handed me a tankard of hot cider. We chatted while I drank the beverage. He smacked his toothless gums together after he took a sip. "Nasty day to be traveling. Where you be headed?"

He seemed a harmless elderly man, so I said, "I'm on my way to Massachusetts."

After taking another sip from his tankard, he again smacked his lips. "The land here is good for farming. Would you be interested in purchasing some from me?"

"Sorry but I'm not interested. If I do purchase any, it would be near my relatives in Ohio. Thank you for letting me dry out."

I reached the Knox's steading at dusk after another twelve miles. The owner took pity on me and agreed I could shelter in his barn. Inside, I found an old rag and used it to wipe down my saddlebags and pack then Beanie before I curried her. Today I managed 40 miles on very slick and muddy roads.

Friday, September 7th

Today I truly left the Ohio valley behind me because the area I now rode through was Pennsylvania. I bought breakfast from Mr. Cracken, then continued east. Miserable weather continued, but at least it wasn't cold enough for snow.

When I reached Washington, I stopped and ate at an inn to dry out. I came upon the Parkinson's homestead eleven miles further east, and this family allowed me to spend the night, helped me dry Beanie, and settle her in their barn. I had gotten drenched and was glad to dry out in front of their hearth.

Saturday, September 8th

The skies finally cleared. I set out early on the trail heading eastward and forded both the Monongahela and Youghiogheny Rivers today. Knowing that I'll soon be crossing mountains, I spent the night at John Neil's Good Irishman Inn when I reached there. Traveling with Nate, we had stayed here and enjoyed an excellent meal.

Today I was appalled to find that his young daughters had spent all day spreading flax while the innkeeper and his wife did much lighter work, bringing food to tables and dusting off crumbs.

"Threshing flax is hard work even for a man. Don't you think it's too much for your young girls?"

"It's harvest time and must be completed as soon as possible."

I thought their reply, while true, was an insufficient excuse but could tell arguing the point wouldn't solve anything, so I ended the conversation.

Sunday, September 9th

The day was clear when I left Neil's place. I headed south and, after passing Chestnut Ridge, I reached Donegal where we'd stopped on our journey out. I wanted to get breakfast, but nobody was home, so I traveled another four miles and found Widow Lockwood's farm. She was kind enough to sell me some food and allowed my horse some grain.

I continued south on Glades Pike trail until I reached Bamer's homestead, about five miles before Somerset, where I spent the night.

Monday, September 10th

It was very crisp this morning in the Glades which are the lowlands between Laurel Hill and the Allegheny Road. Last night, Mr. Bamer said, "The soil here is poor, but small grain does tolerably well even though we have a short growing season. Why, we even had ice thick as window glass on July 14th!"

Set out early in the morning and passed Alleghany Road which heads north. When I reached the foot of Dry Ridge, I bought breakfast at Stotler's Tavern. Followed the top of Dry Ridge along its ten-mile length. The road headed generally due east, and I soon passed through Bedford. Shortly after Bedford, I once again reached the Hartley's home where they remembered me and allowed me to spend the night.

Tuesday, September 11th

Very cold this morning. After crossing Juniata River, I followed the tedious route over the Sideling Hill. With the cold weather I've encountered, I'm glad that I did not delay my departure from Ohio any longer! I traveled 36 miles before I put up for the night at a miserable place. I don't know the name and don't care to enquire.

Wednesday, September 12th

My breath is steaming as I write this. When I reached the summit of Middle Mountain at 9 o'clock, I spotted some flat stones that provide a view of the valley. Today's wind is brisk and chill. I wanted to warm up in the sun's rays and to give Beanie a rest, so I decided to take advantage of this spot.

I've already passed over Tuscarora Mountain this morning. I marvel at the first people to travel across the country this way. It's a bleak crossing. There are only a few scraggly trees which appear to spring from bedrock. Though this route was once traveled by Indians, it took a bold man to make the trail wide enough to be passable for wagons. Once I leave here, I will descend Middle Mountain then travel across North Mountain before I reach Upper Strasburg where I will find a good road.

∞ ∞ ∞

Breakfasted at Skinner's Tavern between the mountains and was glad to be out of the wind. Beanie began favoring her hind quarter as I crossed North Mountain, so I stopped at a smithy in Upper Strasburg and had her shoes replaced. Feeling happy that I'm finished with the mountains, I pressed on until I was seven miles from Carlisle. I spent the night at the Eaken's home and found this family to be civil people who allowed me to sleep by the hearth. I traveled 33 miles today.

Thursday, September 13th

The day was crisp but warmer than what I had encountered in the mountains. I passed through Carlisle then ate breakfast at Bell's Tavern which is five miles past Carlisle. At Harrisburg I forded the Susquehanna River where it is nearly a mile wide.

Beanie still favored her leg, so I stopped when I reached Hummelstown. I stabled her but had second thoughts because the inside of this establishment was dirty. I decided to leave and ordered a stable hand to bring Beanie. While waiting for my mare, Mr. Dearmon, who owns The Irishman's Tavern in Lebanon, arrived and I concluded to go to his place which is six miles away. Traveled 40 miles today.

Friday, September 14th

I ate breakfast at The Irishman's Tavern before leaving. Though the morning was chill, the day warmed up and was pleasant for riding. I reached Reading by dusk and stopped overnight at a tavern. I was able to travel 38 miles.

Saturday, September 15th

Rising at dawn, I headed northeast from Reading. I stopped for breakfast at a Dutch tavern after traveling 14 miles. Though I was very hungry, the food was quite greasy so I could only stomach a little. I reached Bethlehem before nightfall and took a room at an inn. Today I traveled 41 miles.

Sunday, September 16th

I attended church at the Moravian meeting house. The beginning services were in German, and I only understood a few words. Their singing was accompanied by an organ, then there was a short sermon and hymn in English. It was an interesting experience. I paused at the door to speak with the minister before I left. "Is there a meaning for the different colored ribbons worn on the women's bonnets?"

He nodded. "Yes. Females under age 18 wear dark red; unmarried ones over 18 pale red; married women blue; and widows white."

I nodded my thanks. Since we had been unable to tour this town on our way to Ohio, I explored the area then departed Bethlehem at half past two. I stopped for the night when I reached Fair's Inn. This is five miles past Easton over the border into New Jersey. With my late start, I only traveled 17 miles today.

Monday, September 17th

I was able to purchase breakfast from a widow who lived twelve miles beyond Fair's Inn. Six miles farther along the trail, I reached Johnsonburg and stopped to view its courthouse and log jail. Four companies of cavalry are garrisoned here. These men appeared robust and strong, and they rode fine mounts.

Leaving, I headed northeast and passed through Sussex. After crossing into New York, I spent the night at Basley's Pub which lies ten miles northeast from Sussex. I managed 43 miles.

Tuesday, September 18th

After traveling 39 miles, I stopped at Harrison's Inn which is five miles before New Windsor. When I entered the dining room, I saw a familiar face, so I approached two men already seated at a table. "Hello Captain Denny. May I join you?"

"Of course. Do you know Martin Henry?"

"Afraid I haven't had that pleasure." I smiled and we shook hands. After we were seated and I had placed my food order, I turned to the captain. "May I ask why you are so far from Leicester?"

"I met Martin in Palmer, and we are going to Ohio."

I chuckled. "I'm on my way home from there."

Captain Denny nodded. "Joe Willson mentioned you have family there. What can you tell us about it?"

I described what I had seen and where I had been in Ohio. By the time I finished, we were done eating. Martin cleared his throat. "Could I impose upon you to deliver a letter to my father in Brimfield?"

I smiled. "It wouldn't be an imposition at all. Just tell me how to get to your father's home."

Martin retrieved a letter from his saddlebags and handed it to me. In my room, I wrote a reminder in my diary: Letter to Calvin Henry in Brimfield.

Wednesday, September 19th

I set out early, traveled five miles, and ate breakfast in New Windsor. I then took the ferry across the Hudson River and headed northeast to reach Fishkill. Beanie seemed lame again this afternoon, so I stopped early at the widow Vandenburgh's home.

I was entertained by a cellist and met friendly people. When the cellist heard that I was accomplished with the violoncello, he offered to lend me his instrument, but I laughed and declined his offer. Including the ferry, I only traveled 27 miles today because the road was difficult to traverse and the land consisted of steep hills.

Thursday, September 20th

Beanie still favored her hind leg, so it was necessary for me to walk most of the way. Consequently, my progress was slow, and I only managed 26 miles. Setting out I headed generally northeast and bought breakfast at Reasner's Pub. At dinnertime, I couldn't find a tavern, so I stopped at a private home where I was able to buy cider and apples for me, plus grass and oats, for a sixpence. With dusk coming on after crossing into

Connecticut, I found a private home whose owners allowed me to bed down in one of their rooms.

Friday, September 21st

Though I had been very fatigued before retiring because of traveling by foot over mountains and hills upon horrid roads, I spent an utterly miserable night. I got up during the night and lit a candle while I tried to reduce the number of fleas which infested the bed. My effort was not met with success. I laid back down and tried to sleep. Giving up, I departed their home at the crack of dawn.

When I reached Litchfield, I stopped for breakfast at Captain Bradley's home. He thought Beanie had been improperly shod which caused her current lameness. The previous evening a gentleman, who overtook me and professed to be knowledgeable of horses, assured me the lameness was due to a back-tendon sprain. So far everyone I've met has had a different opinion of the cause.

Following the captain's advice, I stopped at the stables and had her shoes once again replaced before heading onward. As I left following Litchfield Street, I noted that the town was flourishing, handsome, and situated on high land.

Beanie continued to favor her hind quarter. When I passed through Harwinton a few miles northwest of Litchfield, another skilled horseman stopped me and assured me he was confident the lameness was in the gambrel joint. I allowed him to apply a poultice to Beanie's hind leg.

When I reached Farmington, I put up for the night at Hull's Tavern after only traveling 31 miles.

Saturday, September 22nd

When I set out late in the morning, Beanie's lameness was not as pronounced. I thought the poultice might have helped. Heading east I traveled ten miles and reached Hartford, Connecticut where I stopped for a late breakfast at Bull's Tavern. From there, I headed northeast and reached Mr. Holton's home in Ellington. Giving Beanie time to continue mending by walking a mile then riding a mile, I only traveled 26 miles.

Sunday, September 23rd

Though I'm close to reaching New Braintree, I decided to remain in Ellington for the day to give Beanie time to mend.

Last night, Mr. Holton invited me to attend church services with him. As I shook out my homespun suit, it had a slight smell of mildew because of the amount of rain I'd encountered at the beginning of my journey. I did my best to make myself presentable then accompanied Mr. Holton to the meeting hall. Two Methodist ministers attended. Mr. Thompson preached during the morning. At noon, a coffin was brought inside. The funeral was said by Mr. Rogers, whose sermon I found inferior to the one given earlier. After this, the corpse was taken to a burying ground and interred. Mr. Thompson read the grave's church service in a solemn manner.

Monday, September 24th

It was chilly when I left Mr. Holton's home early in the morning. I headed due north, crossed into Massachusetts, and breakfasted at Sike's Pub when I reached Wilbraham.

Instead of heading north to take the good toll road to Palmer, I took the eastern road to Brimfield. When I reached this town, I found my way to Calvin Henry's home where I delivered the missive from his son Martin.

From here, I headed north. I reached the west parish of Brookfield just before sunset. There was a regiment of infantry and a company of light horse in parade formation on the plain below the meeting house. I found my brother, Lish, along with many friends and acquaintances, viewing their drills.

I followed the road northeast into the north parish of Brookfield, then took the north road into New Braintree and reached my father's house at 8 o'clock in the evening.

Even with Beanie's lameness, I managed to cover the almost 600 miles in only three weeks on my return trip. It had taken us four weeks going to Ohio.

TWENTY-FIVE

When I arrived home, Father came outside to chat as I took Beanie into the barn, curried her, and gave her some grain. As I worked, I shared news of our Ohio relatives. Finished, I retrieved my musket, saddlebags, pack, and medical kit, then followed him inside the house. I think my father was glad to have me home though he didn't say it with words. While I found some food to eat, he added logs to the hearth, brought in water, filled a large kettle, then pushed it over the flames. I took my things upstairs and retrieved a nightshirt after I finished eating. As I returned downstairs, my father poured boiling water into the tub. It was wonderful to bathe, to change into something clean, and to slip between the covers of my own bed. Within moments, I slept.

∞ ∞ ∞

I woke disoriented. I knew I was in my bed, but the room was different. After a few moments, I realized Lish had moved the trundle to his house during my absence. Its removal bothered me though I hadn't slept in it for over a decade. Then a childhood memory of reaching up to wake John made me smile, and I imagined three-year-old Oramel doing the same to an older brother. Yet, the room, once so cramped by the four of us plus our cousin Phineas, now seemed empty and forlorn with only two narrow beds to fill it.

Father and I walked to my brother's place after our morning chores were done. During my absence, Aunt Hannah had moved into my brother's home so she could help her daughter maintain their household. Both Hannahs greeted me with hugs. My aunt said, "It's so good to have you home. My, you've lost weight. Not to worry, we'll soon put some meat back on your bones."

After grace was said, Lish turned to me. "I've been fattening a sow since you left. I thought to hold a homecoming celebration and roast it this Sunday." He smiled. "We'll invite everyone to come hear of your adventures."

"What a wonderful idea. Thank you!"

Aunt Hannah was seated next to me, and she kept adding more food to my plate. "Please stop. I can't eat another bite!"

Finished eating, Father and Lish took Junior, Danny, and Fred to help get the last of the hay into the barn. I stayed to chat with the women for several minutes after they left.

I needed to replenish my money and wanted to save for the future. I had to take care of business first instead of rushing to see Nabby. I'd been so anxious to reach New Braintree that I hadn't taken the time to wash anything, so there was laundry to be done. Almost everything I owned was grubby, and I wanted my clothing impeccable when I encountered anyone. I was always quite meticulous with my appearance because of my mother's upbringing. She had often said, "Slovenliness is a sign of the devil at work."

I'd often been uncomfortable while traveling because I wasn't used to being covered with grime. Of course, I got dirty doing farm work, but somehow it just wasn't the same. Road dust and mud seemed to get inside every crack and crevice. It also made me itch.

Not one to procrastinate when there was a job to be done, I built a fire in the outside firepit, filled the tub with buckets of well water, and set this to heat. I retrieved my saddlebags and pack from upstairs, took out a bar of lye soap, then did my washing. I had everything pegged to dry before dinnertime.

After eating with my family, I hurried to my apothecary shed because some snake root still needed to be dried. I spread these on my hanging rack. After retrieving my medical kit from the house, I restocked it with willow bark. I spent several hours grinding dried herbs then making potions, salves, and balms. I placed these in my saddlebags and herb pouches in my pack.

Finished, I removed my dried clothes from the line, put them away, and changed into a suit. I sat at the kitchen table and took a few moments to pen a brief letter to Nabby. I wanted her to know I was home, to ask permission to call, and to invite her family to come to the party on Sunday. Though I anticipated visiting the Field family tomorrow, I also wrote a note to Spencer. Then I gathered my things and headed to the barn.

I saddled Beanie and rode into New Braintree. My first stop was the chandlery where I posted my mail then sold the owner some dried herbs. "I'll have snake roots dried by next week. Are you interested in buying some?"

He nodded. "How was your trip?"

"It was good. We're having a potluck on Sunday at Lish's house. He's roasting a pig. Please bring your family. I'll tell you all about my trip then."

He grinned. "We'll be there."

Next, I headed to Dr. Severance's house. It was my habit to visit him first because he lived inside town. His wife showed me into his study.

He grinned. "I'm glad to see you back. My medical supplies have been dwindling."

He purchased most of what I'd brought with me. As he paid me, I said, "I was lucky enough to find some Serpentaria Virginiana. I have it drying in my shed. I'll be able to make tonics next week. Would you like some?"

He nodded. "Of course. How was your trip?"

I smiled. "I'll tell everyone about it on Sunday. My brother will be roasting a pig. Please bring your family to our potluck."

He grinned. "I'll ask the missus to make some apple pies." The look he gave me was incomprehensible. "Have you visited Dr. Blair yet?"

"No. I need to go to Brookfield tomorrow to report back for militia duty. Thought I'd stop at his place on my way home."

He nodded, shook my hand, and followed me to the door. He said, "You should go see him as soon as practicable."

As I rode away, I wondered at his rather odd behavior. *Was one of my few patients ill?*

∞ ∞ ∞

Since I planned to see Dr. John Blair Jr., I changed into a suit after eating breakfast with my family on Wednesday morning. I restocked my saddlebags with medicinals, saddled Beanie, then rode along the southern road to the north parish of Brookfield. When I reached Main Street, I followed it to the western parish. I tied my mare to the hitching post outside the meeting house, went inside, and reported. The duty sergeant checked his papers and said, "Men are already out on maneuvers. They'll finish up this Friday. Enough men have showed that there's no need for you to join them now. Report again in the spring."

As I rode back to New Braintree, I thought about how I could earn more money. If Mr. Willis agreed to my marriage proposal, I needed a better way to support a family.

TWENTY-SIX

Mrs. Blair showed me into the doctor's study. He said, "Ah, there you are. I imagine Doc Severance told you I wanted to see you. Have a seat."

I sat down in the chair across from him and started to open my saddlebag. He said, "No need for you to rummage around. I don't need to buy your medicines any longer."

Shocked, I took a closer look at him. Under normal circumstances, he appeared robust. Today his complexion was pale, and he seemed frail. He noticed my startlement. "Ack. I'm making a muck of this." He coughed. "I can't seem to shake this summer cold."

He looked somewhat embarrassed as he said, "My missus has been after me to take it easy. She thinks I shouldn't be gallivanting around the countryside at night." He sighed. "Last week, when I saw Doc Severance about my condition, we discussed my retirement." He paused and sipped from his tankard. "We both concluded that you should take over my practice because you know everyone around here—," he frowned, "but I still have a concern."

Stunned, I sat there waiting for him to continue, but another coughing spasm racked him. He spit phlegm into his handkerchief and, when he could speak again, he said, "Benjamin told me that you live in your father's house. I see most people in their homes when I make rounds on Tuesday, Thursday, or Saturday, but some patients come here on the other weekdays. So, do you have a place to see anyone who would call on you?"

"To be honest, Sir, I don't know. I didn't expect to be taking over your practice." I paused to think. "My aunt recently moved to my brother's place. Maybe I could persuade my father to allow me to convert the back bedroom into a study since she isn't using the room any longer."

"What if he says no?"

I frowned. Another idea had come to me, one that was unappealing. "I guess I could rent or build a place in town."

He cleared his throat as he examined my countenance. "Benjamin said you were quite a penny saver. Are you willing to take on such an expense?"

"I will do whatever is necessary." I smiled to reassure him of the truth of my words.

"I'm glad to hear it. Here's what we'll do. Come here Monday morning, and we'll go over my books." He paused. "Yes, that'll work out because it's the first of the month. Good time for a fresh start. Then, you'll accompany me on rounds beginning Tuesday, so you'll become familiar with my patients' ailments. I imagine you'll be ready to take over within a week."

Mrs. Blair knocked at the door. "Dinner is ready. Would you care to join us?"

"Thank you, but I'd better not. My family is expecting me. What time do you want me here on Monday?"

"I think 8 o'clock would be good because patients begin arriving a little later."

I nodded and we shook hands. As soon as I crossed the threshold, before I even mounted Beanie, I began praying. My father could prove difficult to sway.

TWENTY-SEVEN

It was after one o'clock by the time I arrived at Lish's home. My father, brother, and the oldest boys had already eaten and gone to harvest the fields. Aunt Hannah had kept a platter of food warming near the hearth and was washing dishes while my cousin put her youngest children down for their afternoon naps.

After I said grace, I asked my aunt to join me at the kitchen table. "I need some advice." She gave me a questioning look as I took a bite of food. "I saw Doc Blair this morning. He's going to retire. I'm to take his place." She smiled, but before she could speak, I continued. "He said I need some place at home to see patients." I sighed. "How do I convince my father to allow me to have a study in the back bedroom? I don't want to spend money to rent a house in town."

She said, "Ah. A beautiful rose with many thorns problem."

"I'm unsure of the best way to approach him. I don't want to start an argument. If Mother were still alive, she would be able to persuade him. I must figure something out by next week."

"Ink, he may surprise you. He really missed you and sorely misses Susannah being near." She smiled. "You won't know until you ask and no use fretting beforehand. Now, get out of here and let me finish washing dishes."

I stood, hugged her, and thanked her for the food. Before I left, she said, "If he says no, I'll see if I can change his mind."

After promising Susannah to deliver a letter to Sarah, I had originally planned to go to the Willson's farm to visit my sister today, but decided I needed to work to clear my mind. Instead of riding to Leicester, I retrieved a mattock and sack from inside my apothecary shed, then rode Beanie to

113

an area close to father's sawmill. A stand of bayberry shrubs stood near the boggy water. First, I gathered the berries and placed those into the bag. My sister, aunt, and cousin used these when making candles. Next, I dug roots from some of the bushes, careful not to remove too much from any one plant. Finally, I harvested leaves for making tea.

I focused on what I was doing while I worked. As my aunt had said, I shouldn't worry about it until I spoke with Father. When I returned to my shed, I portioned some of the berries into a sack that I'd take to Sarah tomorrow. I rinsed the roots, then using a peeler, I sliced and placed these on my drying rack along with the leaves.

∞ ∞ ∞

After Father led our grace and everyone's plates were filled, I cleared my throat. "I have some news. As you know, I went to see Doc Blair this morning. He's going to retire. Both he and Dr. Severance have agreed I should take over his practice."

I smiled and waited while my family congratulated me. "But he also suggested I need somewhere patients can visit me." I glanced at my father. "The back bedroom is empty since Aunt Hannah moved her things here. Do I have your permission to turn it into a study?"

"Hmpf!" With his napkin, he wiped splattered food from his chin. "No. I don't want people traipsing through my home."

I knew better than to argue with him. "All right. I'll find someplace to rent in town." Though I had only eaten a few bites, I was too angry to remain. "Excuse me." I put my napkin on the table and hurried outside.

Ignoring Aunt Hannah's call for me to come back and finish eating, I went up the path and kicked every stone along the way. I saddled Beanie and galloped out of the yard. Without any destination in mind, I sped down our road, heading into town. I recklessly rode through deepening darkness. I was lucky I didn't injure my mare because I didn't pay attention to what I was doing.

I dismounted at the community watering trough, allowed Beanie to drink a small amount, then tied her to the hitching post at Moses's Inn. With slow steps I walked the deserted streets, checking to see if any stores were vacant. Most buildings were two-storied, box-like structures with living quarters above the shop. A soft glow of light showed through many upper windows. None appeared to be unoccupied. It would probably be necessary to build if I were to move into town.

I retraced my steps to the inn and went inside because I didn't want to return until I knew my father was in his bed. A few patrons were seated at tables and called for me to join them. I shook hands, smiled, and invited them to the potluck but kept moving toward the bar. I was in no mood to make pleasant, meaningless chatter.

My first tankard of ale was gone before I realized I'd drank it. As Moses refilled it, I noticed a bowl of hard-boiled eggs, paid for one, and peeled it. My first bite tasted like sawdust, so I pushed it aside. By ten o'clock I didn't know how much I'd drank, but it was much more than normal. I made my unsteady way outside, unhitched Beanie, and led her down the road.

The house was dark when I arrived. I did my clumsy best to curry the pinto before I went inside to bed.

∞ ∞ ∞

I was up, dressed, and outdoors before the cock crowed. Some might deem my behavior childish, but I wanted to remind Father that I wouldn't be there to help with chores if I lived in town. I retrieved the sack of berries from my shed, saddled Beanie, and rode to Leicester. I hoped my sister wouldn't be in one of her strange moods today.

The Willson family was eating breakfast when I knocked at their kitchen door. "Don't stand there like a stranger. Come in, come in." Sarah got up, hugged me, then added another place setting to her table. Joe reached across and shook my hand while Luther smiled as I sat down.

"I wondered when you'd get around to visiting us. You're such a busy man." My sister gave me a pouty look. "Oh, yes. We heard you got back Monday evening." She handed me the platter of food. In a taunting tone of voice, she said, "You must have fought with Father to be here so early in the day."

I shook my head. "No, I haven't. I'm here because I don't want to argue with him." I muffled a sigh and rushed to continue before she could interrupt. "Really, this is the first chance I've had to come here. There was laundry to be done, and I had to report back for militia duty too." I got up and retrieved the sack from their back porch. I grinned as I handed it to her. "I even brought you a present of bayberry seeds." I reached inside my money belt. "Here's a letter from Susannah."

She couldn't hide her smile as I sat down again. "I have more news if you give me a chance to explain."

I told them about Sunday's pig roast then described my housing predicament. My brother-in-law stood up as soon as I finished. "Please excuse us. There's a lot of work to get done before Saturday, because—," with a proud grin he pointed at his son, "he returns to the academy on Monday."

"I'm going to visit with Sarah, but I'll lend you a hand in a bit."

Joe nodded then gave a come-on motion to his son.

As Luther got to his feet, I could see my fifteen-year-old nephew had grown during the summer. I stood up next to him and found he was now two inches taller than me. After the men went outside, I helped my sister clear the table then dried the dishes she washed. As we worked, I answered her questions about our family in Ohio. Finished, she disappeared into her bedroom for a minute and returned with her mending basket. Sarah settled into a rocker and picked up a sock to darn. With a pointed look at me, she said, "Of course you're going to stay for dinner. My men will appreciate your help because they're making roof shakes."

∞ ∞ ∞

I decided to forgo visiting Dr. Field in Oakham after dinner. Instead, I stayed to help Joe and Luther make shingles. I reached New Braintree late in the afternoon.

I'd forgotten it was Thursday, and some pedestrians still visited market stalls. I tied Beanie to a hitching post and went inside the chandlery. I hoped there'd be a post from Nabby. Disappointed there wasn't any, I then walked along the entire square examining the store fronts. My progress was slow because I often stopped to chat with acquaintances. I noticed a few vacant lots, but all two-story shop buildings were occupied. It would be necessary to buy a lot and build if I were to live in town.

Dismayed, my pace was slow as I rode Beanie back to the farm. After I curried, watered, and gave her some oats, I took care of the other animals, thankful the cows had been moved to Lish's barn. Finished, I dumped a bucket of water over my head, washed my face and hands, then hurried down the path. I hoped there wouldn't be a scene with my father. I could hear my nephews splashing water and teasing each other when I neared the house.

I didn't broach the subject of my housing situation during supper, and Father didn't either. I did mention that the Willson family sent their love and planned to be here on Sunday. My aunt stopped me before I left. "Could you please pick some mint? Thought I'd make some of that mint-apple jelly that you love so much."

The kitchen was empty except for my aunt when I returned with the gathered herb. She looked at my sad face then kissed my cheek. "You look like you're toting a heavy weight."

"Yes. A bit. It will take almost every cent I have to build a place in town because there aren't any shops available for rent. I don't see how I can ask for Nabby's hand now. How do I break this news to her?"

She shook her head then sighed. "Might be best to give your father some time to think. Why don't you make yourself scarce?"

"I'll leave tonight and go stay with the Field family." I kissed my aunt's cheek. "I'll be back sometime on Saturday."

∞ ∞ ∞

I stopped by the chandlery to check for mail when I returned to town after staying with the Field family. Nabby's note said her family was unable to attend the potluck and invited me to come for dinner the following Sunday. I had mixed feelings. While disappointed I wouldn't see her this week, I was also relieved. I wondered what I would tell her when we did meet.

Both Hannahs were busy preparing food for the feast when I arrived. Lish and his oldest boys were still at the sawmill. I pulled two sawhorses from the barn and placed these close to the large firepit beside his smokehouse then added wood planks to form a tabletop large enough to hold the pig while we dressed it tomorrow morning. I stepped inside the house. "How many and where do you want the food tables?"

"At least two." My cousin pushed a strand of hair away from her eyes. "I'd say close to the pig table would work the best." My aunt nodded agreement.

I retrieved another four sawhorses from the barn and the remaining planks. I had just shifted the last one onto my makeshift tables when Lish's wagon rolled into the yard. The boys hurried to the barn to do their chores and Father went inside, but Lish came over to chat with me. He squinted at the sky as we walked toward his house. "Looks like the good weather will hold for another day or so. Will you help me chop firewood after supper?"

"Of course."

We washed at the well then went indoors. The delicious aroma of baked apple pie and peach cobbler filled the kitchen. I hoped no one overheard my stomach rumbling over the clatter of dishes being placed on the table but saw my brother's grin.

Father cleared his throat as we sat after he said grace. With a stern look at me, he said, "Increase, your aunt tells me there's no shop to rent in town. Why didn't you say something?"

I stared at his icy blue eyes and shrugged. "Figured it was my problem to handle."

With his chin, he pointed at Lish. "Your brother has offered to help build a partition." He looked down as he placed his knife on top of his plate. "I'll move my things into the back bedroom. You may convert the front one into a study. A wall and doorway should stop people from wandering through my home." He glanced at me. "We'll start work on Monday evening."

"Thank you, Sir. This means the world to me."

∞ ∞ ∞

After eating, I helped Lish chop enough firewood to roast the pig. "I'm surprised you were able to convince Father. It was an admirable thing for you to do. Thank you so much."

He shrugged. "Wouldn't be much of a brother if I didn't lend a hand where I could." He raised his eyebrows and playfully punched my arm. "Couldn't stand to have you so forlorn, moping over your young Miss Willis."

My father had already gone to bed by the time I returned to his house. I tried to make minimal noise as I rushed through my bath. It was late, and I wanted to be up before the cock crowed because there was a lot to be done tomorrow morning. I gave thanks to our Lord for hearing my prayer and for his quick answer before I crawled into my bed.

TWENTY-EIGHT

Knowing everything I wore would get heavily soiled, I dressed in farm clothes then hurried to Lish's smokehouse. My brother had just killed the pig when I arrived. I helped him lift the carcass onto the makeshift table where we dressed it for roasting. Before we were done, Father arrived in his buggy. He called to us, "Hurry up because I don't want to be late!" as he headed indoors to see if Aunt Hannah was ready.

Lish, Junior, and I lifted the spitted pig and placed it on the large tripod. After making sure there were enough larger logs to keep the fire going while we were away, we hurried to clean up and change clothes. By the time I saddled Beanie, my father had left. I mounted and followed my brother's wagon to the Congregational Church. Its bell was pealing, and we were among the last to arrive. I smiled as I joined Sarah, Joe, and Luther in the rear pew.

∞ ∞ ∞

Lish, Joe, and I headed to the firepit to check the roasting progress of our pig. We flipped the spit and added more wood to the fire. The women draped cloth over the makeshift food tables then spread a few quilts on the ground.

Townsfolk began appearing. I welcomed each new arrival and thanked them for coming. Each family brought a large basket filled with food, dishes, utensils, and blankets. My brother's yard was soon filled with friends, and almost every inch of lawn was covered by a quilt. Their multicolored hues and designs made it appear festive.

Lish had been right about the weather holding. It was a glorious, summer-like day. The mouth-watering aroma of roasting meat, along with the laughter of children playing games, floated on the air.

Mrs. Field brought her famous pickled beets. I thought hers were the best I'd ever eaten. Many women added a secret ingredient to their food, and they only shared recipes with their daughters, but sometimes a mother-in-law would teach a favorite dish to her son's wife. My aunt had learned to make scrapple from the elder Mrs. Snow. She would cook today's left-over pork scraps with oatmeal, salt, and pepper, then form this into loaves. Once congealed, it was fried until crispy. This was a treat that I looked forward to eating for breakfast in the upcoming weeks.

Along with fruit and vegetable dishes, the women had brought many desserts: pies, cobblers, cookies, and puddings. Famished, I had just taken a stealthy bite out of a gingersnap when Hannah approached and handed a cherry pie to me. "I made this just for you because I know it's your favorite. I added a dash of nutmeg like your mother always did."

I laughed and kissed my cousin's cheek. Five-year-old Fred came running up to us. "Father says it's time." I glanced toward the smokehouse. My brother stopped carving, lifted his right arm, and joined his index finger and thumb together with his other fingers outstretched. This was a signal that we'd often used inside our mill. I nodded my understanding to him, picked up a serving spoon, and tapped it against a pot. "May I please have your attention everyone?"

It took some time for the crowd to grow quiet enough for me to be heard. "The meat is finally ready." People cheered and started to get up from the ground. I held up a hand. "Sorry folks, but I'm going to be first to fill my plate." My announcement was met by several groans and a bit of laughter. "As soon as I'm done eating, I'll tell my tale."

My plate was full too soon. With such a large variety from which to choose, there wasn't enough room on it to have a taste of everything, and I needed to save room for a slice of Hannah's cherry pie.

Always a bit shy and rather bookish, I was terrified at the thought of speaking to so many people at once. I knew everyone, yet I dawdled eating my food, not wanting to get up and address them. When my plate was empty, I couldn't put it off any longer, so I got up, walked to the tables, then turned to face them.

Every eye focused on me. Speechless, I stood there until I noticed Spencer's smile and encouraging nod. Still nervous, I cleared my throat.

"Ohio was what I anticipated, and yet it wasn't. Its land is indeed lush. I viewed abundant fields of wheat and corn crops. Some forests are so dense and dark, they appear forbidding, yet men are clearing the trees to settle these areas.

"I expected people to still live inside forts, huddled behind wooden palisades. This was not the case. Many houses are like ones built here in Massachusetts. In fact, my Uncle Rufus's home is similar to the large one he owned in Rutland. Ore mines, mills, and shipyards are being built."

My brother-in-law handed me a tankard filled with hard cider. I paused to take a sip. A voice near the back called, "Tell us about the Indians!"

"I really can't say much about them. I only saw a few at the trading post in Wheeling, Virginia. Some males had feathers in their long hair, and all wore a loin cloth and fringed moccasins or boots. The squaw's dresses were made of buckskin adorned with beads and shells.

"Many frontiersmen also wear clothes made of buckskin. My brother John said it was more durable. I didn't believe him—," I waited for their laughter to subside, "until I joined my brother-in-law Jonathan's survey near Gallipolis. By the time I returned to Susannah's home in Belpre, my breeches were tattered from walking through brambles. My sister grows flax to make linsey-woolsey cloth and used some to patch my clothing.

"The farm and dairy the Stone family started there is thriving and so are their six children. She has many customers for her milk and cheese. They plan to build an impressive two-story home and hope to have it completed by next summer."

Once started, I found it easy to continue. I told them we had stopped at Newgate, recounted its deplorable conditions, and how its prisoners were treated. I spoke about the Governor's dinner and described the lovely evening ball I attended. I mentioned missing the packet boat and the flea-infested home. When I regaled them with the story of the drunkard who chased me for over a mile, they laughed.

I wasn't used to speaking so loudly and had often paused to take a sip from my tankard. By now my voice had become hoarse and throat sore. "The fireflies tell me it's past time to stop."

My audience laughed.

"Thank you all for coming. Please come get a second or third helping. The tables are still laden with food."

As they started to rise from their quilts, Dr. Benjamin Severance also stood up then waved his hands high in the air. In a loud, carrying voice, he said, "Attention please. I need to speak for a minute or two."

The adults settled back down to listen. He waited for their confused chatter to stop. "As some of you know, Dr. Blair hasn't been in the best of health. No need to look around. He isn't here. John has decided to retire." He paused until it grew quiet before he continued. "Increase has agreed to take over his practice."

This announcement was greeted by several cheers. I overheard someone say, "Now Increase will be able to get married." Within moments, I was surrounded by friends who offered congratulations. I shook their hands, smiled, and thanked each one for coming.

When just relatives remained, we carried leftover food inside then took down our temporary tables. Aunt Hannah shooed us out of the kitchen. "I'm tired. Washing up can wait till the morning."

Sarah, Joe, and Luther hugged us and departed for their home. The rest of us settled into porch chairs and chatted about the evening. Trying to stifle a yawn, I said, "Doc Blair expects me to be at his place by eight. I need to get to bed."

TWENTY-NINE

Monday, October 1, 1798

Mrs. Blair came outside as soon as I stepped on the porch. At my puzzled look, she said, "I don't want him to overhear me. I think John needs more rest, so I want you gone by three o'clock. I'm sorry that sounded rude." She lifted her apron and wiped away tears. "But he strenuously objects to taking an afternoon nap. I hope you'll help me convince him to do so."

"Yes ma'am. I'll do my best."

She turned, led the way to his study, and left me standing in its doorway. The doctor was seated at his desk with a large ledger open. Several smaller ones were stacked beside it. At my tap on the doorjamb, he removed his pocket watch and glanced at it. "Ah. There you are. Right on time. Close the door." He pointed at a chair across from his desk. "Bring that over here and sit down."

"This large one is my account book where I keep track of outstanding fees." A coughing fit racked his body. After it ended, he moved the ledger closer to me. "Take a few minutes to examine it as I'm sure you'll want to have a similar one."

The open page was titled September 1798. The first column was narrow and had a list of dates. The next one was wider. It included the patient's name and medical service he had performed. The last column was also wide. In it, he listed what had been received as payment. He had drawn a line through paid accounts and noted "pd" in the right margin. It was a simple system. Yet, with a brief glance, he could see who still had an outstanding debt.

I immediately recognized it as the same process used by Spencer Field though some abbreviations differed. I ran my index finger down the page, looking at how many patients paid with goods, not cash.

Dr. Blair handed the smaller books to me. "These are the medical histories of the patients who may come here today and those we'll visit tomorrow. I want you to read each of these while I finish updating my accounts. Please move to the other side of my desk."

I opened the top ledger and noticed the first date was in 1793. I glanced at the first page of several others and each began with entries for that year. Upon reflection, I nodded to myself. The town didn't have a second physician for almost two years because Thomas Fletcher had stopped practicing in 1791.

After the date, John had noted the patient's ailment or symptoms, then his diagnosis and treatment. While each book was for one family, member entries were comingled. I thought it might be better to have an individual page for each one but didn't make any comment to him.

Dr. Blair continued to have coughing fits which often interrupted my concentration. Patients coming into the entryway then fidgeting while they waited didn't help.

At precisely nine o'clock, he got up from his desk, handed me the patient's ledger, and called the first one into his study. He introduced me then explained that I was taking over his practice, that I would do today's exam, and that I would begin seeing patients at my place on Monday, October 8th. *He hasn't discussed this with me. How can he tell them when I'll be ready?* Startled, my mouth opened then closed as I realized it would be best if I didn't contradict him.

He resumed his seat behind the desk and watched while I worked. I checked each person, prescribed remedies, then added notes to John's medical histories. By the time Mrs. Blair announced dinner was ready, no one remained in the waiting area. As we walked to the kitchen, I noticed the doctor's cheeks were blotched and sweat beaded his forehead. *He shouldn't be working; he should be in bed.*

We returned to his study after eating. I picked up the next ledger to peruse it. I had finished reading two more when Mrs. Blair rapped on the door and said, "It's 3 o'clock and time for your nap."

I glanced up and saw his nostrils flare. An odd sound issued from his mouth. He slammed his fist on the desk. "Why do you insist on treating me like a child?!"

"Oh dear. You've forgotten we have a guest."

A look of mortification, then his face flushed. He said, "Increase, please return at eight tomorrow."

Their argument continued as I made my way to the door.

∞ ∞ ∞

I ordered strap hinges at the smithy, stopped by the chandlery to purchase ledgers, then visited the tailor's shop to order a new suit. After stabling Beanie in the barn, I changed into farm clothes then moved Father's furniture from his bedroom into the empty one. Finished, I hitched my pinto to his wagon. She snorted her displeasure at being treated in this fashion, but the mare I'd given my father wasn't there and he'd sold his old nag to the tannery.

My nephews had stacked lumber near the sawmill entrance before I arrived, and they helped me load the wagon. Lish stopped the blade and joined us. "Where's Father?"

"Didn't expect you here so early. He went to have a pint. My boys can help you unload. After I lock up, I'll join you."

Because it looked like rain before morning, we placed the cedar planks and keg of wooden pegs in the shelter of the back porch then hurried to Lish's home for supper.

I don't know if Father had changed his mind, if he didn't like how I'd arranged his furniture, or if he had gotten into an argument at the tavern, but he was in a foul mood when we started work.

"I think it would be easiest to turn the window into a doorway, then enclose—"

Father didn't give me a chance to finish. Like a child, he stamped his foot. "No! I don't want my front bedroom destroyed."

I opened my mouth but didn't get a chance to utter a word.

He raised his voice. "It will be done my way, or not at all!" He pointed. "We'll create a vestibule here."

This required us to build two walls to close the area off from the rest of his home, and the resulting room near the existing front door would be very narrow. I'd be lucky to fit a bench into it.

Father worked for only an hour, then went to read his Bible. It was late by the time Lish and I joined a doorway to the hall's frame. He said, "I'm too tired to continue. We can finish the walls tomorrow."

∞ ∞ ∞

A nearby clap of thunder woke me. Dressed in farm clothes, I trudged through rain to help with the morning chores. After breakfast, I put Beanie between the traces on Father's covered buggy before I hurried indoors to change into a suit and my good boots.

Mrs. Blair answered my knock. She glanced outside and smiled. "Oh, I'm so thankful to see you came in a buggy. I didn't want John fiddling with his in such a downpour!"

The cold rain fell aslant. Worried the doctor's breeches would become soaked, I offered the blanket to him so he could cover his legs. He pushed it back at me. "Don't you go fussing over me too. I'm not an invalid!"

"Sorry. I don't want to be drenched and thought you wouldn't too."

With a huff, he draped half the cover over his lap. I adjusted my half, then clucked to Beanie. "Which home is first, Sir?"

"I generally go to the farthest one out then make my way back toward home. Of course, I change my route if someone is extremely ill and needs immediate attention." He coughed. "There's no one like that today."

I followed him inside the home when we reached our destination. Though I already knew the family, he still introduced me then told them I was taking over his practice. He then sat in a chair and watched while I examined the patient. Since I had read the medical history, I was aware of Dr. Blair's diagnosis, but I still asked questions, determined this was only a minor, common complaint, and agreed with the doctor's previous assessment. After giving the mother a fresh vial of balm from my kit and instructing her to apply it to her son's rash three times each day, we departed.

Our next stop was at the home of a recent widower who complained of tiredness along with sore legs and feet. When I looked at the man's throat, I noticed his gums were very red. I thought over the previous treatment, frowned, and glanced at the doctor. *How will he react to my having a different diagnosis?*

To confirm my suspicion, I asked the gentleman about his recent eating habits. I nodded as he described his diet. "I believe you're suffering from scurvy because you haven't eaten any fruit and vegetables lately. You can't just have meat and potatoes. You'll begin to feel better as soon as you add those back to your diet."

I saw John's scowl and flared nostrils as I picked up my medical kit, but he waited until we were inside the buggy before he berated me. Phlegm spluttered from his mouth along with his words. "You're a whippersnapper! What possessed you to contradict me? You told him I was wrong!" A coughing fit shook his body. He pulled his handkerchief out and wiped the spittle away. "Scurvy?! Why on earth would you say that?"

I delayed speaking until he stopped coughing and grew a bit calmer. "From the redness of the man's gums."

His clenched jaw revealed my answer didn't satisfy him. *How do I explain without upsetting him more?* "Dr. Field suggested I suffered from a touch of scurvy during my time in Ohio. It's been on my mind since our discussion." The rigid cords of his neck began to loosen as I described how miserable I'd been while on my brother-in-law's survey trip, subsisting only on meat and potatoes, and how I hadn't felt better until I had peaches when I arrived in Gallipolis.

∞ ∞ ∞

It was close to one o'clock when we returned to his home. He'd remained silent after our diagnosis dispute. Yet, his glowering sideways glances every time we returned to the buggy made me uncomfortable. I wanted to escape his company, but Mrs. Blair stood in the doorway, watching for our arrival. "You're soaked through. Let me take your cloaks." She draped our garments near the fire then bustled around the kitchen adding hot food to her already set table.

John's dinner prayer was interrupted by a coughing fit. His wife frowned, glanced at me, but didn't say anything until he finished saying grace. "I do hope you like stew Mr. Mathews."

"I do indeed, ma'am. It's perfect for today's weather."

After ladling some into my bowl, she handed me a basket filled with slices of oatmeal bread. "I made plenty so please feel free to have more."

Silence filled the room, broken only by the sound of John slurping his food or by his frequent cough. When he gave a barking sneeze, Mrs. Blair said, "I think you need to rest."

Stew splashed as he thumped his spoon into the bowl. "Don't tell me what to do!"

I hoped my footsteps were silent as I grabbed my cloak and fled their house.

∞ ∞ ∞

Wanting to get the woodwork completed, I didn't want to take the time to visit Spencer in Oakham, so I decided to talk matters over with Doc Severance. With a puzzled look, he stood up from his desk and extended his hand. "What can I do for you?"

I groaned. "I tried to put my best foot forward but afraid I'm now at sixes and sevens."

He resumed his seat then motioned for me to sit across from him. "I upset Dr. Blair today because I gave a different diagnosis than he'd given to a patient."

Benjamin raised an eyebrow and said, "Tell me exactly what happened."

When I explained, he sighed. "He's always been a bit irascible." He thought for several moments. "Here's what I think you should do in the future. Instead of giving a conflicting diagnosis, ask John for a consultation, then allow him to tell the patient."

I immediately saw where I had misstepped and nodded my understanding. I stood and shook his hand. "Thank you for your excellent advice."

∞ ∞ ∞

I started work on the doorless wall. Starting at the bottom, I placed each plank horizontally and pegged it to the wall frame. I had completed the entryway side and started on the other side of this wall before going to my brother's home for supper.

After we ate, I followed Father back to his house. As soon as he saw the new wall, he stopped walking. He turned and glared at me. "What were you doing?"

"I thought—"

"That's the whole problem. You weren't thinking!"

I glanced at Lish and Junior. Both of their expressions were puzzled. "Sir, I don't understand what's wrong."

"You dolt! Look around the room. Does this match?" With an exasperated sigh, he turned and stalked away.

I glanced at the main living area. Only the upper area of each wall had horizontal planking. The bottom half had vertical.

My brother and nephew helped me gently tap out each dowel as we took down what I had built. We damaged a few of these pegs. Too short for vertical placement, we set the planks aside. I hoped each could be reused because Father would be even more livid if any lumber was wasted.

Lish measured and cut the wood to the correct height. Junior held each one as I bored the holes with an auger then glued and pegged it into place. It was almost eight o'clock by the time we began adding back horizontal planking. Within a short time, we had both sides of this wall completed.

I thanked my brother and nephew for their help and went upstairs after they were gone. Before I changed into my nightshirt, I prayed the rest of the week would be better. Today had been horrendous. Sliding between the sheets, I thought about what I would say to Dr. Blair tomorrow morning.

THIRTY

Wanting to smooth things over between us, I began my apology as soon as I stepped into the doctor's study. "Sir, I'm sorry for my behavior yesterday. I realize I should have consulted you before giving your patient a different diagnosis. I will consult with you in the future."

He glared at me. "Make sure that you do!" He motioned me to sit across from him and pushed several small ledgers toward me. "These are people likely to come here today."

I opened the first one. "Sir, I love your idea of keeping patient histories. May I please borrow these to copy?"

"No!" He huffed, gasped, spluttered, then coughed. It took several minutes for his breathing to return to normal. "Why should you benefit from my hard work?!"

How childish! It would be beneficial for the patients! I didn't argue. Instead, I turned my attention back to reading. His continuing animosity puzzled me. *Lord, please give me the strength to get through the next few days.*

As soon as the last patient was seen, I fled the confines of his study. Refusing to remain for dinner, I made an excuse of pressing business to Mrs. Blair who sighed then nodded.

I hitched Beanie to the porch railing when I reached my brother's home. My aunt looked shocked at my arrival. She'd been washing dinner dishes, so she dried off her hands then came and hugged me. "Didn't expect to see you until supper."

"I know, but I'm hungry. Are there any leftovers?" I sat at the table. "Just couldn't stand to stay at the doctor's house another minute today. He's so hostile!"

Aunt Hannah fixed a sandwich, along with sliced cucumbers and tomatoes to the side, and handed me the plate. Before I finished eating everything, she added a slice of apple pie.

I kissed her cheek. "Thanks. Well, I'd better get on with the woodworking."

After changing into farm clothes, I cut enough lumber to complete the vertical planking for the second wall. Finding it difficult to place these by myself, I hitched Beanie to the wagon then hurried into town. The small vestibule would be dark when both walls were completed. I had decided it, along with my future study, needed to be whitewashed.

Though it was almost closing time, the chandler was still helping a customer when I arrived. I loaded two large bags of lime into the wagon then returned inside to pay for those plus another and a five-pound sack of salt.

I parked near the front door when I returned and carried these bags into what would be my study. I drove the wagon into the barn, unhitched and stabled Beanie, then hurried to Lish's place for supper.

Father finished making the door which couldn't be installed until I pick up the hinges from the smithy tomorrow. My brother and nephew helped me complete the second wall. Father went to bed before we finished.

"Tomorrow I'll whitewash this and the study too. Lish will you help me make furniture for my office?"

"What are you thinking you'll need built?"

He and Junior followed me into the other room. "Though I'd like a proper desk, I could make do with a table for now. I need another one for examining patients. So, two tables plus two—" I paused to think "—better make that three chairs and a bookcase. Oh yes, a small bench to fit inside the vestibule."

Lish nodded. "All right. Since you'll be painting, we'll save you a trip and bring back enough wood for everything tomorrow night."

"Wonderful! Thanks again." I picked up the oil lamp after they left, carried it to the kitchen table, then retrieved my small ledgers from upstairs. Since Doc Blair wouldn't allow me to copy his medical histories, I wanted to jot down what I recalled while the details were still fresh in my memory. Though exhausted, I worked until almost midnight, then lit a candle, blew out the lamp, and went upstairs.

∞ ∞ ∞

Someone was pounding on the front door. I struggled with the flint, but finally got the candle lit and rushed downstairs.

A stocky man stood outside. "Mrs. Blair said I was to wake you. Need you to come quick. There's been a stabbing."

"Come in while I grab my medical kit and get dressed."

When I returned the man was pacing the small area, sweat beaded his forehead. "We've got to hurry, Doc, or my brother will die!"

"I'll have my mare saddled in another minute."

"No!" He wrung his hands together. "Took so long going for Severance then Blair, don't think he'll make it! You'll ride behind me."

I blew out my candle and followed him into the moonless night. I didn't have any idea where we were going when we galloped out of the yard. This was a reckless act, and I prayed the horse wouldn't break its leg before we reached our destination.

The constable was there when we arrived at Moses's Inn and was questioning the patrons. The quick-thinking barman had wound a tourniquet on the man's upper arm after placing him atop a table.

My unconscious patient had a deathly pallor because of the amount of blood he'd lost. A glance at his arm revealed a severed artery. The barman held a lamp aloft as I threaded a needle. "Where did you learn about tourniquets?"

He said, "I was a sailor and saw it done onboard ship. It saved a man's life though he lost a leg."

"Your action may have saved his too." I splashed whiskey into the wound, then sutured the brachial closed. While I worked, the peace officer approached and asked questions of the man's brother who told him the argument started over an ongoing water-rights dispute.

When I finished, the constable turned to me. "Doc, can he be moved to the jail?"

The brother erupted. "Why would you jail him? He's the victim!"

"It will be up to the Justice of the Peace to decide this matter. The assailant is already in custody. If you don't calm down, I'll put you there too!"

The brother huffed but nodded. The constable raised his eyebrows at me because I hadn't answered. "Not yet. He lost a lot of blood. Unsure if he'll survive. Best not to move him until he wakes."

The peace officer settled into a chair to wait and the brother joined him.

"I need to make rounds in the morning, so I must rest. Come get me if his condition worsens."

I turned and walked out.

∞ ∞ ∞

Father did the morning chores, then came inside, stood at the bottom of the stairs, and yelled. "Increase, it's time for breakfast."

Disoriented, I started to put on farm clothes, realized my error, then dressed in a suit. I saddled Beanie and rode to Lish's home. My family was already eating when I arrived. I sat down at the table and filled my plate as they passed dishes to me. Father said, "Don't forget to pick up the hinges today."

"I won't, Sir. I need to make several stops in town." I gobbled my food then departed before the others left for the sawmill.

Doc Blair was waiting in his buggy. He glanced at his pocket watch. "You're late!"

"I'm sorry, Sir. Got called out—"

"There's never a good reason to be late!" He glared at me.

I was barely inside his shay before he clucked to his mare, and we rolled out of his yard. *It can't be more than three minutes.* I hoped my action was surreptitious as I checked my own watch which read four minutes past eight.

I somehow managed to get through the day. He had remained peevish throughout our house calls. As we drove into his yard, he said, "The missus is expecting you to stay for dinner."

The thought of staying to eat and making idle, polite chatter appalled me. "I cannot remain. There's too much to be done to have an office ready by Monday."

He huffed. "I told her you would make an excuse, but she insisted you'd eat with us."

Though I knew it would cause further upset, I shook my head, mounted Beanie, and left him to take care of his buggy and mare. As I rode away, I pondered how I could make amends with Mrs. Blair.

∞ ∞ ∞

My first stop was the smithy to pick up hinges. My next was Moses's Inn where I found out last night's patient had been moved to a cell this

133

morning. I indulged myself by buying and eating dinner before heading to the jail.

The same constable was on duty, answered my knock, and led me to the cell. The wounded man was feverish though there wasn't any sign of an infection. I handed the peace officer pouches of chamomile tea and ground willow bark and asked him to brew a pot. When he returned with a tankard, I made sure my patient drank it all. "Send a messenger for me if his condition worsens."

The tailor's shop was the last place I visited in town. I wanted to make sure my new suit would be ready in time. It was almost complete, but the tailor needed to make an alteration to the waist because I had gained a few pounds. "Will I be able to pick it up on Saturday?"

"Yes, yes. I'll have it finished before noon tomorrow."

∞ ∞ ∞

I put a large kettle of water over the fire before I went upstairs and changed into farm clothes, then headed into the barn to find a paint brush, ladder, and an old bucket. I carried these into the vestibule, poured warm water then salt into the pail and stirred until the salt dissolved before adding lime. I kept stirring until there weren't any lumps, and my mixture was the consistency of flapjack batter.

It didn't take long to coat the small entryway, but the whitewash kept thickening, so I had to often stop painting to add more water. Two coatings of whitewash brightened the narrow room. I was starting on the second in my study when Lish and his boys arrived with lumber. I hurried outside to help them unload the wagon and was shocked by what I found. "You brought maple? Does Father know?"

"Yes, he knows." Lish chuckled. "He's mad, but he'll get over it. Afterall, it's supposed to be my mill, so I should be able to give you what I want."

We stacked the lumber on the porch, then carried Father's woodworking bench, sawhorses, and tools from his barn into the study.

"Come inside a minute. The vestibule looked so much better I decided to add a second coat to the study too. Just started on that."

My brother followed me indoors. "Danny's old enough to give you a hand with painting after we eat while Junior helps me. Once you finish, I'll send them home."

Father was indeed upset. After he said grace, he didn't say another word during our meal and remained at my brother's when we returned to his house. The first thing Lish and I did after supper was add the strap hinges and install the door. With my eight-year-old nephew's help, it only took an hour to paint my study with a second coat of whitewash. "Thanks for your help, Danny."

"You're welcome." He turned to his father. "Need help with anything else?"

Lish said, "You'd better get home and do your schoolwork. Junior go with him and get yours done too. Your mother will harangue me again if you don't. She was really upset yesterday. Oh, before you go, bring me the glue pot from the barn."

My brother had measured and chalked enough wood for both tabletops then left his oldest son to saw each one to the proper length while he used an auger to bore holes. I wasn't as experienced with carpentry as my brother and was afraid of damaging any wood, so I applied glue then used a mallet to tap each peg into place. After I placed two boards upon the sawhorse, Lish helped me align the holes and pegs, then tap these tightly together. It was extremely late by the time we joined the second tabletop together.

"Since one of these will serve as my desk, any idea how we could make it look different than a regular table?"

Lish nodded. "We could make one with a crossed trestle base." At my puzzled look, he said, "The legs would be angled, like this—" he crisscrossed his forearms "instead of upright."

"Ah! That sounds perfect."

After he departed, I cleaned the paint brush and whitewash bucket then returned these to the barn. I lit a candle and blew out the oil lamps we'd used to light the study. Because of being called out last night, I was too exhausted to write another patient history. Instead, I went to bed but had a hard time falling asleep. I lay there worrying about completing the two tables, chairs, bookcase, and bench before Sunday. Then it occurred to me that I needed to think about what I would say to Nabby's father. This kept me awake for several hours.

∞ ∞ ∞

135

Before I left Lish's home after eating breakfast, I pulled Aunt Hannah aside. "Please keep some dinner warm for me. I don't wish to eat with the Blairs." She nodded, and I kissed her cheek.

When Mrs. Blair answered my knock, I asked her to step outside a moment. "Please don't go to the trouble of making food for me to eat today or tomorrow. I need to complete building furniture for my study or I won't be able to see patients starting next week." She frowned and her mouth opened, but I continued before she could speak. "I've still got tables, chairs, a bookcase, and a bench to make and it's already Friday. Been up late every night this week doing woodworking." I could tell she was a bit disgruntled, but she nodded her understanding.

The doctor snapped his watch closed when I entered his room and closed the door. "Good morning, Sir." He didn't answer. Instead, he pointed across his desk at a chair where he had placed several small ledgers. I picked these up, sat in the chair, opened the top one, and read the medical history.

Though I could hear patients fidgeting in the waiting area, he didn't open his door and call the first patient into the room until precisely 9 o'clock. Without a word to me, he resumed his seat behind his desk.

I did my best to ignore his coughing fits as I worked throughout the morning. Several times I found it necessary to ask a patient to speak up because I couldn't hear their words over the noise he made. I was relieved when the last patient was examined. Mrs. Blair knocked on the doorjamb. "John, your dinner is waiting."

"Have a good day, Sir. Ma'am. See you tomorrow." As he spluttered, I hurried out to Beanie, thankful that I'd somehow made it through the day filled with rancor.

I rode Beanie at a gallop to Lish's home. Though my aunt wasn't in the kitchen, she'd left a plate of chicken and dumplings warming on the hearth. She walked into the room before I was done eating. "You're earlier than I expected."

I finished chewing a bite of food. "Rushed to get here. There's still so much to do before Sunday, and I know curious people will show up first thing Monday morning. Thank you for keeping dinner warm. It's delicious!"

I got up to rinse off my empty plate, but she took it away from me. "Go on now. I'll take care of this."

After stabling Beanie and giving her feed, I went upstairs to change clothes. I completed the parts for one table, then glued and joined the base together. Unsure of how to make the other one, instead I worked on chair pieces. Once I had cut each plank to the proper length, I used great care to drill holes with an auger, worried I would crack a board. My mind sometimes wandered to thoughts of Nabby or her father, but I swatted those away. *There's still so much to get done! Concentrate so you don't mess up!* These thoughts were often repeated as I worked through the afternoon. When I heard Lish's wagon rumble past, I hurried to his place to eat supper.

I had hoped my father would come help us, but he stayed at Lish's home. My brother and Junior helped me move a tabletop onto its base, then we pushed it into a corner of the room. As we did this, Lish said, "I've been thinking 'bout your desk idea all day. I imagine you'd like it built so it can be broken down and taken with you if you move."

"I hadn't given it any thought, but that would be splendid."

He nodded, moved to the workbench, and picked up the chalk. "Here's what we'll do." He sketched how the x-shaped legs would each have a mortise in the middle. A plank with tenons at both ends would brace the legs. He smiled when I nodded my understanding. "All right. I'll get started. Junior, you can saw the lumber for me, but I'll do the angle cuts."

I lit the lamps, then sat on the floor and used the plane to smooth the cut edges of each chair piece. I was gluing pegs when Father walked into the study. "Junior, your mother says it's past time you were in bed." He took the handsaw from his grandson, glanced at the chalked diagram, nodded to himself, then started work. "Lish, your hands are now steadier than mine. I'll let you make the angle cuts."

From the corner of my eye, I saw my brother's proud grin. It wasn't really a compliment, but it was close. With his off-hand words, Father had just admitted my brother was the better carpenter.

These two men worked well together, so I left them to it. By the time I assembled two chairs, each was working on carving out the mortises and tenons. "Thank you both. It's too late to keep going tonight. I'm exhausted."

Father put down his tools and left. Lish smiled. "With his help, got a lot farther than I thought could be done tonight. Won't take long to finish it tomorrow, but don't think we'll have time to make both a bookcase and a bench."

I sighed. "I can make do without a bookcase. Must get the bench done. You know some people won't want to pay my traveling fee, so they will come here Monday. Others, like Mrs. Utley, will be nosy. Got to have someplace for them to sit."

He patted my shoulder. "I'll do what I can."

I smiled. "I know you will. Thanks again."

After he left, I lit a candle and blew out the lamps. Upstairs, I managed to write one medical history before I gave up because my eyes kept closing. I changed into my nightshirt, blew out the candle, and immediately slept.

∞ ∞ ∞

The air was crisp, giving a hint that fall was fast approaching, as my father and I walked to Lish's home after finishing chores. While we ate, I asked permission to use the shay since I needed to pick up my new suit. Father grunted but nodded.

I hitched Beanie to the buggy before I rushed inside to change clothes. I checked my watch before I clucked to her. *Good, I'm early and should arrive before he comes out.* If I drove, I could depart as soon as we returned to his home. Doc Blair was startled to see me ready and waiting. I didn't acknowledge his grumbling as he climbed onboard.

Other than telling me which home was the next to be visited, he didn't speak to me. I was grateful to find it wasn't yet eleven o'clock when we visited the last patient. As I drove into his yard, I said, "Thank you Sir for your continued patience and for introducing me. Now, I must be off because there's much that needs to be done. Thank you again."

He huffed, then climbed down. Without saying a word, he turned and went inside.

On the way back into town, I stopped to see a widow who kept bees and bought two large chunks of beeswax. My family was already eating when I arrived after picking up my new suit, so I sat down and ate dinner with them.

I took the suit upstairs and changed into farm clothes before I took care of Beanie and put the buggy away. I stored one wax chunk in my apothecary shed then carried the other into my study and placed it on a completed tabletop.

I measured then sawed enough lumber pieces to make the third chair then did the same for a small bench. After smoothing the cut edges of each piece with a plane, I returned to boring holes. I had assembled the last chair when I heard the wagon drive past.

My father was in a good mood because the sawmill had been busy with customers. After we had eaten then returned to his house, he boasted, "All the cedar shakes and shingles in stock were sold today. Even the leftovers. Many men have faith in Isiah Thomas's *Almanac*. It predicts this will be a harsh winter."

He and Lish continued work on the crossed-leg base for the trestle table. Junior helped me with the bench. I had planned to make it backless, but Father nixed that idea while my nephew and I were still joining it together. "People will sit for a long time waiting to see you. You should give them something to lean against."

Disgruntled, I nodded. I knew better than to argue with him but making a back meant I wouldn't be able to build any bookcase in time. For several minutes, I thought about what to do before I moved over to the workbench. I picked up the chalk and sketched. "Father, I don't want to waste the wood I already cut for the rear legs. If I saw off another two inches from each, I could use those as braces between two boards to form a back like this."

He came near me, glanced at my drawing, then nodded. I computed the length necessary for the new hind legs before I measured and chalked two planks. I did the same for the two back boards. Because my nephew had already cut the excess from the two braces, I planed the edges of those smooth and let him continue using the hand saw to cut the other planks. When he finished, I handed him the plane. "Please do the two back boards first."

He nodded, and I picked up the auger to bore holes. When Junior finished smoothing the plank edges, Lish sent him home. "It's late. Though tomorrow is Sunday, you still need to do chores at dawn."

"But—"

Lish gave his son a stern look. Junior immediately set down the plane and headed home. My brother turned to me. "Ink, give us a hand threading the brace."

I held one side while Father held the other as Lish inserted the tenons in the mortises. Once we moved and centered the tabletop on this base, my brother chalked lines for the small braces to be put on its underside.

We flipped it over and placed it on the workbench. Father's forehead was beaded with sweat. "That's enough. I'm going to bed."

After he left the room, Lish said, "I'm going to use cedar for the braces since it won't be visible." He retrieved a plank from the back porch. "Help me finish this, then I'll help you."

After he had sawn the proper length, he chalked a line down the center of the plank. "Hold it while I cut."

Next, he chalked where we should drill on each brace and the table. "We'll make the holes deeper on the cedar side than on the maple."

I nodded, handed him an auger, then retrieved the glue pot and pegs. It didn't take us long to finish adding the braces. We turned the tabletop over and placed it on its base. I paused to admire his handiwork. "Thank you. It's a simple, yet distinctive design. You should be proud. Do you know how much I appreciate this?"

Lish shrugged. "That's what family is for." He playfully punched my arm. "Thought about what you'll say to old man Willis tomorrow?"

"No. I've been too worried about getting these done in time. Probably won't sleep tonight."

He said, "It's late and I'm tired. We'd better get on with it."

It was after midnight when we finished the bench. Lish helped me carry Father's workbench and tools to the barn then departed. I returned to my study and applied a heavy coat of beeswax to the furniture. I blew out the lamps and carried a candle into the kitchen. It was too late for a bath, so I dipped a rag into cold water and washed my upper torso before I went upstairs.

Exhausted, I should have been able to fall asleep. Instead, I tossed and turned, mulling over what I could say to Mr. Willis. I hoped starting my practice would persuade him that I was a suitable candidate for his daughter's hand. My nerves tingled when I thought of seeing Nabby. *Has he managed to convince her to marry Sam Utley instead? Surely, she would have written about it in her note or was she waiting to tell me in person?*

It was almost dawn. I gave up, got dressed, lit my candle, carried it downstairs. In the study I used it to light the lamps then searched for a clean rag to wipe off excess wax. I heard the rooster's call as I finished buffing and polishing the furniture. I was still unsure what I would say to Mr. Willis.

THIRTY-ONE

I put my knife and fork on my empty breakfast plate and started to rise from the table. Aunt Hannah said, "Please wait a moment, Ink. I know you're going to church in Oakham then on to visit the Willis family today." She smiled and nodded to her daughter. "So, Hannah and I thought we should give you our present now."

My cousin had gotten up when her mother nodded. She now returned to the kitchen with a large bundle in her arms. She smiled as she handed it to me. "We made this ticking for the entryway bench."

Astounded, I beamed with pleasure. "Thank you both. It must have taken you days to make! This means a lot to me." I kissed both Hannahs on their cheeks. "I wish I could linger, but I must hurry, or I'll be late to church."

My aunt said, "Go on. Good luck today!"

My cousin grinned and echoed her mother's words.

I put the cushion on the vestibule bench before I rushed upstairs to change into my new suit. A glance in the mirror revealed my hair was a mess. I combed out the snarls then clubbed it with a black ribbon. I nodded to my reflection as I tied my new cravat, then bounded down the stairs.

Reaching the road to Oakham, I set Beanie to canter but slowed her to a walk just outside of town. I hitched her to the post as the deacon came out to close the doors. I took off my tricorn hat, then brushed past him and took a seat in the last pew.

I tried to concentrate on the church service, but my thoughts were in turmoil. Anticipation, anxiety, desire, and dread waged war inside me. *Lord, you know I wish to marry Nabby and will do my utmost to be a good husband to her.*

Please help me make her father understand this and allow us to marry. But, in this, as in all things, may Your will be done. With my prayer, a peaceful feeling settled over me.

∞ ∞ ∞

A servant came out and led Beanie to the stable. Another stood in the doorway, took my hat and cloak then showed me to the formal dining room. I was surprised to see Nate and his wife Lucy there. Nate came and embraced me in a bear hug. He whispered, "My children have been sent to eat in the kitchen. Can't have them breaking fine china!"

Mrs. Willis smiled at me and motioned to the chair to her right. "Mr. Mathews, please come sit next to me."

As I moved to where she directed, Nate's wife moved to my right with Elijah seated between her and Mr. Willis. Nabby was seated across from me with Nate to her right, then their sister Lucy between him and their father.

Seated, we held hands as Mr. Willis said the prayer. Mrs. Willis nodded to a servant. "We're ready to be served."

Nate asked about my trip back home. I answered then asked about his. Each time I glanced at Nabby she gave me an encouraging smile. I replied to questions from both Mrs. Willis. My hands grew cold and clammy as we continued eating because Mr. Willis's countenance continued to remain impassive. He hadn't said two words during the meal. When I placed my napkin next to the empty dessert plate, he said, "Mr. Mathews, follow me."

I hoped my gulp was inaudible as I stood up. "Thank you for the enjoyable meal and conversation, Mrs. Willis."

She smiled then shooed me away. A fire blazed in the hearth of his study. Unlike my last visit, today I was grateful for its warmth. Mr. Willis seated himself behind his desk and looked at me.

"Sir, my prospects are better than the last time we spoke." Pride filled my voice. "Since last Monday, I now have a medical practice." I glanced at him, and he nodded for me to continue. "Sir, Nate will attest that I gave your words much consideration during our trip. I vow I'll listen to Nabby's advice regarding matters that will affect her life."

He frowned. "My daughter and her eldest brother hold you in much admiration. I don't understand what they see in you, but I will allow..." His upraised hand wiped the beginnings of a grin from my face. He cleared his throat. "You may call upon Nabby. This does *not* mean that I agree to a marriage. You have yet to prove your worth to me." He glared at me. "Above all, I don't want my daughter uprooted and taken to live so far from here."

"Sir, I can't say for certain whether or not I'll move to Ohio. The future is unknown, but any decision like this will be up to Nabby."

He scowled and motioned for me to leave.

Nabby wore a shawl and waited near the front door with an expectant look on her face. She handed me my hat and cloak. I followed her outside then took her hands in mine. "Your father did not agree to our marrying." She looked crestfallen, so I gently brushed her cheek with my fingertips. "But he did say I may call upon you."

With a delighted squeal, she said, "We'll convince him yet!"

"I would love to see you daily, but I cannot." Her lips started to turn down. "Please don't frown. Let me explain dear one." She gave me an inquiring look. "My father has allowed me to open my medical practice in his home. Tomorrow will be the first day I'll see patients there."

Nabby released my hands and clapped. "That's wonderful news!"

I shared her smile. "Yes. I worked hard all week, first building walls then furniture, but I didn't have time to make a bookcase. I must do that as soon as possible." I sighed and took her hands in mine. "I'm unsure how I'll find time to keep up with my apothecary work along with a medical practice, so I doubt whether I'll be able to visit during the week. May I call upon you next Sunday?"

Her smile was radiant. "Of course. I'll tell them to expect you for dinner." She stood on tiptoes and placed a chaste kiss upon my cheek. "I'll see you then."

"Know you'll constantly be in my thoughts dear Nabby." I removed my entwined fingers from her hand and brushed an errant strand of hair from her brow. "Please give my best regards to Nate."

She nodded. I approached a servant who stood nearby holding Beanie's bridle and waiting for me to mount. With a grin and a jaunty tip of my hat to Nabby, I turned and rode away. Only then did I allow my disappointment to show. *Dear Lord please guide my footsteps and words to convince him of my worth.* I would offer up this refrain many times each day during the following weeks.

THIRTY-TWO

After stabling Beanie, I hung my outerwear on its peg near the back door then headed to my room upstairs. I picked up the ledgers and my medical kit then carried these downstairs. Father was seated in his rocker near the hearth. He had retrieved a lamp from the study so he could see to read his Bible. I nodded to him then opened the door to the vestibule. He raised his voice. "You know you shouldn't work on the Lord's day."

Because I didn't want to argue with him, I said, "Yes, Sir. I won't."

I thought the study needed to be made ready before morning and prayed the Lord would forgive my transgression. I lit a candle with my pocket flint then the remaining oil lamp and got to work. I did my best to be quiet as I polished then positioned the furniture. I set the trestle desk where I'd be able to look out the front window then placed one chair behind and two chairs in front. I put the lamp on one corner of it then stacked my ledgers on another. I shifted the other table into the corner farthest from the door.

Finished, I examined my domain. It didn't look much like a doctor's office because it lacked a bookcase to hold medical texts, ledgers, and remedies. With the room closed off from the rest of the house, my study was chilly. A few rag rugs could rectify this problem. I recalled seeing some for sale at the chandlery. He was a kind man and allowed widows to sell their items from his shop.

I retrieved the inkwell, a quill, and some paper from the kitchen mantle then centered these on my desk. The room was as ready as I could make it for tomorrow. I picked up my polishing rag and beeswax, lit a candle, blew out the lamp, closed the door, and went upstairs.

∞ ∞ ∞

After eating breakfast, I hurried back to change into a suit. I heard voices in the vestibule as I headed upstairs. Finished dressing, I checked my watch and found it was only a quarter to eight.

Three people sat on the bench when I opened the vestibule door. Cloaks were draped across their laps. Mrs. Utley stood up. "You need somewhere for us to hang our things."

I nodded. "Thank you for the suggestion. I'll see to it as soon as I'm able." I looked to the other two female patrons. "Who was here first?"

Both pointed toward Mrs. Utley who said, "I was."

Her answer didn't surprise me. She was the eldest and nosiest of these ladies. She made gossiping an art, always the first to know of any happening inside town. Her version sometimes differed from the actual event.

"Mrs. Utley, please follow me."

It was a cloudy morning, so I lit a candle then the lamp. While I did this, she draped her cloak over one chair then sat in the other. "What's ailing you?"

She sighed. "It's my ankle acting up again, Doc. It's awfully painful today."

"Please go sit on that table." I retrieved my medical kit then realized I needed another chair for when I examined patients. I picked up my chair and placed it near her. By this time, she had rolled down her sock. I unwrapped the binding around her ankle. The area was blotchy and slightly swollen. I applied calendula salve, rebound it, then returned the chair to my desk and sat down.

I thought she was Benjamin's patient because I didn't recall seeing her name in Doc Blair's ledgers. I also knew her family could afford to pay traveling fees. I wrote an invoice for my services as I waited for her to again seat herself across from me then passed this to her. "Here's my bill. Would you prefer I send it to your husband?" She shook her head as I handed her a vial of salve. "Apply this cream first thing in the morning and again before bed. Thank you for coming to see me. I hope I've alleviated some of your misery. Now, would you prefer to schedule Tuesday, Thursday, or Saturday for your house call?"

The only visible sign that my words had perturbed her was a quick shake of her head. She glanced at the paper, then reached into her coin purse and placed money on my desk. "It's not necessary to send your bill to my husband. My ankle feels so much better, I'm sure there's no need to call upon me. Thank you for your time. Have a good day."

I spent a few moments entering information in my large ledger after Mrs. Utley left. I did not start a patient history for her because I knew she'd only come to satisfy her curiosity.

After I finished, I opened the door. "Who was next?"

The other two women who had been waiting when I arrived also had superfluous complaints. Like Mrs. Utley, they were just nosy neighbors. Every time I entered the vestibule after taking care of a patient, there were three people sitting on the bench. This constant flow continued all morning.

Some of the elderly didn't really need medical care; they wanted a listening ear. Though aggravated at this waste of my time, I treated all patients with the same courtesy as my mentor Dr. Field would have provided.

It was late morning when the widower who I'd diagnosed with scurvy came to see me. "Just stopped by to thank you, Doc. I took your advice and now I feel like a new man. Don't think you need to keep making house calls at my place."

"Hold on. Let me take a look at you." After he was seated on the table, I examined his mouth and looked closely at his gums. "Much better. Promise me that you'll continue to eat fruit and vegetables."

"You bet I will."

I nodded. "Good. Then, I won't need to keep seeing you."

∞ ∞ ∞

It was one o'clock when I opened my door expecting to find more patients. Instead, Aunt Hannah stood there with a basket over her arm. She said, "I chased them away because you need to eat your dinner."

She set her basket on a chair, removed a large bowl filled with stew and a half loaf of bread, then placed utensils and a napkin next to it. I sat down at my desk, and she took a seat in an empty chair.

My aunt's face showed concern. "How was your morning?"

I took a bite of stew before I answered. "Busy as I expected. The gossipmongers were here before I got back." I broke a small chunk from the loaf and popped it in my mouth. "Tastes so good."

Aunt Hannah smiled. "Do you plan to keep your apothecary business going?"

"Yes, because it'll bring in extra coins." I sighed. "At first I wasn't quite sure how I'd juggle it—" I paused to take another bite of stew "but now I have an idea."

She raised an eyebrow. "Tell me."

"Thought about going to Worcester today to order new visiting cards. I'd like to keep my afternoons free to do apothecary work. These cards would state my available hours, and I could pass one out to each patient. I know this isn't normally done, but it's the only thing I think will work."

She stood and gathered the dirty things. "Sounds like a good solution. Well, I'll leave you to it. See you for supper."

After she left, I took a sheet of paper, thought for several minutes, then designed what I wanted printed.

Dr. Increase Mathews

Office Hours	House Calls
Monday, Wednesday, Friday	Tuesday, Thursday, Saturday
8 a.m. till Noon	by Appointment

Available for any emergency

I placed this in my money belt, blew out the lamp, then put on my hat and cloak. Saddling Beanie, I decided to stop by the blacksmith shop in town before riding to Worcester because it would take the rest of the afternoon to go there and come back.

The smith didn't have any J hooks available but promised that he would be able to forge three by tomorrow afternoon. He would shape these with a pointed end to be hammered into the wall. I also ordered four wall sconces to be picked up on Friday.

Thankful the chill wind was at my back, I hurried to my brother's home after seeing the printer who promised the cards would be ready by Saturday. My family was already gathering around the table.

Once the platter of food was passed, Lish turned to me. "Guess you didn't have time to start on the bookcase. I'll come give you a hand with it."

"Thanks. I need another chair made first."

He chuckled. "Oh, I see how you are. Anything else?"

I grinned. "Not that I can think of now, but I'll try to think of something else for you."

∞ ∞ ∞

Thanks to my brother's help, my study was almost complete. Late Thursday evening, he helped me position the bookcase behind my desk then helped me carry down my medical textbooks and put these on the top shelf. Lish followed me to my apothecary shed where we retrieved several jars and vials then placed these on the middle shelf.

"Are you done now? Got something else for me to slave over?"

I saw his teasing grin and decided to tease back. "A few wall sconces would be nice." At his startled look, I said, "I ordered those from the smith. Well, really don't need your help anymore. I can't thank you enough for all you've done for me."

After he left, I surveyed the room. On Tuesday afternoon I had purchased three braided, oval rugs at the chandlery. One went under my desk; one put under the chairs in front; and the smaller one placed in the vestibule. I had also bought two oil lamps, an inkwell, and paper. I had picked up the coat hooks and installed those behind the front door in the entryway. The smith would have the wall sconces ready tomorrow, and I would put two on the wall near my examining table. The other ones were for the vestibule. I positioned a lamp near the edge of the polished bookcase. Hoping I'd have enough light in my study during the long, dark days of winter, I blew out the lamps and went to bed.

THIRTY-THREE

T he remaining days of October flew by as I settled into my new routine. Frost had changed tree leaves to glorious shades of gold, orange, and red. I hadn't noticed Mother Nature's beauty until Nabby pointed it out to me as we walked through her father's orchard after eating dinner on the last Sunday of the month. Her younger sister Lucy followed us at a discreet distance. Though I wanted to wrap an arm around Nabby's waist, I was only able to entwine my fingers with hers. I stopped walking, turned to face my love, and took her other hand in mine. "Won't be long until snow falls. What will we do when it's too cold to walk outside? Don't think I've had any success impressing your father."

"We'll sit and hold hands in the front parlor. If you sometimes give me a kiss—" Nabby blushed, "Lucy won't tell. You know she likes you and is favor of our wedding."

I pulled her closer and placed a tender kiss upon her cheek. She wore an impish smile as she stepped back. "So, now you want to woo my father." Her melodious voice filled with laughter. "Nate said I should tell you that Father enjoys a fine cigar though Sarah will only allow him to smoke in his study. His birthday is November 17th, and I hope you'll make an exception to come calling on that Saturday."

Because seeing patients and working in my apothecary took up so much time, I'd been unable to visit her except on Sundays. "His birthday party will be at noon?"

She nodded.

"I'll clear my schedule and plan to be there unless I'm called out for an emergency."

This time it was Nabby who pulled me closer and embraced me. Lost in her gaze, I wished my fingers were the wind which gently rustled her auburn tresses. Lucy coughed and we stepped apart.

With the last rays of sunset lighting our way, we turned and slowly made our way back to their grand house.

∞ ∞ ∞

I rode Beanie to the Field's home. It had become my habit to visit this family after calling upon Nabby. After exchanging hugs with everyone, I turned to Spencer. "May I have a few minutes of private conversation?"

He raised a bushy eyebrow, nodded, then led the way to his study. He poured us a tot of peach brandy, settled into the chair behind his desk, then arranged the pieces on his chess board. "White or black?"

"Doesn't matter as you usually beat me whichever color I choose." I moved a pawn after he made his opening gambit. "I don't think I've been able to change Mr. Willis's opinion of me one iota. Today Nabby mentioned her father's upcoming birthday and that he likes fine cigars. This sparked an idea." I moved a bishop to counter his knight. "Excuse me, I haven't carefully thought this through yet." I paused. He nodded and waited for me to continue. "Uncle Rufus enjoys Havana cigars which he orders from Boston. He says these are the finest smokes, so I'd like to purchase some before the party. I know our chandler doesn't carry those, and I doubt I'd find any in Worcester. I'm afraid if I order from Boston, the package won't arrive here in time." I moved my queen to block his checkmate, then crossed and uncrossed my legs.

"Please stop fidgeting. You're thinking of making a trip to Boston?"

"Yes, but I'd need someone to cover for me." I glanced at him. "I know Jack has been accompanying you on house calls. Do you think he would be capable of taking my place for a week?"

Spencer's look turned pensive. I shifted my feet. "He can stay at my father's house while I'm gone, and he'll have access to my patient histories. I'll make sure each is updated before I leave. I'll also inform everyone Jack will take care of them in my absence."

"When do you propose to go?"

"Mr. Willis's birthday is on the 17th, so I'm thinking to leave on Monday the 12th to be able to return on the 16th. I'd like Jack to cover for me on Saturday too."

His face remained thoughtful, so I said, "There's another purpose too.

I want to buy a betrothal ring to give to Nabby on Christmas, but I want to show it to her father first to clearly demonstrate my intentions. I hope this will persuade him."

Spencer smiled. "Well, it's really up to Jack to decide." He opened his door and called his son into the room. After the matter was explained to him, Jack radiated excitement. "Yes, yes! I'd love to help you out."

"Thank you both. I appreciate this."

∞ ∞ ∞

After I examined my last visitor on Monday, I rushed to Lish's home. They had already eaten, and the men had returned to the sawmill. Aunt Hannah washed dishes while I ate leftovers that she'd kept warm on the hearth. "Don't wait for me at suppertime. I'm going to visit Sarah, and I'm sure she'll insist I stay."

My aunt grinned. "I bet she will. Give her my love."

I kissed her cheek. "Will do."

∞ ∞ ∞

It had been weeks since I visited my sister's family. I found her kneading bread in the kitchen. I kissed Sarah's cheek and wiped a bit of flour off her forehead. With a pouty look on her face, she turned the dough over and pushed her fist into it. "Oh, the busy doctor has found time to visit. He must need something."

I suppressed a sigh. "Would you really want me to come calling after 7 o'clock at night? I don't normally complete my day's work until then."

"Excuses, excuses." She turned to me and smiled to take the sting out of these words.

I cleared my throat. "Actually, I would like your help. I suppose I could do this without you, but I would appreciate your advice."

She used a forearm to push back an errant strand of hair. "Go on."

"Still trying to convince Mr. Willis I'm suitable. He made a fortune making and selling munitions during the war. I'm afraid he thinks I'm only interested in Nabby for her dowry, but I love her for herself." I paused to fill a tankard with cider and took a sip. "His birthday is coming up, and

Nabby told me he enjoys fine cigars. Uncle Rufus said Havanas are the best. I decided to journey to Boston to get some."

Sarah said, "I don't see how you need my help."

I laughed. "Not with that! I want to buy a betrothal and wedding ring while there. Something that would impress him, yet not be ostentatious. Rings Nabby would be proud to wear." I cleared my throat. "So, I'd like you to come with me and help me choose. I need a woman's guidance."

She pondered my question for several minutes before she shook her head. "You're asking too much. Who would take care of my family? I also don't want to sit in an uncomfortable coach for so many days."

"Wouldn't a neighbor be willing to help out? If you agree to go, I'll persuade Father to let us use his buggy. It will be faster than going by coach. Oh, please, please? You've always said you wanted to see Boston."

Sarah frowned. "I don't know enough to make a decision. When do you plan to leave? When would we return?"

I noticed her change in pronoun and grinned. "We'd leave two weeks from today and return on Friday the 16th. There's plenty of time to make arrangements." I made my face look disappointed. "I could ask Aunt Hannah, but I really wanted my dear sister to come with me."

My disappointed look hadn't fooled her. She laughed. "You rascal! Your dear sister indeed!" She grew thoughtful as she shaped the dough into loaves and brushed melted butter on top. It was several minutes before she said, "Joe will decide. If he says yes, I'll ask Mrs. Lewis if her eldest daughter Emma could stay here while I'm gone."

The delicious aroma of baking bread soon filled the room. Laden with textbooks, my nephew arrived home from Leicester Academy. My sister turned to her son. "Luther, go fetch your father before you do your chores."

A few minutes later Joe entered the kitchen. After he was seated at the table, Sarah explained the purpose of my trip. Her face and voice revealed her excitement. "He wants me to come along and advise him. Do you think it would be all right for me to go? Maybe Mrs. Lewis's daughter could come over to cook for you?"

My brother-in-law glanced at his wife's face shining with anticipation. Joe's pensive frown curved into a smile. "I suppose. That is if you can arrange something with her."

Sarah took off her apron then put on her cloak and bonnet. "I'll go find out right now."

Joe waited for her to leave before he said, "I'm not very keen on this idea of yours, but it's been years since I've seen Sarah so animated about anything."

"Yes. It has boosted her spirits. Thank you for saying yes."

He stood up. "Well plenty of work to be done, and there's still some daylight left to do it. You staying for supper?"

I nodded.

"See you then."

I thought about offering to lend a hand, but I was still wearing a suit. Wanting to keep busy, I checked to see if the bread was done by tapping the bottom of each loaf. A few minutes later I removed these from the oven and set one on the cutting board. I was looking through Luther's books when Sarah came inside wearing a huge smile. "It's all set. Of course you're staying for supper." She pegged her cape and bonnet then put on an apron. Sarah bustled around the kitchen muttering to herself. "Let me see. Yes, plenty of fried chicken and baked beans left from dinner. Not enough time to bake a pie." She turned to me. "Go get some apples and sweet potatoes from the cellar. I have just enough time to bake those."

It took two trips to get everything she wanted. While she finished washing dirt off the potato skins, I peeled and cored the apples with a knife. She hummed as she poured a bit of water into a baking dish and brought it to the table. As I placed the fruit inside, she dotted each one with butter then sprinkled maple sugar over the top.

Both men came inside. Sarah turned to them. "Going to be another half hour or so. Joe you have time to go smoke outside. Luther start your schoolwork."

My brother-in-law picked up his pipe and tobacco pouch from the mantle, then went out. My nephew sat on the bench across the table from me and opened his Latin text. "I have a test on Wednesday. Could you please quiz me on my parsing, Uncle Ink?"

I nodded, moved to sit beside him, and asked him questions. A short time later my brother-in-law returned. Luther carried his books into his room, and I helped Sarah set the table.

My sister's excitement was palpable while we ate. "Will we have an entire day in Boston?"

"We should arrive early morning and maybe spend the night there."

"Do you think we'll have time to visit historical sites like the Puritan Meeting House or Stone Chapel?"

I paused to think. "Probably. If we leave at dawn on the 12th, we should have plenty of time to do so."

Sarah glanced at Joe, then nodded.

∞ ∞ ∞

Father gave his grudging agreement to my use of his buggy when I broached the subject at breakfast on Tuesday morning. I did have to point out that he only used his shay on Sundays and that I should be back by Friday. With his consent, everything was arranged for my trip.

I was careful not to reveal my plans to Nabby when I called upon her. I didn't want to dash her hopes if her father didn't give his consent.

Like a child counting down the days until my birthday, I marked off each one on my calendar.

THIRTY-FOUR

I hitched Beanie to the one-horse shay an hour before dawn, filled my canteens, then put oatcakes and dried apples in my saddlebags. When I reached the Willson's farm in Leicester, Sarah put on her bonnet and cape, kissed her family, then picked up a covered basket from the table. Outside I assisted her into the buggy, covered our laps with blankets, and we set out for Boston.

At first our pace was slow because we had to travel behind farm wagons and carts. I turned Beanie onto the post road when we reached Worcester. This road was almost empty of farm traffic, so I allowed my pinto to canter past a slow-moving coach. Sometime later, we stopped by the side of this road to eat the packed food and I fed my mare some oatcakes and apples. Sarah and I ate an early supper at a pub in Marlboro, and it was after dusk when we stopped for the night in Weston.

A light dusting of snow covered the ground when Sarah and I left the inn on Tuesday after eating breakfast. We reached Boston before noon. After stabling Beanie, I carried our things to adjoining rooms at an inn, then we went to a pub for refreshments. I asked the owner if he knew the shop location for William Holmes Silversmith. He said, "It's not nearly as close as Revere's. It's located near the Neponset River's southern end. I'll draw you a map."

When he brought our meal, he handed me a sketch with directions to reach Ann Street, and I decided it was too far to walk.

After we were seated in our buggy, I said, "Our first stop will be at Revere's shop even though Nate warned me that his prices are high and that many apprentices make his pieces. I figure looking there first will give me an idea of what price would be reasonable."

Sarah nodded. In a few minutes, we reached Paul Revere's smithy which had some lovely jewelry, but the prices were indeed steep, especially for apprentice pieces. We followed the written directions to the other shop, then entered and looked around. I liked a gold heart-in-hand ring and the design of a filigree heart band. Both were simple, yet stylish pieces.

"May my sister try on these two? I'd like to see how they look together."

William Holmes removed these two rings from the showcase and handed them to Sarah.

After she put these on, she smiled and said, "They look lovely together."

Her response clinched my decision. "Would it be possible to carve initials on this one?" He nodded. "What is the cost and how soon could we return to pick these up?"

Holmes said, "I could have it ready by morning." On a sheet of paper, I wrote down the initials to be engraved. We dickered over price but soon mutually agreed upon $20. While I was busy haggling, Sarah had wandered over to a counter which contained brooches and necklaces. I moved next to my sister. She pointed at a heart-shaped brooch that had caught her eye and whispered, "It looks so elegant. Any woman would be proud to wear this. Would make a perfect bridal gift."

This piece was also made of gold with gems that contained every color of the rainbow and changed colors with the light. I motioned for Mr. Holmes to join us. "What are these stones?"

He smiled. "Those are dichroic tourmalines that I purchased from a Ceylon trader who doesn't come here very often. Since those are so difficult to obtain, I'm asking $35 for that piece."

"Would you consider $30 for it?"

After he reflected for several seconds, he accepted my offer. I paid him the $50 and told him we would return at 9 o'clock tomorrow.

Our next stop was at a tobacconist where I bought a box of Havana cigars and ordered another to be delivered before Christmas. When we returned to the shay, it was almost dusk and the day had grown chilly, so we returned to the inn.

∞ ∞ ∞

Mr. Holmes had the rings ready when we arrived on Wednesday morning. I'd been afraid our initials would be too small, but his engraving was perfect. He placed the rings and brooch into boxes. As he handed these to me, I said, "Your work is beautiful. I will recommend you to my friends."

From there we drove north to Faneuil Hall to see a merchant who sold glassware items. I ordered and paid for a baker's dozen of both apothecary jars and small stoppered-glass vials to be delivered by post.

I smiled at Sarah when we stepped outside the shop. "My business is done, and we can go wherever you want."

My sister's steps slowed as we walked back to the buggy. I turned to see what had caught her attention and saw a beautiful fringed shawl. It was the same color as the ribbon on her bonnet. I bustled Sarah into the shop. Though she protested it cost too much, I paid a half dollar for it. "My thank you for coming with me." I helped her drape it over her cloak. "This green is a perfect match to your eyes!"

Sarah smiled then looked over her shoulder to see her back in a mirror. "It's so lovely. Thanks."

After stabling Beanie, we ate dinner at our inn. Because I picked at my food, my sister gave me a quizzical look. "What's wrong? It's not like you to eat so slow."

Nervous, I cleared my throat. "I'd like to support the Federalists by going to their theatre on Federal Street." At her raised eyebrow, I said, "It's become quite acceptable to attend. I've read that John Quincy Adams is one of the trustees. Earlier this year, a fire damaged the building, but it recently reopened. The proprietors have encountered financial difficulties since the opening of Haymarket which is run by Jacobian Republicans."

Sarah said, "So?"

"I want to take supper at Mahony's Restaurant then attend a performance tonight. I've wanted to go to one and think it will prove an interesting experience. You may stay here tonight if you don't want to go, but I'd like you to come with me."

My sister's face remained expressionless for several moments. At last she smiled and nodded. "It will make a memorable evening."

I was thrilled by her answer because I didn't want to leave her alone in our rooms at the inn. I'd been afraid that she would stubbornly insist upon remaining here and say it would be too sinful.

After we finished eating, we went on a walking tour. We passed through the park and followed Beacon Street to view the new statehouse which architect Charles Bullfinch had completed in January. Red brick archways supported regal stone columns which adorned the upper level. A massive wooden dome with a pinecone on top completed the edifice. Sarah said, "It's breathtaking."

I nodded. "Magnificent. Fills me with pride."

We continued until we reached the corner of Tremont Street. Here we stopped to gaze at Stone Chapel which had been known as King's Chapel before the war. Built in 1754, this imposing red brick structure had a Georgian style of architecture.

Our pace was slow as we walked the city streets. When I had last visited, many buildings had still shown damage received during the British occupation. One such was the Meeting House. Completed in 1729, this large brick building with a clock tower, belfry, and tall steeple was where the Boston Tea Party had been launched. The British had gutted it, filled it with dirt, and used it as a horse-riding arena. Since then, it had been restored. Most of Boston was now rebuilt and again thriving.

After paying a half dollar for two gallery tickets at the box office on State Street, we leisurely made our way south on Devonshire and within several blocks reached Franklin Street.

We ate supper at Mahony's on the lower level. I tucked Sarah's hand into the crook of my arm and escorted her up the grand staircase to the assembly area. This room glowed with candlelight from enormous chandeliers and from exquisite free-standing girandoles along its walls. When we arrived at the top, Sarah gasped. "I never imagined anything like this. It's so sumptuous."

I patted her hand. "I believe Charles Bullfinch hired the Skilling brothers to design the columns, medallions, and pilasters. It's quite elegant."

An attendant took our tickets, handed us a program, then led us to our seats. Sarah glanced at the paper. "First, a three-act comedy. Then, a ballet pantomime."

Ushers snuffed out candles while an orchestra tuned their instruments. When they stopped playing, an expectant hush filled the room. Within a few minutes the performance started. Soon my older sister's staid manner cracked. She raised a hand over her mouth to hide her merriment. It was wonderful to hear her giggling as she had as a child. The nearby audience joined in her infectious laughter.

A damp and misty fog enveloped us when we left the building. With quickened steps we hurried back to our inn. Sarah turned to me before she entered her room. "Thank you for convincing me to go. May I keep the program as a memento?"

"Of course. I'm glad you enjoyed the evening." I kissed her cheek. "I'll see you early in the morning."

∞ ∞ ∞

Before we finished eating breakfast, I ordered a packed lunch that we could eat while on the road. The morning was chill, and a thick fog blanketed the city when I drove Beanie out of the stables. The heavy mist turned into cold rain shortly after we left Boston. I said to Sarah, "We're lucky the rain is at our back or we'd get drenched."

It was past mid-day when I parked the buggy by the roadside so we could eat our lunch. I also fed Beanie the last of the oatcakes and apples. We stopped for the night when we reached Westboro. I tipped the stable hand. "Please take good care of my mare, rub her down, and give her extra oats."

∞ ∞ ∞

The cold rain continued falling on Friday morning. It turned to sleet before we reached Worcester. We stopped at a pub, not only to eat dinner, but also to dry out our clothing. Then we pushed on to reach Leicester. I was thankful to see the lights of my sister's home. Sarah insisted I should spend the night. Hungry and soaked through, I did not argue.

After our things were draped near the fire, Joe said, "I asked Emma to keep enough food warm for both of you. Come eat and tell us all about your trip."

My sister's eyes glowed as she showed Joe and Luther her new shawl before she sat down to eat. She beamed with pleasure at their compliments. Sarah was more animated than usual, and her voice became passionate when she talked about our theatre outing. She was so joyous that I remained silent and smiled as I watched her. My nephew turned to me. "Did Mother help you pick out rings?"

I smiled at him. "She gave me wonderful advice and helped me find a perfect bridal gift." Fearful it would be bad luck to show my gifts before I had Mr. Willis's approval, I refrained from retrieving the boxes from my vest pockets.

Exhausted, I went upstairs to sleep in what once had been my niece Melissa's bedroom.

∞ ∞ ∞

Saturday, November 17, 1798

Cold rain combined with sleet fell as I drove back to New Braintree after helping the Willson men with their morning chores then eating breakfast. I stopped at my brother's home to tell both Hannahs I was back. I chatted with them for several minutes then stabled Beanie in father's barn and returned the buggy to its place. I curried my mare and gave her oats before I went indoors.

I started water heating for a bath, then checked to see if Jack Field was in my study. He wasn't there so I left a note to let him know I was back and would see him this evening.

After checking my watch, I rushed through my ablutions, dressed in my best suit, and transferred the various boxes into my pockets. I wasn't sure if I'd be able to show my gifts for Nabby to Mr. Willis today, but I wanted them on hand just in case.

THIRTY-FIVE

I rode Beanie through a mix of snow and sleet. The road to Oakham was slick so I let my pinto set her own pace. I checked my watch when I arrived and was glad to see I was a few minutes early. At my knock, a servant came out and led Beanie to the stable while another took my damp cloak then escorted me to the front parlor.

This room was empty, but Nate appeared within a few moments. I reached out to shake hands, but he pulled me into an embrace and patted my back. In a low voice, he said, "No need to look for my wife. She isn't here. Lucy so wanted to be here to celebrate my father's sixtieth birthday, but little Charles has a cold. Besides, she's again in the family way, a good reason for her not to come out in this awful weather."

I clapped his back. "Congratulations. Are you hoping for another boy?"

He said, "I don't really care. I just want this one to be healthy enough to grow up!"

Nervous, I cleared my throat and glanced at the open doorway. I murmured, "This may seem a bit audacious, but I went to Boston to purchase bridal gifts to impress your father because I'd like to give Nabby a betrothal ring for Christmas."

Nate smiled. "Do you have these with you?"

I patted my vest pockets. "I do, but I'm not sure this would be a good day."

He chuckled. "Father should be in a magnanimous mood. Don't think you'll find a better day. Have you been practicing your chess game?"

Sadly, I shook my head. "Haven't been able to play much with Spencer, and he's the only one who plays a decent match. Besides, my medical practice keeps me too busy." I felt my pockets again. "I'm such a dolt. I

161

left his birthday present in my cloak. Could you ask a servant to bring it here?"

Nate nodded and left the parlor. He returned with a servant who carried my wrap. I reached for it as Nabby appeared in the doorway. Her smiling face changed to one of concern. "Oh my! Tell me you haven't been called out!"

I chuckled. "No. Jack Field is seeing my patients today. I simply forgot to get this from my pocket." I pulled out the box and gave my cloak to the servant.

She smiled. "Thank goodness! Sarah sent me to tell you dinner is ready."

I smiled and shook hands with the Willis siblings and their spouses in the dining room. Mrs. Willis said, "Everyone please take your seats."

I added my cloth-wrapped package to the others atop a sideboard, then turned. Vashti smiled. "You're over here next to me, Doc."

I took my seat between her and Chloe. I was delighted to find that Nabby sat across from me between her brothers-in-law Martin and Silas who sat opposite of their wives. Mrs. Willis motioned to a servant to pour wine. As soon as everyone had a full glass, Nate stood up. "Happy Sixtieth Birthday, Father. May you have sixty more blessed years."

Everyone applauded his toast then took a sip of wine. In unison they raised their glasses and said, "To your health."

The table had been set with so much silverware, plates, and bowls that I didn't know which to use. I watched the sisters then did what they did. Several types of vegetables followed two different fruit servings then the main courses began. In addition to roast turkey and trimmings, there was ham, roast pork, and roast beef. I had never eaten so much at one sitting, so I refused the pork and beef when it was offered to me by their butler.

When everyone finished dining, servants cleared the table then placed the presents in front of Mr. Willis. He was in jovial spirits. Like a child, he gave each one a tiny shake before he opened it. His gifts included a mahogany walking stick with a carved ivory head, a black wool cloak, ascots, hose, and several boxes of fine cigars. My package was the last one to be opened. His eyes gleamed with pleasure when he found these were Havana cigars. "Who gave me this?"

"I did, Sir."

He nodded. The servants returned his gifts to the sideboard, then cut the cake and gave a slice to each person. When everyone finished, Mr. Willis smiled at his wife. "Please tell the cook our meal was excellent."

He stood up after she nodded. I saw him place my box in his pocket before he left the room. The other men also stood, and Nate motioned from me to come. I followed them to the parlor. Their butler served whiskey to each man then stood near the doorway. Mr. Willis said, "That will be all. Each man can serve himself if he wants more."

The man nodded and said, "Very good Sir." He left the room.

Mr. Willis downed his drink then motioned for his eldest son to follow him out of the parlor. Betty's husband, Luther Hayward, and Molly's husband, Gideon Howard approached and introduced themselves. While I had met many of Nabby's relatives before starting my trip, I hadn't met these two men when I was in the Bridgewater area.

I listened while the others discussed politics. They disagreed over the Sedition Act which had been passed by Congress in July because the French continued to harass our merchant ships in both Atlantic and Caribbean waters.

Martin said, "My brother Daniel says the Jacobians are going to cause trouble. Through his many correspondents, the Judge has heard the Republicans who own newspapers plan to sue themselves, so they'll be thrown into jail."

Gideon said, "Wonder how much Jefferson is paying them to do so. He'd do anything to make Federalists look bad."

Luther said, "You've got to admit the Sedition Act as it was written goes too far. That's why the Jacobians will do this!"

I noticed Nate in the doorway, trying to get my attention. He motioned for me to join him. When I approached, he said, "Father is enjoying one of your Havana cigars. I suggested you'd like a game of chess." He smiled. "The rest is up to you."

THIRTY-SIX

Nervous, I fidgeted with my cravat as I walked to his study. I thought I'd find the elder Mr. Willis seated behind his desk, but this was not the case. As I raised my hand to tap on the door, he said, "Don't just stand there. Come in and close the door."

I did as he bid me, then joined him at a game table placed near the fire. As I sat down, he said, "Black or white?"

"I'll take black Sir."

I helped him set the pieces. He moved the queen's pawn forward. As we played, I tried to formulate how I could broach the subject of marriage. Because of this, my performance was lackluster, and he had me in checkmate in less than fifteen minutes.

"I know I can do better. How about another match Sir?"

He nodded and lit another Havana. I concentrated this time, and our game ended in a draw. He took his last puff from the cigar and stubbed it out. "We'd better get back to the parlor or else Sarah will have a conniption."

"May I have a few more moments of your time, Sir?"

He gave me a quizzical glance but nodded.

"You may think me presumptuous, but I desire to prove I'm worthy of marrying your daughter. To this end, I've purchased gifts to give Nabby upon your approval."

Though he frowned, he motioned for me to continue.

I pulled the boxes from my pockets. "I went to Boston and purchased rings plus a bridal gift." I quickly opened these and placed them before him. "With your permission, I'd like to give Nabby the betrothal ring for Christmas."

I think his hand moved with unconscious volition as it reached out and picked up the heart-shaped brooch. He cleared his throat. "I've never before seen anything like this. What are these gems?"

"Those are dichroic tourmalines from Ceylon."

He nodded but continued frowning. At last he said, "I'm still not happy that you may remove Nabby so far from home, but I'm tired of being badgered by her and Nate. I give my consent, but Sarah will be the one to set the date and make wedding plans."

"Thank you, Sir. I'm so grateful you've accepted my troth."

He grunted and stood up. "Nabby is not to know until you give her the gift at Christmas."

I nodded and followed him to his front parlor. The women had joined the men, and Sarah frowned when we entered. "How could you be so inconsiderate?"

Mr. Willis rushed to move beside his wife, drew her aside, and whispered in her ear. Nate stared at me expectantly. I grinned and raised my thumb. A broad smile lit his face and he opened his mouth to speak. At a quick shake of my head, he did not say anything.

Nabby approached. "Nate told me you were playing chess with Father. How did you do?"

"He dealt me a severe loss in the first, but—" I smiled and gazed into her green eyes, "we came to a draw in the second match."

"Well done. You were in there a long time. Did you speak of anything important?"

I was saved from answering her question because a servant appeared with my outdoor things and handed those to me. "Sorry Sir, but a man says it's urgent that you go with him."

THIRTY-SEVEN

The man standing outside said, "I went to Doctor Field's home, but he was out. I hope you don't mind but Mrs. Field thought I might find you here."

I nodded, mounted Beanie, then followed him through the falling snow to his home. It was long after dark by the time I returned to my father's house. I stabled Beanie, then stomped my feet outside the back door after getting as much snow as I could off with the boot scraper. Jack hurried into the kitchen as I entered. "I've been getting worried." He reached for his cloak and hat.

"No. I can't let you go out there. Your mother would never forgive me if anything happened to you riding home."

He started to argue, but I shook my head. "No, and that's the end of it. There's already over a foot on the ground. I barely reached here and wished I had a lantern. You must wait until morning when you can see where you're riding. You don't want to break your horse's leg, do you?"

Jack muttered something under his breath then nodded.

∞ ∞ ∞

The miserable weather continued. My sister Sarah and her family did not come for Thanksgiving because the roads were too nasty to travel the distance from Leicester. Over two feet of snow had fallen within a few days, the temperatures had dropped, so none had melted. The next few weeks were devoted to caring for my patients. So many people became ill, I was glad my apothecary was well stocked. I didn't have time to make new remedies and didn't have a chance to visit Nabby until the second Sunday in December.

Nabby approached as I handed my hat and cloak to a servant. "It's been so long since you've visited. By now, I thought you'd changed your mind about me."

I started to apologize then noticed her impish grin. She came close and placed a chaste kiss on my cheek. She whispered, "Before he left, Nate told me Father finally gave his approval."

I murmured, "I was ordered not to tell you."

Her green eyes sparkled as she took a step back and answered me in a soft voice. "I haven't let on that I know, and I won't!"

She placed her hand in the crook of my elbow and led me to the dining room. As we entered, she said, "Look who's finally taken the time to visit us."

Mrs. Willis said, "We thought you might come today." The table had been laid with six place settings. She smiled and motioned for me to take the seat to her right. Nabby took the chair across from me with Elijah to her left and Lucy next to me. Mr. Willis said grace, then the butler served us. I said, "I've been worried. Did everyone make it safely back to the Bridgewater area?"

Mrs. Willis said, "We received a letter from dear Vashti last week. The roads became impassable. They were forced to spend several nights at an inn, but they eventually reached home." She stopped to take a bite of food. "I'm so glad they followed one another, so we know they all arrived safely!"

Chest puffed with pride, Mr. Willis said, "I just know that was Nate's doing. He'd make a fine general."

Because I agreed, I said, "He certainly would Sir."

"Mr. Mathews would you like a match when we finish?"

"Yes, I'd very much enjoy doing so. I haven't played a game in weeks."

A few minutes later I followed him to his study. After he was seated at the game table, he lit a Havana. "How did you know to get this kind of cigar?"

"Israel Putnam gave a box of those to my Uncle Rufus who said they were the best he ever had. He now has boxes of Havanas shipped from Boston to his home in Ohio."

He nodded and made his opening gambit. "Sarah has decided upon a late April wedding for you. This will allow time for the marriage banns to be read in both churches. We will arrange for these banns to be read at the Unitarian Church in Worcester on the last three Sundays in March." He stared at me a moment. "You will, of course, accompany us to worship then."

"Yes, Sir and I will arrange for our banns to be read at the church here in Oakham for the April Sundays."

He took another puff from his cigar. "Sarah wants the wedding to take place in our home. She thinks the last Thursday would be best."

"I haven't any objection. I'll arrange for Dr. Severance to see my patients."

He now focused his concentration on our chess match and did not speak again until the game came to a draw almost an hour later. He said, "You'd better go along and see Nabby. She has a gift for you."

I left him in his study and joined the others in the front parlor. Nabby smiled and moved over so I could sit between her and Lucy on the settee. She reached over to pick up a package from a side table. "I know I probably won't see you until next Sunday, and your birthday is this coming Wednesday. So here is my birthday gift a few days early."

I grinned at her and opened the present. I stood to drape a heavy, navy-blue muffler around my neck. "This is perfect. Mine got caught in my saddle and ended up with a hole poked into it. It's quite a sorry looking thing now."

Nabby crinkled her nose and gave me an impish grin. "Yes, I know. Can't have my doctor looking so raggedy."

I chuckled. I wanted to kiss her but refrained. "Thank you so much."

Mrs. Willis said, "Happy Birthday. How old will you turn?"

"Twenty-six, Ma'am."

Elijah stood up. "I'm going to see if Father would like a decent match."

His stepmother frowned as he left the room. Within a few minutes, she said, "Please excuse me but I need to check on the servants."

With only her sister left as our chaperone, I kissed Nabby on her cheek. I brushed a strand of auburn hair away from her green eyes. "Thanks again dearest one." I placed an arm across her shoulders and pulled her a bit closer.

Lucy coughed. "What will Sarah say if she comes back and sees you two like this?"

Nabby's nose crinkled while she laughed. "Oh, Lucy! It's not as if we were bundling. Please don't be such a prude." Still, Nabby removed my arm and moved slightly away.

We then talked about the weather and my patients. The warmth of the fire made me drowsy, and I could not stop yawning. Nabby said, "I can see you're exhausted, so I order you to get some bed rest. Isn't that what you tell your patients?"

I laughed and said, "I'm fine."

She frowned. "So why are there dark circles around your eyes? Straight home with you. No stopping to see the Field family today."

She rang a small bell. When a servant appeared, she said, "Please get Mr. Mathews's things."

The woman returned with my hat and cloak then departed. As I put on my outerwear, Nabby said, "Come here a moment." She stood on tiptoes to wrap the muffler around my neck.

I pulled her closer and mumbled. "Do you know how much I've missed you?"

"I missed you too."

I gave her a thorough kiss on her lips and ignored Lucy's coughs. Two long minutes later, Nabby stepped back and grinned up at me. "Will you be here next week?"

"I'll do my utmost to be here, dear one."

Thoughts filled with our lingering kiss; a smile remained on my lips during my five-mile ride back to my father's house.

THIRTY-EIGHT

I found a present on my seat when I arrived at my brother's home for breakfast on Wednesday. After Father led our grace, Lish said, "You never seem to make it on time to have dinner with us, so we thought we'd give you our birthday gift this morning." His face glowed with pride. "Junior, Danny, and Fred helped make it."

Inside the package was a wooden plaque. "Dr. is out" had been fire etched into one side of its wood. Holes had been drilled near the top with a bit of rope threaded through.

My smile was enormous. "It's perfect. Very thoughtful of you to make this. It's an excellent way to let people know when I'm unavailable. Thanks to all of you!"

The boys beamed with pleasure when I asked each one what they had done. They laughed and pointed out the section they had worked on. My father scowled because he still believed that children should not speak at the table.

My aunt and cousin handed me their gifts of knitted wool socks. "I really need these too. With the continuing cold weather, I've been tempted to wear two pairs of socks. Now I'll have enough to do so. Thanks again."

I coughed to clear my throat. "I've been remiss in sharing my news. Been afraid of jinxing my luck." I could feel my cheeks flush. "I won't be here for Christmas dinner because Mr. Willis has finally given his consent. I'm to take dinner with their family and present Nabby with my betrothal ring."

Father harrumphed. Lish reached over to pat my shoulder. "Congratulations!"

Both Hannahs bustled over to kiss my cheek. My aunt said, "When will the wedding be?" Her daughter echoed her question.

"In the spring. The last Thursday in April if all goes smoothly."

Father stood up from the table. I glanced at my watch. It was a quarter to eight. I kissed the women then followed the others outside. When I returned to my father's house, I placed the socks on the stairs and the plaque in my study, then called my first patient into the room.

∞ ∞ ∞

After eating breakfast with my family on Christmas morning, I changed into my newest suit then rode to the Congregationalist Church in Oakham. Elated that today would be a glorious day, I ignored the brisk nip of the wind and falling snowflakes.

I hitched Beanie to a post inside the lean-to shelter. The deacon greeted me, shook my hand, then ushered me to sit next to Mrs. Field in their family pew.

Reverend Tomlinson sermonized about the significance of this holiest of days. Unbidden, thoughts and images of Nabby floated in my mind, and these disturbed my concentration. I must have grown antsy because Mrs. Field lightly placed her hand on my arm. I flushed scarlet and returned my attention to the homily.

The snow had stopped but a strong wind still whipped flakes through the air. Shivering, I followed the Field family outside. Spencer couldn't resist teasing me. "I bet you were thinking of your love today. You were almost as fidgety as a young boy. You're giving her the ring today?"

Face red, I nodded.

His wife said, "Well you can tell us all about it when you visit later today."

I frowned. "Don't think I have time to come today. I'd like to return to New Braintree before my sister heads home to Leicester. Now that Sarah and I are on better speaking terms, I'd like to keep it that way. I'm sure she'll be anxious to hear what Nabby thought of her ring. I'll visit you as soon as I can."

We exchanged hugs and said, "Happy Christmas!"

∞ ∞ ∞

A servant led Beanie to the stable. Another answered my knock, took my outerwear, and showed me to the front parlor. "Sorry Sir. The family hasn't yet returned from church. We expect them momentarily."

She left me alone. Too nervous to sit, I wandered the room, examining its contents. A garland of pine boughs and holly decorated the mantle, above which was a large landscape painting. This was a scene of a seaside in winter. A coating of snow covered its beaches with a thick storm cloud overhead.

I resumed pacing. A crystal bowl filled with pinecones stood on a side table near the hearth. I picked one up then quickly replaced it as I heard a flurry of activity in the foyer.

I whirled toward the doorway and saw Nabby's smile as she entered. "I'm sorry we're late, but the road to and from Worcester is awful. Have you been waiting long?"

I shook my head. She approached the fire and put her hands out to warm them. Lucy joined her. "Sarah has gone to tell the servants we're ready for dinner."

"Has it started snowing again?"

"Thankfully, no." Nabby's lips turned down. "We've had more than enough to last us through this winter. I swear I don't remember this much snow so early in the year."

Elijah poked his head into the room. "Sarah says everything is ready."

I placed Nabby's hand in the crook of my arm then we followed her brother to the dining room. While I led Nabby to her seat, I noticed wrapped packages atop the sideboard, but did not add mine to the stack.

None of Mr. Willis's other children had come from Bridgewater, so there were only the six of us seated at the table, and I took the chair across from Nabby. Today's meal was much simpler than the feast we'd had for his birthday. I did accept a second helping of roast turkey and stuffing.

After we ate pumpkin pie, the servants removed the dinnerware then placed the presents in front of Mr. Willis. While they did this, I surreptitiously added my box of Havana cigars to the pile. Eyes crinkling in the corners, he said, "My are all these for me?"

His children laughed. Lucy said, "You know they're not Father."

"Then you must tell me!" He picked up a round bundle. "Who is this for?"

Nabby said, "It's for Sarah from both Lucy and me."

The package was passed to the other end of the table. He continued to pick up and question each one. Soon, everyone had gifts in front of them. "Well what are you waiting for? Lucy, you go first."

When she unwrapped all her presents, he called for Elijah to go next. When Elijah finished, he looked at Nabby. I stood up before he could speak and rounded the table. I smiled at Nabby and said, "My gift isn't with the others because I need to ask you something first." I pulled the small box from my vest pocket. "Will you do me the honor of consenting to be my wife?"

She stood up on tiptoes to wrap her arms around my shoulders. "Oh yes, Ink. Yes!"

She kissed me. Mr. Willis coughed. "Enough of that. Open your present."

Nabby took the box out of my hands and removed the lid from its top. A radiant glow lit her face. "Oh, it's so beautiful!" She handed the ring to me. "Please put it on me."

As I slipped our betrothal ring on her finger, I whispered, "You're the best present I'll ever receive." I gave her a chaste kiss and returned to my seat so she could finish unwrapping her gifts.

When it was my turn, I opened the single package before me. Inside, I found a blue vest. Nabby blushed and said, "I wasn't sure of your size, so I had the New Braintree tailor make it for you. He assured me that he had your correct measurements. I added the embroidery."

She had detailed the outlines of two pineapples in gold thread, one to either side of the buttons. Her craftmanship was exquisite. I said, "I'm sure it will be a perfect fit. Thank you."

When Mr. Willis opened my box of Havana cigars, he smiled. "Thank you, Increase. Would you care to join me for a chess match?"

"Sorry, Sir but I cannot today. I need to spend time with my family too."

He grunted then picked up the cigar box. "Elijah?"

"Coming." His son followed him out.

Mrs. Willis said, "Well, I guess we'll go into the drawing room now. I'm sure the staff are anxious to eat their holiday meal."

She glanced at the butler as she stood up. "Please see to it."

The man nodded. "Of course Madam."

We had only been seated in the front parlor a few minutes when Mrs.

Willis stood up. "I'm afraid you must excuse me because I need to give the servants their gifts." She glanced at her stepdaughter. "Come along Lucy."

I noticed shock on her face as Lucy stood then followed the older woman from the room. Nabby giggled as she turned to me. "Oh, the look on my sister's face! She doesn't yet realize that we can spend time alone together now that we're officially engaged. I'm sure Sarah will explain."

She placed both hands on my cheeks, pulled me closer for a kiss. When we drew apart, she said, "The ring is perfect. It was so thoughtful of you to have our initials put inside."

"Why did you select blue fabric for my vest? I usually pick black cloth."

With a saucy smile on her lips, she said, "You should always choose blue. It brings out the color of your eyes."

I kissed the tip of her pert nose. We spent a few more minutes cuddling and kissing on the settee before I stood up. "I'm sorry but I must go. I hope to see my sister before she heads home." I pulled her into an embrace when she stood.

With a teasing, pouty look, Nabby said, "Barely betrothed and he's off to the arms of another woman."

"You know the only arms I want to be in are yours!" We shared another lingering kiss before she rang the bell to summon a servant.

∞ ∞ ∞

I stabled Beanie then hurried upstairs to retrieve my gifts before I headed to Lish's home. Sarah, Joe, and Luther were putting on their cloaks when I arrived.

"I rushed to get here before you left. Please stay for another five minutes to open your gifts."

My sister frowned. "You know the animals don't like to be kept waiting."

Joe said, "Another few minutes won't hurt them dear."

They returned their outwear to the pegs by the back door then resumed their seats at the kitchen table. After hanging up my clothing, I passed out my presents without saying a word.

Sarah stared at me when I sat down. "All right, Increase. You haven't said anything about Nabby. Did she like her ring?"

My answering smile was enormous. "Yes, thanks to you. She said it was beautiful. Now please open your gifts."

My presents included lengths of ribbon and lace for the women, new cravats for the men, Brown's *Weiland* for Luther, and wooden toy soldiers for the older boys. For Lish's younger sons I had purchased Kendall's *Keeper's Travels in Search of His Master* which was a story of a dog trying to make its way home. I was sure they'd enjoy having this book read to them during the long winter nights.

As soon as all packages were opened, Sarah stood up. "We really must go now." She stared at me a moment. "I expect you to come visit soon."

I nodded, kissed her cheek, then shook hands with Joe and Luther.

THIRTY-NINE

The unusually cold weather continued; the snow didn't melt. The almanac had been correct in predicting a harsh winter. I was kept so busy caring for patients that I didn't visit the Willson family until the end of February. Finished with my last house call by late morning on a Thursday, I rode Beanie to Leicester then stabled her in their barn.

Sarah and Joe were eating dinner when I arrived. As I pegged my cloak, muffler, and hat, my sister added another place setting to the table. She glanced at me. "I won't scold you for not visiting sooner. I can see the dark circles under your eyes. It's been a miserable winter."

I joined them at their table. "Where's Luther?"

"I packed food for him because I don't like him walking home through this cold." She ladled my bowl full of hearty stew then passed this to me. "Bread?"

"Yes, please." I took a spoonful. "Delicious!"

Joe pushed the butter plate closer to me. I grinned at him as I slathered some on my slice then took a bite. "You make great bread. I've invited Nabby to attend church with our family on the tenth of next month and would like you to be with us."

My sister said, "Of course, we'll come."

I said, "Have you heard that Dr. Blair passed away a few weeks ago?"

They nodded. Joe said, "Our Reverend mentioned it during church service."

I said, "At his funeral, Doc Severance told me it's been ages since so many people were sick at one time. He's just as tired as I am. Can't wait for spring to get here."

Sarah said, "Speaking of spring. When exactly is your wedding?"

176

I grinned. "Two months from today. It's the last Thursday in April."

My sister glanced at her husband. Joe stood up. "Excuse me. Some tack needs mending. I'll be in the other room."

Sarah stared at me for a moment before she spoke. "There's no easy way to say this. A new bride should not be brought home to a dirty house." She fidgeted with her wedding ring. "Both Hannahs and I discussed this on Christmas day. They told me the house hasn't been thoroughly cleaned since our aunt moved out. They've only had time to give it 'a lick and a promise' every other week. Nothing has been done to our mother's standard of cleanliness."

At a loss for words, I nodded for her to continue. She cleared her throat. "I've already discussed this with Joe who has agreed to my absence for a few days this spring. When I come, the Hannahs and I will give the house a thorough cleaning, replace those old curtains, and sew new bedding linens and a quilt for your larger marriage bed."

I blushed and pulled at my cravat. "I hadn't even thought of buying a new bed yet."

Sarah laughed at my discomfort. "Well you certainly don't want to sleep in a single! You don't need to worry about buying one. At Christmas, Joe and Lish made plans to build you a bedroom set. Luther and Junior will help them. Oh, I almost forgot to ask you. What's Abigail's favorite color?"

"I don't know. I'll have to ask her. Just so you know, she prefers being called Nabby."

"Tell Aunt Hannah when you find out. We'll decorate your room with it."

I started to stand up, but my sister raised her hand to stop me. "I'm not done with you yet." She waited for me to sit. "Now then. When was the last time the interior rooms got painted?"

"I just did the study and the entryway this fall."

A long, exasperated sigh accompanied her frown. "You men can sometimes be such dolts! I'm asking about the rest of the house."

"Oh! I helped Father when I moved back from the Field's home."

She gave me a pained look. "How long ago was that?"

"Let me think. About three and a half years."

Sarah scowled. "Better than I thought, but you still must redo everything before you bring your wife home. The house should be sparkling clean."

"I'll have it done before we marry."

"You better! Tell our Hannahs I'll arrange to come on the last Wednesday in March and spend three days. This way you can start painting as soon as we finish cleaning and you'll have all of April to do it." She paused. "I'm curious. Do you plan to sleep in Aunt Hannah's bedroom?"

"Oh!" I thought for a moment. "No, I don't want to be directly above Father. He snores louder than a hibernating bear. Though my room is across the hall, I sometimes have trouble falling asleep. Guess I could move my current bed and the other one into the room across the hall."

"What happened to all the other beds?"

"Lish moved those to his house for his sons."

Sarah stood up. "These dishes aren't going to wash themselves."

I gave her a hug and kissed her cheek. "I appreciate your advice. I've been too busy to really think about how marriage will change my life. Can I help you with anything?"

My sister smiled. "No. You need to go home and get some rest."

Sunday, March 10, 1799

My family had already gone inside the church. It was a warm and pleasant spring morning, so I didn't mind standing outside while I waited. Anxious, I worried. *I hope Father will be in a good mood and everything goes well today. Will Nabby like my family?*

When the Willis sisters arrived, I assisted them down from the carriage then escorted them to my family's pew. There had been a murmur of conversation when we entered. The congregation grew quiet when the reverend stepped up to the lectern. During the service, he preached against any form of slavery and asked us to pray for God's guidance to come down upon the people who settled in the new territory. Fire and brimstone would be sent against those who allowed the practice of slavery to continue. The people living in the new territory should not allow their lands to become infected with this abomination of life. We should not follow George Whitefield's philosophy that legalized slave ownership. These people were not dogs to be fed scraps from the master's table; they were people who should be able to follow their own God path in life. It was a stirring sermon, and I would reflect upon it often in the days ahead.

As we stood outside after the service, I introduced Nabby and Lucy to the New Braintree congregation. While we were occupied, my family hurried back to finish dinner preparations. When we reached my brother's home, I assisted the ladies down from the carriage. I told their groom he was welcome to join us for dinner, but he declined.

The men had set up a makeshift table under a maple tree, and the boys were bringing out chairs from their home and from my father's house too. Indoors, I introduced Nabby and Lucy to my family. I had worried because Father still seemed upset that I wasn't marrying someone from our religious sect. Today, he surprised me by taking Nabby's hand in his. "Welcome to the Mathews family, Miss Willis."

Nabby shyly smiled up at him. "Thank you. Please call me Nabby."

She and her sister asked if they could lend a hand then carried out plates and flatware. Lish carved a large ham while the ladies carried dishes laden with food to the table. Once we were seated, Father asked God for his blessing upon our growing family and the food. Aunt Hannah turned to Nabby. "My dear, what's your favorite color? Ink was supposed to ask but, if he found out, he didn't tell us."

I frowned. "Sorry I've had other matters on my mind and completely forgot."

Nabby smiled and reached over to pat my hand. "Light green, like an apple."

Junior seemed a bit smitten with Nabby because he stammered and blushed whenever she asked him a question. When we'd finished eating, Sarah turned to me. "Would you please play the cello?"

I retrieved the violoncello from my father's house and started with a rousing march then finished with my favorite hymn, *Amazing Grace*, which everyone joined in singing. After this, the ladies began taking the dishes into the house. Nabby started to rise to help, but my cousin Hannah said, "Go take a walk with Ink."

Carrying a dish, Lucy followed them into the house. I picked up the instrument in its case and led Nabby to my father's house. After putting it away, I gave her a tour. "I plan on painting and whitewashing the interior soon so everything will be fresh for you."

Nabby nodded. "I want to see where all the magic happens."

When I gave her a quizzical look, she said, "Dr. Field has told us that you create the best medicine in our area. He said you have a magic touch."

I blushed at this compliment and took her to the apothecary shed. She was interested and asked a lot of questions, so I explained the use of each herb. She fiddled with the mortar and pestle. "Do you make your medicines out here in winter?"

"It was so cold this year that I took my equipment and worked in the kitchen. If we move to Ohio, I'd like to build an apothecary next to my office, so it will be heated."

"What kind of home do you imagine we'd have there?"

"Let's go for a walk while I explain."

We followed a path that wound behind the barn and stopped at the pond to watch a frog that was jumping from a log into the water. I took both of her hands in mine and pulled her to sit down on the grass. "To answer your question, I'll build a two-story log house to start. Have I told you my brother wants me to go into business with him?" When she shook her head, I said, "John supplies provisions to many general stores in the territory. He'd like for me to open and operate one. The store and my medical office would be on the lower level, and our living quarters would be upstairs."

I gazed into her green eyes. "This would only be a temporary measure. I want to purchase land near a quarry because I'd like to build a large stone house for you. Do my plans meet with your approval?"

Nabby glanced down at her ring as she smiled. "Sounds wonderful."

I pulled her into an embrace. We kissed for several minutes before I noticed the position of the sun. It was past time for us to head back. Lucy was already waiting inside their carriage. I gave Nabby a chaste kiss and helped her board. I stood waving until the vehicle was lost from sight.

∞ ∞ ∞

After I finished making house calls on Tuesday, I went to the tailor's shop. He took measurements and pinned black cloth to my body for a long frockcoat, which would be single breasted with gold buttons, and for black breeches with two gold buttons at knee level. I had brought along the blue vest that Nabby had given me for Christmas. "I also plan to wear this for my wedding."

He said, "Then, I suggest a light color for your shirt and hosiery." He showed me several bolts of cloth, and I selected a white one. "Would you prefer a cravat or a jabot?"

"Can a jabot be made of cloth instead of lace?"

"Of course Sir. Do you require a new hat?"

Though my father would call me a dandy, I decided upon the latest style of top hat to be made of the same black cloth with a gold ribbon as trim. I gave him a down payment and agreed to return by the second week of April to try on my clothes to ensure a perfect fit.

My last stop was at the elder Mr. Willson's cordwainer shop. "Increase, it's good to see you my boy. Joe said you'd probably come in soon. What can I do for you?"

"I need a pair of new black dress shoes Sir. I'd like the buckles to be gold."

While I knew his apprentice would do the work, he had me sit in a chair while he took my measurements. He smiled at me before he stood up. "Will have these ready before mid-April. Does this suit?"

"That would be perfect." I paid him and left.

FORTY

Sunday, March 17, 1799

When I arrived at the Willis home, their groom had already brought out the carriage, and the ladies were boarding. A servant came and led Beanie to the stable. I followed Mr. Willis inside, and we sat opposite the women. Nabby gave me a quick smile, then looked down at her clasped hands. Mr. Willis opened his Bible and sat reading it silently. No one spoke. It seemed an extremely long ride to Worcester due to the silence.

When we reached our destination, Mr. Willis exited first and held out his hand to help the ladies down. I followed the family inside to the second row of pews. The church was quiet with only an occasional cough to be heard. Seated next to Mrs. Willis, she gave me an encouraging smile. During the service, I followed her lead: I sat when she sat, stood when she stood, and knelt when she knelt. When the congregants turned their heads to stare at me as our marriage banns were read, my cheeks turned red. I hated being the center of attention. Especially in a crowd of strangers!

I found it quite interesting that the reverend's speech emphasized each person's duty to society and was not a fire-and-brimstone sermon. The hymns were led by a choir with everyone joining in their song. At the end of service, the congregation gathered on the steps. Now I heard people chatter as they exchanged news. Mrs. Willis turned to me. "Did you enjoy our service?"

"It was pleasantly different."

Mr. Willis brought the reverend to meet me. "This is my future son-in-law, Dr. Increase Mathews. He practices in New Braintree."

I shook his hand, smiled, and made polite conversation for several minutes. I'm unsure what words were even exchanged because my mind was focused on being introduced as a future son-in-law! My ear-to-ear grin probably made me look ridiculous. Yet, I could not contain my pleasure. Nabby smiled and came to stand beside me as the reverend moved away to greet other worshipers. After this many parishioners approached us to offer their well wishes.

We were soon seated in their carriage heading to Oakham, and our return seemed rapid because everyone chatted. After we ate dinner, I played chess with Mr. Willis. Near dusk, Nabby and I went for a walk.

I held her hand as we wandered through their orchard. Nabby abruptly stopped and kicked at a clod of dirt. "What's on your mind dearest one?"

"I'm so sorry, Ink!"

Puzzled, I searched her face for any clue of what she was talking about. "What do you mean?"

She bit her lip. "We both wanted a small wedding with just our immediate family." Nabby scowled. "Sarah has gone crazy with sending out invitations. Just because she's the great-granddaughter of Peregrine White is no reason to invite all these people I don't even know. You'd think we lived in Boston with its high society who put on airs." With tears in her eyes, Nabby grabbed my other hand, brought both up to her mouth, and kissed them. "I don't dare complain to Father about her arrangements. I'm afraid he'd call off our wedding! Please don't be upset."

I wiped a tear from her cheek. "It's not your fault." A smile quirked my lips. "I can be a circus performer before an audience if it means you're my wife at the end of the day."

Nabby laughed. "Oh my! Will you be John Rickets who dances a hornpipe on horseback?" She scampered away.

I emitted a low growl and chased her. When I caught up, I swept her into my arms and tickled her. Our laughing embrace turned into a lingering kiss. We broke apart when we heard Lucy calling us.

"Nabby, Sarah says it's time for you to come inside. It's too dark."

Absorbed in kissing, neither of us noticed that night had descended. I took my leave from the family shortly after we returned indoors.

∞ ∞ ∞

As promised, Sarah and both Hannahs descended on the house at the end of the month for a thorough cleaning. They dusted every room, shined flatware to a high gloss, removed and washed each dish from every cupboard. I helped the women carry all our bedding outside and pin it on the line. They gave these a thorough beating. They washed each room's ceiling and walls with lye soap. Last, they scattered fresh herbs around the house to inhibit insects from building nests. The rooms were now ready for me to paint.

∞ ∞ ∞

As I returned from breakfast early on April 1st, Jack Field arrived. He had volunteered to care for my patients, so I could work without interruptions unless something came up that he couldn't handle.

I had set several large buckets of milk on the back porch a few days ago, so it would have time to curdle. Using a cheesecloth, I strained out the whey from one bucket, then wrung the cloth to remove any excess. Setting this aside, I mixed lime with salt and water in another large bucket, stirring the mixture until it reached the desired consistency. I broke the curds into fine bits before adding this and a measured portion of green dye to the mix. I kept stirring until all lumps were gone and the color was even.

The upper walls of the kitchen and main room had previously been a Federal blue, so it took two coats before I achieved the apple-green color I desired. After eating dinner, I mixed another batch of milk paint before heading upstairs to do the larger bedroom. I spent another two days whitewashing ceilings, wainscoting, and trim then did the smaller upstairs bedroom. Except for moving the two beds into the other room, the house was now as ready as I could make it for my future bride.

∞ ∞ ∞

When I returned to the tailor's shop to try on my wedding outfit, one minor alteration had to be made which was completed in just a few minutes. After the tailor bundled my clothing, I paid him the balance due. I dropped my package before I reached the door. He chuckled. "Wedding jitters. You're not the first gentleman to drop his purchase."

Mr. Willson had my shoes ready when I arrived. He grasped my hands and said, "Try them on. I made these myself because it was for your wedding."

The shoes fit snugly but didn't bind or pinch. "Perfect. Thank you, Sir for doing the work yourself."

∞ ∞ ∞

Late in the afternoon on the last Monday in April, Lish and Joe brought my nuptial bed along with a large bureau. They helped me move the existing single beds and chests into the smaller room before we carried their wedding gift up to the larger bedroom. "The furniture is beautiful. I can't thank you enough for your kindness. I know your love went into making each piece. I'm sure Nabby will thank you too."

Once again, the ladies descended upon the house, now with their gifts of linen and bedding. I was surprised to see they had made a feather mattress and pillows. Lish and Joe disappeared while Sarah and Aunt Hannah made the bed. The men returned carrying a large oval mirror in a scrolled, wooden frame. Lish said, "Where do you want this?"

Aunt Hannah glanced at my sister. "It should go above the bureau. Don't you think so dear?"

Sarah smiled. "It would be perfect there." She tugged on a pillowcase before she turned to me. "Now, you're to stay out of here until the wedding. Can't have you mussing things up. You'll just have to put up with Father's snoring for a few days."

Aunt Hannah glanced around. "I'll bring over vases of lilacs on Thursday morning."

I looked around then smiled as I kissed their cheeks. "Thank you. The bedroom looks wonderful. I'm sure Nabby will be pleased with everything you've done. I know I am!"

∞ ∞ ∞

With my small bed now in the room directly above Father's, I tossed and turned. Not only did his snores bother me, I was also too excited to sleep. I lay there mulling over what life would be like with Nabby. I realized things would change with my marriage, but I never imagined how much or how quickly it would change.

FORTY-ONE

After I finished my round of house calls and stabled Beanie, I took a bath then went upstairs to dress. Wearing his best clothes, Lish arrived a short time later. "I've made our travel arrangements. You and I will take the one-horse shay. Father has agreed to drive the remainder of our family to Oakham in our wagon."

His announcement eased my mind because I really hadn't wanted to ask for the Willis's stableman to drive us back here in their coach. "Thanks. Here take this." I handed the wedding ring to Lish, and he put it in his pocket. I slipped the package with my dower gift into the right pocket of my blue vest. I combed then clubbed my hair with a black ribbon.

I struggled to attach the jabot, so Lish helped arrange it then held up the frockcoat for me to don. As I inspected myself in the mirror above the dresser, I wished I had just purchased a new cravat. When I put on the top hat, Lish said, "You look like a fop!"

I grinned at him. "It's not the top hat. It's this cursed collar I'm wearing. Though it's not made of lace, I think it's too frilly."

I heard the wagon rumble out of our yard. With a critical eye, I looked around the bedroom, and everything looked perfect. As I put away my discarded clothing, Lish said, "Hurry up or we'll be late."

Lish had hitched Beanie to the chaise before coming upstairs, so we climbed aboard and drove to the Willis's home. When we entered, Reverend Tomlinson motioned for us to join him near the foot of the staircase.

Increase Mathews and Abigail Willis were joined in marriage at her father's house, in Oakham, Massachusetts by the Revd. Daniel Tomlinson. My wife was the daughter of Mr. Nathan Willis, who was born and lived in Bridgewater from whence he removed to Oakham about the year 1796.[2]

The family's harpsichord had been moved from the front parlor into the foyer, and a hush fell as one of Nabby's older sisters began to play. Lucy walked sedately down the stairs, and a cry of "Ah" was heard when Nabby appeared at the top of the stairs next to her father. He beamed at her and kissed her cheek before they started down. When they reached me, he took her hand and placed it over mine. The music stopped. Reverend Daniel read a brief blessing then asked us to exchange our vows. I was so bedazzled by Nabby's beauty that Lish had to pat my shoulder three times before I realized he was trying to hand me the ring. I slipped the wedding band onto her finger. She murmured, "It's so beautiful!"

We exchanged a short kiss then Reverend Tomlinson said, "I'm proud to announce Dr. and Mrs. Increase Mathews."

We were immediately surrounded by well-wishers. I did my best to respond, but I was engrossed by Nabby's looks and couldn't help staring. Her dress was in the latest French style. An apple-green gown gathered just below the breasts with a clinging narrow skirt and a round low-necked bodice. The lace around her neckline was a cream color and an apple green ribbon was wound through the curls of her auburn hair.

I'm unsure how much later it was when my sister Sarah came near and gave me a huge hug. She murmured in my ear. "I want to copy her dress. Maybe it would bring some fire back into Joe's eyes." She laughed and handed me a plate of food from a buffet which had been laid out in the dining room.

Servants brought in a cask of whiskey and bottles of elderberry wine. Once everyone had a beverage in their hand, a round of toasts began. Some were quite suggestive. Nabby blushed. I admit that my own cheeks did the same.

Mr. Willis announced that it was time to open our presents. Surprised, I wondered whether this was a family or religious tradition. He made a great show of presenting me with a cheque for Nabby's dowry. Startled at

---

[2] Direct quote from the Mathews Family Record contained in Increase's published journal.

the large amount written on it, I stammered as I thanked him. I was incredibly surprised to receive cheques from various members of the Howard family. Nabby and I opened many wrapped gifts, and each one was met with a burst of applause. We received flatware, cookware, dinnerware, and all types of linens.

Feeling my family's discomfort because they hadn't brought gifts to be opened, I said, "Lish and Joe please come forward." When they came near, I said, "This is my brother Elisha and brother-in-law Joseph Willson. These men handcrafted beautiful furniture for us. Their items include a bed, bureau, and mirror."

After they were applauded, I said, "Aunt Hannah, Sarah, and Hannah please join me." When they complied, I said, "My aunt, sister, and cousin have sewn a feather mattress plus pillows, many fine bedding linens, and also a marriage quilt."

This announcement was met with another round of applause. The women gave me a grateful smile and nod. I was still the center of attention when I reached into my vest pocket to retrieve the dowry package. An expectant hush fell.

I gave Nabby a kiss on the cheek as I handed her my gift. Nabby's eyes gleamed with pleasure when she saw what was inside. She gently removed the brooch and held it up to the light. Besides exclamations of "Oh!" I heard the word "beautiful" repeated many times. Her eyes danced as she said, "Please pin it on me."

Fingers like thumbs, I tried to find some spot to place it and blushed when my hand brushed her breast. Our audience was laughing, and several men made lewd comments. Lucy relieved my distress when she approached with a green ribbon in her hand. Once pinned to this ribbon, I tied the brooch around Nabby's neck. She said, "It's so beautiful. What are these gems?"

"Those are dichroic tourmalines."

She turned around in my arms and gave me a kiss that took my breath away. As soon as I stepped back, she was immediately surrounded by admirers. Two servants entered with a large package and placed it at my feet.

Nabby broke away from them and came to stand beside me while I unwrapped it. I was astounded to see a black walnut medicine chest and marveled at the interior's twenty-six drawers with a top shelf filled with apothecary jars. It also had sliding panels in the back which provided more storage. The exterior doors included a brass keyhole and key. There were tears in my eyes as I took Nabby in my arms. "It's exceptional. I love you." I pulled her into my arms and kissed her. This was greeted by cheers.

Another round of toasts began. I whispered, "When can we leave?"

She said, "Soon."

Nabby went to cut the enormous cake her Aunt Rhoda Lathrop had made, and servants passed slices to everyone. A short while later, Nabby ushered her aunt out to her carriage. When my wife came inside, she said, "Now we can leave anytime we wish."

Lucy appeared with a small sack which she handed to her sister. As we left the house, Mr. Willis reached out to shake my hand. As he kissed Nabby's cheek, he said, "I expect to still see a lot of my daughter."

I nodded. Nate grinned as he patted me on the back. "I know you'll take good care of my sister."

Nabby exchanged hugs with the rest of her family then I assisted her into my father's buggy. As we drove to New Braintree, Nabby said, "I'm so glad it's over. Was it too much of a circus for you?"

My smile quirked as I said, "It did feel like a bit of a stage performance because there were so many people. I wasn't expecting gifts either. Is that a religious tradition?"

"No. My relatives decided to provide for a future household just in case we move to Ohio." She cleared her throat. "Did you pick out my gold brooch yourself?"

"I cannot take credit. My sister Sarah pointed it out to me."

"Tell me about the gemstones."

"The jeweler said those were rare because of being imported from Ceylon."

Nabby fiddled with her rings. "I confess I've been anxious for weeks wanting to see your dower gift. I overheard Father telling my stepmother how it impressed him and changed his mind."

I chuckled. "I knew you'd love it, and I was indeed trying to impress him. By the way, Sarah wants to copy your bridal dress."

She said, "I'm pleased to hear this. I noticed your father's stern frown at my appearance. I'll lend her my gown so she can make a pattern."

"Don't worry about Father. Fashions are changing." I laughed. "Lish said I looked like a dandy."

She giggled. "You looked dapper."

"What gave you the idea to purchase a medicine chest for me?"

"Why do you think I asked to visit your apothecary shed?"

"You're a sly fox."

She grinned her serene smile as we drove into father's yard. I kissed her cheek. "Please go inside. Make yourself comfortable while I take care of things out here. Our room is the large one upstairs."

She nodded, picked up her sack, and went indoors. I stabled Beanie then put the chaise away next to the barn. I prayed while I worked. *Lord, please let me be a good husband to my wife. I do not want to be a disappointment to her.* I entered the house. With a nervous clearing of my throat, I went upstairs where Nabby awaited my arrival.

FORTY-TWO

I awoke early in the morning and stared at my sleeping wife. *Thank you, Lord, for giving me such a beautiful and willing life partner.* Her eagerness had matched my own as we consummated our marriage.

I heard my father stirring in his downstairs room, but I remained in bed, enchanted by her beauty. The door slammed as he went out and it woke Nabby.

I brushed a strand of hair away and leaned forward to kiss her. "Father went out to do chores, and I must go help him. When we finish, we'll go to Lish's house. Since my aunt moved next door, it's become a habit to eat our meals over there."

She nodded but also frowned as I got up to get dressed in farm clothes. "This needs to change. I would rather fix our breakfast here each morning, then later go over to assist both Hannahs with dinners and suppers. They have enough to do with getting the boys ready for school without worrying over making breakfast for us too. This will also make it easier for you to take care of your morning patients."

"I've got to rush to help him. Go on over to Lish's place once you're dressed."

∞ ∞ ∞

As we ate, Nabby smiled at my family. "I want to thank you all for making our bedroom so wonderful and comfortable. It made me feel welcome." She paused to eat a bite of food. "Would you mind if I fix breakfast for my husband and father-in-law starting tomorrow? Once I clean my house, I'll come over to help you with dinner and supper preparations."

My aunt glanced at her daughter who nodded. "Whatever works best for you, my dear, is fine with us."

Nabby smiled. "Thank you. My father's servants will arrive with our presents and the rest of my things in a little while. I'll return after I unpack everything."

My cousin Hannah smiled. "Let us know if you need any help with it."

Nabby and I walked back together. I kissed her cheek before heading upstairs. "I need to change. I'll be back in a minute."

When I returned downstairs, Nabby was in the entryway chatting with my patients. She smiled as I opened the door. "See there he is. I told you he'd only be another minute." She closed the door behind her.

Two hours later there was a soft rap on my door. "Yes?"

Nabby stepped into the study. "Doctor, I'm sorry to interrupt you, but I thought while Father's men were still here it might be easier to have them bring the medical chest inside your room."

I put down my quill and smiled at my wife. "Great idea. Where do you think it should go?"

"Somewhere close to hand. Maybe over there under the side window?"

When I nodded, she pointed out where it should be placed to the men who now stepped into the room. "Please be careful setting it down. I don't want any of the apothecary jars to get broken."

After they left the room, I finished writing notes for my last patient before I called the next one into my study.

∞ ∞ ∞

The kitchen table was covered with our presents by the time I finished seeing patients. I glanced at my watch then hurried upstairs to change clothes because the others would already be eating. I noticed some minor changes while I dressed. Nabby's brush, comb, and a small mirror now rested atop our bureau, and she'd placed fresh lilacs into the vases.

I ran down the path to my brother's home. Nabby got up from their table, retrieved a plate of food from the hearth, and placed it in front of me. I smiled my thanks to her, then bowed my head and said a silent grace.

I had only taken two bites when Father and Lish stood up. "We need to get back or we won't get that order finished in time."

As the door closed behind them, Nabby said, "Aunt Hannah was kind enough to come help me put away my things and showed me where the linen closet is." She stood up and hugged my aunt who had gotten up to clear away the men's dishes. She sat back next to me and patted my hand. "I'm sorry I left our kitchen such a mess, but I wasn't sure where to put some of our presents. There are too many duplicates to be put into the kitchen. Aunt Hannah suggested those could be stored upstairs in the smaller room until we move to Ohio."

I grinned at her. "Oh, and I bet you expect me to cart everything up this afternoon."

She smiled her impish grin. "That would be wonderful if you're not too busy dear."

Together we followed the path back to the house. I had waited until we were alone to ask her what I found puzzling. "Why were you so formal when you knocked on my door?"

Her green eyes glinted as she smiled. "I will always call you Doctor when there are patients who will hear me."

I had picked up a package from the kitchen table when there was a knock. I shrugged my shoulders when Nabby glanced at me. My aunt and cousin stood on the porch. With my free hand, I held the back door open for them. "Why on earth did you knock?"

The younger Hannah blushed. "We didn't want to intrude. We thought you might be kissing."

Aunt Hannah said, "The boys are napping so we thought we'd come see about stocking your larder. This way Nabby can give you a list of what's needed before you leave for your house calls in the morning. I know the bin is empty because I didn't want it full of weevils, so here's a small bit of flour." She handed the sack to Nabby.

My cousin said, "We'll also help her sort out what should be stored upstairs."

I put down the present long enough to kiss both women then took it upstairs. The women chatted as they worked while I carted packages. I was thankful my relatives were helping Nabby get settled.

∞ ∞ ∞

On Saturday morning after my father left for the mill, Nabby hesitantly said, "I've been thinking about church services. Maybe we could alternate our attendance and spend every other Sunday with my family. This would really please my father. He does like playing chess with you."

193

I readily agreed to this change, kissed her cheek, and left to make house calls.

∞ ∞ ∞

We were in our bedroom later that evening. "Why do they call you Nabby instead of Abby?"

"Nate called me Nabby to make me mad. Somehow the name stuck, and I no longer mind it."

We spoke of other inconsequential things, but we were soon discussing politics. I was surprised to find that my wife had very firm views. "I've often discussed politics with my family. I believe every woman should know what's going on with the world."

∞ ∞ ∞

Our life soon settled into a routine. Nabby got up when I did and fixed breakfast while I helped with the morning chores. This change allowed me time to get ready and be available in my study before any patient arrived. I spent most afternoons working in my apothecary. In the evenings I read medical journals or sometimes played the cello while my wife did the mending.

Nabby succeeded in charming my father, and he allowed her to use his buggy whenever she wished to visit her parents. She helped the other women fix our meals when she wasn't gone.

∞ ∞ ∞

Nabby raised her voice. "Ink!"

I had been absorbed in reading *The Medical Repository*. "Yes, dear?"

She huffed. "I've asked you three times to stop and pick up flour tomorrow."

"Sorry. Yes, I'll get some for you."

"Tell me why you were so engrossed that you didn't even hear me speak to you."

"Dr. Samuel L. Mitchill's August 11, 1798 letter to Dr. Andrew Duncan of the University of Edinburgh. He discusses his findings on the need for cleanliness in clothing due to the body's perspiration. I was struck by his sentence, '*Garments, too long worn, without being cleansed from time to time, often grow rotten and infectious as they grow nasty.[3]"*

I smiled at my wife. "My mother was a stickler about cleanliness. She said slovenliness was a sign of the devil. Because of her, we took weekly baths and she did laundry every Monday. When my aunt came to stay, the women argued about cleaning." I laughed. "Mother insisted it was her household and things would be done her way."

I frowned. "You know some of the patients smell like they haven't taken a bath in months, maybe years."

Nabby's nose wrinkled. "Yes they do."

"Dr. Mitchill mentions a soldier who marched through extreme heat then was imprisoned without a change of clothing. This man quickly became feverish. The doctor feels that yellow fever cases, which infected many sailors in the West Indies, was due to the uncleanliness of the sailors on board their ships. He states these sailors never left the ship, so they did not encounter infected people while on shore. In one of his concluding remarks, the doctor stresses, *'the same means that will cleanse a shirt will purify a ship or a jail[4]*.

I finished reading the article then said, "I think Dr. Mitchill is correct in his findings. Many men were sick at the Newgate jail because they live in such deplorable conditions. It was so dark, dank, and odoriferous that I couldn't wait to get outside."

Nabby shuddered. "Please don't tell me anymore or you'll make me ill!"

∞ ∞ ∞

On my way home from making house calls in early July, I stopped at the general store for supplies and mail. The latest edition of *The Medical Repository* had arrived and there was a letter from my sister.

When I went to my brother's home for supper, I read Susannah's letter out loud. She had miscarried in January. Jonathan had laid the foundation for their new home in March. Her letter was also filled with political news. The first representatives for the Ohio General Assembly had taken office. The first delegate to Congress had been a closer decision than anyone had anticipated. Eleven electors had cast their ballots for William Henry Harrison while ten had voted for Governor St. Clair's son. In February,

---

[3] Page 167 of *The Medical Repository*, Volume III. Minor changes for spelling.
[4] Page 170 of *The Medical Repository*, Volume III. Minor changes for spelling.

Harrison had journeyed to Washington which was the new location of Congress.

Though I was aware Harrison had been elected, I still let out an excited whoop because I'd been unaware how close the political contest had been. Susannah sent congratulations to Nabby and me then ended her letter with love to all our family.

As we walked back to Father's house, Nabby took my hand. "Please explain Ohio's land prices."

"With the current price at $2.00 plus the large amount of land required to be purchased, only the rich can afford it. Harrison hopes to reduce this cost, to reduce the land requirement, and to institute better credit terms for purchases."

She nodded as she picked up her mending basket. "When do you think we will leave for Ohio?"

"I suspect it will probably be sometime next year because I need to wait until the current laws are changed. I have faith that Harrison will succeed."

∞ ∞ ∞

Nabby confirmed my suspicion later that evening. I had noticed changes in her body but waited for her to tell me. She sat down on the side of our bed instead of climbing under the covers. I saw her pensive look and sat next to her. She entwined her fingers with mine before she spoke. "Dearest, I think I may be in the family way."

"This is wonderful news. I'm incredibly happy to hear it."

She gave me a tremulous smile. Her reaction worried me. "Darling, what's wrong? Don't you want a baby?"

Nabby stood up, crossed over to our bureau, and fiddled with her brush and comb before she turned to face me. "Of course I do. It's just come too soon. People will be counting their fingers. You know what they'll think."

I stood up and embraced her. "Let them count all they like. We know better and will prove them wrong!" I cleared my throat as I gazed into her green eyes. "Was your last monthly in April?"

Her cheeks flushed redder than a strawberry. "Sometimes I forget how observant you are. Yes. The end of April though it wasn't as much as usual. I had nothing in May or June."

I grinned. "So, we can look forward to our baby arriving in January.

When will you tell your parents and my family?"

Nabby returned my grin. "I'd like to visit them tomorrow. Can we tell yours afterward?"

I nodded before I kissed her.

∞ ∞ ∞

I finished my work in the apothecary before Nabby returned, so I retrieved *The Medical Repository.* I read Dr. Jeremiah Barker's letter about his documented use of lime, magnesia, and alkaline salts in cases of patients with dysentery, yellow-fever, and scarlet fever in the Portland area. He'd been successful when the patients received alkaline remedies early in their treatment. Wine, cinnamon, opiates, and leeching proved to have disastrous effects, sometimes fatal. Alkaline remedies provided relief and cure. Nabby drove into the yard. I put down my reading and went to greet her.

I returned to the house after stabling my father's horse and putting away the buggy. In the kitchen, I pulled Nabby into my arms. "Have I told you lately that I love you?"

With an impish grin, she said, "You usually wait until we're upstairs." She blushed and reached for my hand. "Father was pleased with the news of an upcoming grandchild."

"I'm thrilled. You're amazing! You're at ease in everything you do on this farm. You have a good relationship with everyone and have charmed my father."

Nabby's smile beamed her pleasure. "My mother taught me how to run a household." Her smile became sad. "She was a wonderful woman, and I still miss her." She gave her head a tiny shake. "We didn't have servants until Father married Sarah and we moved into a fine house to please her."

This led us into a discussion of indentured servitude and slavery. Nabby said, "A few of Father's servants are still indentured, but some have finished their term of service and elected to stay with our family."

"The first time you attended my church the reverend preached against George Whitefield's philosophy of legalized slave ownership. Do you remember?"

She nodded. "Go on."

"As I prayed that night, my Bible opened at Exodus: 21." I cleared my throat. "What is your opinion of slavery?"

Nabby shook her head. "I think it's wrong to hold anyone against their will. I'm against perpetual servitude."

I let out a deep breath, not realizing I'd been holding it. "I'm relieved to hear you say this. While in Ohio, I doctored a runaway slave named Johari. The poor man had so many whipping scars, his back resembled a patchwork quilt." I paused a moment. "Never thought about what slavery was until I encountered this man. Now I'm firmly convinced it's wrong."

Nabby kissed my hand. "I love that you showed him such compassion. Did Johari get safely away?"

"I know he was sent on from my sister's farm. Don't know if he escaped slave catchers and made it to Canada." I sighed. "Slavery is becoming an issue in Ohio. The original Northwest Territory laws prohibited it, but I overheard many pro-slavery sentiments. So many men from Virginia, Kentucky, and Tennessee have settled there, I can only hope that the Ohio legislature will have the sense to follow the law's original intent."

When I pulled her closer, I felt the swell of her belly. "Would you be willing to help slaves hide from catchers?" Seeing the slight downturn of her lips, I continued. "I promise that I'll do nothing to put you or our child in danger. I would never hide them inside our home. Whatever I do will be covert."

Nabby nodded. "Of course it will be dangerous, but it's the right thing for us to do."

FORTY-THREE

In late September, I picked up a letter from my brother at the general store. Outside, I quickly scanned John's missive. I unhitched Beanie and headed back to the farm but stopped before I reached it. I let my mare graze while I reread it.

The beginning was cheerfully breezy with news from the Territory and with best wishes on my nuptials. The second half contained a shocking confession, and I read through this portion three times trying to make sense of its contents.

In a previous letter to me, John had written –

"...my old bachelorship has not rendered me altogether insensible to the charm of the fair and I shall make short work of the marrying business some of these days..."[5].

At the time he had written these words, I thought he'd been charmed by a member of the fair sex and had expected to receive news of his marriage, but this hadn't happened. I'd anticipated being introduced to someone during my trip, but John had not made mention of any woman while I was in Ohio. In fact, he deflected my question when I brought up the subject.

Now, he confessed to fathering a four-year-old son. He wrote that Johnny's mother had passed away during his birth. John did not reveal the

---

[5] Direct quote from the John Mathews April 15, 1797 letter to Increase Mathews: Samuel P. Hildreth Collection, Volume 3, No. 2. Minor changes for spelling, grammar, punctuation, and clarity.

mother's name. He wrote that they had met while he was the provisioner at Gallipolis.

I paced the roadside as I continued reading. He begged me not to be offended by his actions because he had intended to marry this woman. Events had conspired against him. He had lost touch when her family moved from Gallipolis and settled on the new lands granted to the French. She had not informed him of her pregnancy. By the time John had found her family in the new French settlement, she had already died.

He was determined to "do right" by Johnny. Once he obtained land and built a home, he would bring his son to live with him. He begged me to keep this information a secret from our family, especially our father. I realized I'd misunderstood Monsieur Bureau when I visited Gallipolis. When he said, "Johnny is good," he was speaking of my nephew, not my brother.

I decided I would pray for guidance, put the letter in a pocket, and remounted.

After stabling Beanie, I walked to my brother's place for dinner. I was so late that Father and Lish had already returned to the sawmill. I thanked Nabby as she placed the kept-warm plate of food in front of me. My aunt was washing dishes, so I didn't mention the letter to my wife.

Finished eating, I went to work in my apothecary. As I ground herbs, John was on my mind. I prayed for guidance. I did not like the idea of keeping such an onerous secret from my wife. If I believed my Congregational teachings, the birth of this child was predestined. The passage of John 8:7 came to my mind. I should not judge my brother harshly as the Lord had said, "*Let him who is without sin cast the first stone*".

My brother lived in the new territory and its laws were unresolved. Since the Revolutionary War, even here in Massachusetts, capital punishment and public lashings were no longer administered, instead hefty fines were charged against those who were convicted of practicing sexual misconduct.

I'd been so lost in my thoughts, I didn't hear Nabby come inside. She said, "My you're really pounding those herbs today! Is anything bothering you?"

"Yes." I retrieved John's letter from my pocket. "This upset me." I handed it to her. "Please read this with an open mind."

Nabby shuffled through the pages twice before she looked up at me. "How has this affected you?"

"I've been praying and decided I can't judge my brother harshly. His intentions were good."

She nodded. "What do you intend to do?"

"Immediately burn this and keep his secret."

She agreed that it would be best to keep John's secret from the rest of our family. I kissed her and thanked her for being so understanding.

FORTY-FOUR

The months passed by quickly because our days were filled with chores and my medical practice. Nabby had sometimes been moody as winter approached and her girth increased. "How can you possibly love me when I look like a silly goose waddling my way around?"

I had kissed then patted her stomach. "You're beautiful. Every ounce of you."

With the first snowfall, I worried about her walking alone to my brother's home. This led to an argument in front of my family when we entered the house. "If I hadn't had your arm today, you would have slipped and fallen. I'm not always here to keep you safe."

"I'm fine. I didn't stumble at all. There's no need for you to be so upset."

"Aunt Hannah please tell her I'm right. If she falls, she could cause damage to herself or our baby."

Nabby's face flushed with anger and she opened her mouth. Aunt Hannah spoke before she could. "He's right honey. I'm sorry we didn't think of this before. We can just as easily come there to cook the meals."

This arrangement made things a bit more difficult for my aunt and cousin, but I was grateful they did this without any complaint.

Nabby suffered some teasing about her large belly at the Christmas feasts at both family homes. We were both surprised and touched when Lish presented us with a cradle. Made of hickory, he had embellished it with two angels he had hand carved near its top. Most of the gifts we received were for our child, so Nabby rearranged our clothing and filled two drawers of our bureau with baby things. Most of these items had been made by my wife.

Tuesday, December 31, 1799

My footsteps were slow and heavy as I walked to the house after stabling Beanie. The women glanced up from their supper preparations and saw my ashen face. Nabby said, "Whatever is wrong?"

I sat down before I could collapse. "Feel like the world has ended today."

"What?!" and "Why?" came from all three women at once.

"Get Father and Lish. Once were all together, I'll tell you the unbelievable news."

My cousin had Junior fetch his father from next door. Lish was speaking as he came into the kitchen. "Supper is early. I didn't expect to be called—"

He broke off his words when he saw my face. My father entered, grumbling about being woke up if supper wasn't ready.

I turned to him. "Everyone needs to sit down to hear this."

Father frowned at being ordered but took his place at the table.

"I went to see Dr. Field today. He was reading yesterday's issue of *Oracle of Dauphin and Harrisburgh Advertiser* when I arrived. He subscribes to this Philadelphia newspaper, and he handed it to me without saying a word because I wouldn't have believed him if he'd told me."

Tears filled my eyes, but I didn't brush them away. "The great man is dead. Our first President passed on December 14th. The story outlined his illness and funeral arrangements."

I glanced at the others. Each one's face showed distress except my Father's showed confusion. He said, "It can't be right. There wasn't any word in the Boston paper. No one in town mentioned this."

"It will probably be in their edition tomorrow. They must have gotten this news too late to be printed today."

The women stood up and returned to supper preparations. Lish said, "Washington was a fine man. Our country wouldn't exist today without his foresight and leadership."

I nodded because I agreed with his sentiments.

∞ ∞ ∞

We were alone in our bedroom, and Nabby's look was thoughtful as she brushed her auburn hair. "Do you really think the world is ending?"

"No. It was only my grief talking." I joined her near the bureau and took her in my arms. "There has been talk of doomsday for centuries. Martin Luther said the world would end in 1600. Cotton Mather made three predictions for this century and each one was wrong. Back in 1780, my family thought the end days had come. Don't know what caused the strange weather we had back then, but the world hadn't ended."

I kissed Nabby to reassure her. "I think the 1800s will be wonderful for us. Our baby will be born next month. I hope we'll move to Ohio sometime later in this upcoming year." We kissed again. "Our future appears bright."

THE END

BOOK CLUB DISCUSSION

In 1798, Increase was already aware of Dr. Jenner's smallpox discovery. Why do you think it took so long for other doctors to accept this treatment?

Elisha married first cousin Hannah Snow. How many states now have laws which regard this type of marriage as illegal? Why shouldn't first cousins marry?

Increase wanted to travel by boat but ended up going on horseback. Have you ever booked a trip then later had to change your plans? Were you ever so determined to go somewhere that you found an alternate solution?

Robert Parkman has been described as a sick young man, told to take this trip to improve his health. Can you think of another famous man who received similar advice? Since this is before the industrial revolution, what do you think caused Robert's illness while in New England?

A Pennsylvania Dutch tavern owner who treated his wife and daughters as servants appalled Increase. Did you find his attitude surprising? Did you think any other 18th century man would feel this way?

Traveling through the mountains was treacherous, and Robert Parkman's horse was injured. Have you ever done anything dangerous? Looking back, would you do it again?

Do you think John mailed the quoted letter to Lish? Do you think it was never sent and just got buried in his business records?

Why was it so important for Ohio settlers to own land near a waterway?

A ball was a much anticipated, rare occurrence. The women followed rules of etiquette based upon their New England upbringing. How has society changed today?

Many farmers, especially those who lived west of the Appalachians, thought the whiskey tax was unfair. Was this unpopular tax ever repealed? Have we had similar laws?

Increase approached strangers and spent the night with them. Would you consider approaching a stranger to ask for assistance? What kind of reassurance do you need before you would book time at a bread and breakfast?

While doing easier work, the parents of young daughters gave them the onerous task of threshing flax. Do you think anything similar occurs today? Do some people still treat their children as servants?

Several people made suggestions about Beanie's lameness. Have you ever taken your vehicle in for service, had repairs made, then found out it was something different causing the problem?

Mothers sometimes taught younger relatives how to make secret recipes. Have you ever made a special one given to you by an older relative? Did it turn out the same way as theirs? Or did it take some practice to achieve the desired result?

A law was passed to abolish theater, gambling, horse racing, and cockfighting in 1778. Most ministers preached against these events saying it was a sin to attend. Do you think Increase and Sarah would have gone to a Boston play? If not, why not?

Increase never refers to his father's house as home. After you leave your parent's place, does it ever feel like home again?

Both of his older brothers had illegitimate children. Do you think this was unusual for this time? How has society changed?

AUTHOR'S NOTES

When I first read Dr. Increase's diary as a teen, the names of people that he mentioned were meaningless. At first, I created fictional first names for these because his Journal only referenced some people as Mr. Someone.

My research enabled me to fill in many of these blanks. For example, Mr. Parkman who journeyed to Ohio. I'm confident his first name was Robert because research led me to Parkman, Ohio where I found a Robert Parkman had been an early Ohio settler. The Geauga County history published in 1880 states his first trip to Ohio was in 1797, but I think the year should have been recorded as 1798. Increase doesn't mention Mr. Parkman again after they arrived in Wheeling which makes sense because Robert would have traveled north from there.

I have assumed that the Mr. Tomlinson mentioned near the beginning of his Journal might be the Reverend Daniel Tomlinson's older brother, Levi, who later settled in Ohio.

Some of the early Ohio histories quote Increase's diary and imply he was interested in some of the women he met while there. From the beginning of my writing journey, I believed he was already enamored with Abigail before he traveled to Ohio. Further research seemed to confirm this belief.

Abigail Willis had two brothers, Nathan born in 1765 and Elijah born in 1777. I thought it likely Nate was the one who traveled with Increase. As I did more research, this made sense because both of Nate's wives had relatives who settled in Ohio.

I relied on Mitchell's *History of the Early Settlement of Bridgewater in Plymouth County, Massachusetts Including an Extensive Family Register* for information about Abigail's family. Some of the people mentioned by Increase at the beginning of his Journal were his future in-laws!

It was easy to find out the cost for flatboats, but I estimated the cost for a keelboat. Increase never mentions purchasing a horse nor that it was any special breed. I couldn't resist bringing in a Morgan since it was a new breed at that time, though he wouldn't have purchased one near Bridgewater.

A transcript of his actual diary is appended, so you can see Increase's actual words. While writing, I followed Increase's route and noted any differences in footnotes. With the advent of railroads in the 19th century and the subsequent creation of interstates, much of the landscape and surrounding areas were changed. I heavily relied on Google's maps and used a distance calculator to check consistency with the Journal's mileage. I removed some surnames from the Journal to protect the descendants of those mentioned in an unfavorable manner and footnoted the removals.

The original Putnam wooden home in Marietta is now contained in a wing of the Campus Martius Museum which also includes the Ohio Company Land Office. Rufus's home is the only remaining structure of the fort.

Muskingum Academy was completed in April 1797 and was the first institution of higher learning in the Northwest Territory. It was the forerunner to Marietta College which was established in 1835.

The description of John Mathews was based upon *Massachusetts Soldiers and Sailors of the Revolutionary War*, Volume 10, which records he was 5'2" with light complexion. It's unclear whether John mailed the offensive letter to his brother Lish. It could have been buried in his papers and forgotten. The only certainty is that it is contained within the historian Samuel P. Hildreth Collection at Marietta College.

Many times Increase did not note the departures of the men with whom he traveled. Mr. Parkman disappears from the Journal after Increase reaches Wheeling. He doesn't say if Nate Willis accompanies him to Marietta, but Willis is mentioned in the party that goes out to explore from Marietta on August 1, 1798, then he isn't mentioned again. Mr. Edward Tupper joins his boat trip but is not mentioned again after Gallipolis.

From July 18th to August 1st, Increase doesn't record what he did, so I filled in this gap with parties and the Governor's dinner to introduce Ohio's political climate. Rufus was later elected to the territorial legislature. Increase and his relatives probably discussed this topic.

There is a headstone for Sophia Tupper Willis in Marietta, Ohio. I used this fact as the basis for why Nate made the trip, but I doubt she was exhumed and reburied there.

Increase stayed for a week with Susannah before taking the packet boat to Gallipolis but fails to record his activities. I took this opportunity to bring up the Stone family's abolitionist activities. The house Jonathan built in 1799 does have an upstairs hidden room used by runaways. I thought Susannah and Jonathan would have helped even before their new home was built. Increase was also later involved in abolitionist activities, but I'm unsure to what extent. I hoped to journey to Ohio to determine this, but the pandemic occurred.

I don't know the purpose of Edwin Tupper's August 13th trip to Gallipolis, but it is possible that he was checking to see if the June 25, 1798 Congressional land grant recipients were going to relocate from Gallipolis to the Scioto County of Ohio. Andrew Craigie did not visit the territory. I brought him into the story to explain why Edwin and Increase missed returning to the packet boat on time.

Levi Whipple wasn't mentioned in his Journal. Since Increase, Levi, and Uncle Rufus later form a partnership to purchase land, I thought Increase would have met him during this visit, especially since Levi had arrived there in early spring.

Tuft's anniversary history of New Braintree revealed Dr. Increase Mathews practiced there in 1799 and Dr. John Blair Jr. practiced from 1793 to 1798. According to the town's vital records a John Blair died on February 7, 1799. I moved Increase's takeover of Dr. Blair's medical practice a few months forward. This is the only record I found about what Increase did when he returned to Massachusetts other than the wedding and birth information in the family record. Since he does return to Ohio in October 1800, it seemed likely he had already decided upon settling there. Because of this lack of information, I could only imagine what might have happened in his life.

I estimated the cost of the bridal gifts based upon the ounce cost of gold in 1798 as noted on the University of Missouri *Prices and Wages by Decade 1790-1799*. The cost of Sarah's shawl was also obtained from there.

I had already written an imagined almanac prediction of a harsh winter when I later found confirmation of the early New England blizzard. Noah Webster had even commented about this weather.

John Mathews did father an illegitimate son. The mother's name and nationality are unknown. Contained within the John Mathews Collection at Marietta College are letters between John and John Peter Romaine Bureau in Gallipolis. In an August 23, 1805 letter, Monsieur Bureau approves of John's idea of sending his son there for schooling. Based upon the fact that John wanted his son to be fluent in French and sent him to school in Gallipolis, I thought the child's mother might be from France. I know Increase meets Johnny later in Ohio, but I thought John would have confessed his transgression before his younger brother returns there.

While I have read David McCullough's *The Pioneers: The Heroic Story of the Settlers Who Brought the American Ideal West* and Robert Ernest Hubbard's *General Rufus Putnam: George Washington's Chief Military Engineer and the "Father of Ohio"*, these works are not listed in the bibliography. My research was already complete by the time I read these and nothing from either novel was added. However, while reading the work about fourth great-granduncle Rufus, I was reminded there is another Benjamin Franklin Stone.

Susannah and Jonathan's son Benjamin "Ben" Franklin Stone was born in 1779 in **Brookfield**, Massachusetts. Ben's grandfather was also named Jonathan. The other Benjamin was born in 1782 in **Rutland**, Massachusetts. His father was Israel, and his grandfather was John. This Benjamin lived for a time with Rufus's daughter Susanna Burlingame, traveled with the Putnam family to Marietta, and also lived at Belpre. Dickinson's *History of Belpre* records Susannah and Jonathan's family on page 22 and the Israel Stone family on page 23 as living inside Farmers' Castle in 1792.

In later life, this other Benjamin wrote about early life in Ohio. When I first read his autobiography, I was extremely confused because the names of his siblings were different than our Stone family. Through research, I found he wasn't related to our family and haven't been able to find a link between these Stone families.

There will be another book in this family saga trilogy. Increase returns to the frontier along with his wife and infant daughter, and this novel will be about his life in Ohio.

Diane Hildebrandt
Writing as Trana Mathews
January 2021

ABOUT THE AUTHOR

Dear Reader,

If you enjoyed reading *Dr. Increase*, please, please, please write a review on Amazon or on Goodreads. (Yes, I am begging!) By doing this, you will help others find this book when they search for historical fiction. Please suggest my novel be read by your family, friends, and coworkers and recommend it to your book club. If you don't want to post an "official" review, please send me an email and I'll post your comments on my website. Thanks for your assistance!

This is the sequel to *The Mathews Family: Mathews Family Saga Book 1*. There will be one more book in this family trilogy. To find out more about me, please visit my website at http://tranamathews.com

Amazon: https://www.amazon.com/Trana-Mathews/e/B0842WSPCG/
Goodreads:
https://www.goodreads.com/author/show/19960446.Trana_Mathews
Facebook: https://www.facebook.com/Trana-Mathews-101609848128774

You may send questions to me on Goodreads and Facebook or send an email to diane@tranamathews.com.

Thanks in advance,
Diane Hildebrandt
Pen Name: Trana Mathews

ACKNOWLEDGMENTS

Sincere thanks to Linda Showalter, Special Collections Associate at Marietta College, for furnishing the transcripts of personal letters from the Samuel P. Hildreth Collection. This information provided valuable insight into the family dynamics. She also added *The Mathews Family: Mathews Family Saga Book 1* to the college's Special Collections.

I'm indebted to Willis Adams Bailey and Margaret D. M. Fulton for the transcription and 1932 publication of Increase's diary in a pamphlet distributed to family members.

Special thanks to Patricia Woodruff for allowing me to use her grandmother's first name as part of my pen name. As my first beta reader, Pat always encouraged me to keep writing and has provided wonderful advice. I also acknowledge and thank my beta readers Julie Briscoe, Tammy Mathews, Betsey Staley, and Linda Truelove for reading and providing suggestions. I am blessed to know such wonderful people.

DIARY OF A JOURNEY FROM MASSACHUSETTS TO THE OHIO COUNTRY, 1798

Dr. Increase Matthews,[6] the writer of the diary describing a journey from Massachusetts to the Ohio Country and return in the summer of 1798 which is printed in this article and also of the first part of the family record which follows the diary, was born at New Braintree, Worcester Co., Mass., 22 Dec. 1772, a son of Daniel and Huldah (Putnam) Matthews, and died at Putnam (now a part of Zanesville), Ohio, 6 June 1856, in his 84th year. He married first, at Oakham, Worcester Co., Mass., 25 Apr. 1799 (intention recorded at Oakham 7 Apr. 1799), Abigail

---

[6] The likeness of Dr. Increase Matthews which forms the frontispiece in this reprint has been reproduced from a photograph of a portrait by James T. Barton, painted, it is believed, about 1845 and now owned by Edward Spencer Sturges of Chicago. The frame of the portrait was carved by Miss Marle Stuart Nye from logs of the house that Dr. Matthews built in 1802 on the banks of the Muskingum River, in the town of Springfield, later called Putnam and now a part of the city of Zanesville, Ohio. Miss Nye, formerly of Putnam and now living in Columbus, Ohio, carved the frame when she was working in Cincinnati as a pupil of Benn Pitman and Henry L. Frye.

Willis of Oakham, who was born, probably at Bridgewater, Plymouth Co., Mass., 20 Aug. 1777, and died at Springfield (afterwards Putnam and now a part of Zanesville), Ohio, 14 June 1802, aged 24 years, 9 months, 25 days, daughter of Nathan Willis, a native of Bridgewater, whence he moved to Oakham about 1796; and secondly, at Marietta, Ohio, 23 Mar. 1803, Betsey Leavens, who died at Putnam 3 July, 1852, in her 77th year, daughter of Capt. John Leavens. Dr. Matthews's father, Daniel Matthews, Jr., was a great-grandson of John Matthews of Charlestown, Mass., who died 28 July 1659, and his mother Huldah (Putnam) Matthews, was an elder sister of Gen. Rufus Putnam, the founder of Marietta.

In the summer of 1798, the year before his marriage, Dr. Matthews made the journey from Massachusetts to the Ohio Country and return which is described in the following diary. In the autumn of 1800, with his wife and infant daughter, he went back to the Ohio Country, and, after living for a while at Marietta, moved with his family, in the spring of 1801, to Zanesville. In the same year Gen. Rufus Putnam (Dr. Matthews's uncle), Dr. Matthews, and Levi Whipple purchased the land that now forms the Seventh and Ninth Wards of Zanesville, and laid it out as a town, which they called Springfield, the name being changed later to Putnam. Dr. Matthews, after living for about a year in Zanesville, moved across the river to the new town, and resided there for the rest of his life. He was the first physician to settle permanently on the Muskingum River above Marietta. He established the first drug store and was one of the five original members of the first church organized in Muskingum County.

In 1798 Dr. Jenner's discovery of vaccination was announced to the medical world; and, when smallpox broke out in Putnam in the autumn of 1809, Dr. Matthews procured vaccine virus and vaccinated himself and his family. In order to overcome the popular prejudice against vaccination and to demonstrate its efficacy, he took his two little daughters, Abigail and Sarah, aged respectively seven and six years, who had been vaccinated, into the house and up to the bedside of a patient very ill with virulent smallpox. The children did not take the disease, and their father's faith in the protecting power of inoculation was justified. The rest of the villagers then submitted to inoculation.

Possessing large landed interests and having a taste for agriculture, Dr. Matthews withdrew from the active practice of his profession as other physicians settled around him. He sent to Spain for the first merino sheep brought to Ohio, and they were delivered in Washington, D. C., and transported to Putnam in a wagon by a man sent to Washington for that purpose. He was a man of many accomplishments and had more than the usual amount of energy characteristic of the pioneers. He was a skillful performer on the violoncello and an entertaining talker. He enjoyed telling his grandchildren that he remembered the ringing of the bells in celebration of the adoption of the Declaration of Independence — the earliest distinct recollection of his childhood days. He was held in the highest esteem by all his fellow townsmen, who could not fail to recognize the simplicity and purity of his life. He was buried in Woodlawn Cemetery, which is now in the city of Zanesville and was a part of his original purchase from the Government in 1801.[7]*

---

[7] This sketch of the life of Dr. Matthews is based on the family record that follows the diary and on a paper prepared by Mrs. Margaret D. M. Fulton and included in a pamphlet entitled "The Pioneer Physicians of the Muskingum Valley," by Edward Cone Brush, A.M., M.D., which was read by him before the Ohio State Historical Society, at a meeting held at Columbus, Ohio Mar. 1890.

Diary of a Journey from Massachusetts
to the Ohio Country, 1798,
by Dr. Increase Matthews,
with a Matthews Family Record

Published diary cover from 1932

Diary Kept by Dr. Increase Matthews on a Journey to the Ohio Country, 1798[8]

Monday June 4th 1798. Set out for the Ohio country from Oakham. Intend going to Bedford[9], from thence by water to Alexandria in Virginia, from thence to Redstone on the Monongehala[10], thence down the river to Marietta. Put up at Miller's Tavern in Mendon. Expenses .21. Found Mr. Saul and his daughter at the tavern, spent the evening very agreeably.

Tuesday morning the 5th. Very rainy. Set out at 8 o'clock. Put up at Raynham. Expense 1.04.

Wednesday 6th. Expenses .62 Arrived at Mr. Chaddock's in Rochester at 12 o'clock, took dinner and walked to Mr. Willis' five miles.

Thursday June 7th. Went to the wharf in company with Mr. & Mrs. Tomlinson, Mr. and Mrs. Chaddock, and Mr. Willis. Sailed out in a boat and had an agreeable time. Expenses .25

Friday, 8th. Went to the forge.

Saturday, 9th. Went to Fair Haven with Mr. Willis. On the road called with Doct. Foster to see a family sick with the small-pox. One of the family caught it in the natural way, and came home and had it very favorably. The rest were inoculated, and the symptomatic fever had just acceded. Doct. Foster says he

---

[8] The original manuscript of this diary, preceded by the words "Increase Matthews' Property May 28th 1798," is in the possession of S. C. Belknap, a resident of Maine. It was copied by Mrs. Margaret D. M. Fulton, and a transcript of her copy has been used in preparing the diary for publication.

[9] Bedford is located east northeast of New Braintree while the Mendon destination is south southeast of New Braintree. Increase must have meant New Bedford which is located on Buzzards Bay. Originally called "Bedford Village", the town was incorporated in 1787 as "New Bedford" because there was already a Bedford incorporated in Middlesex County. Increase apparently didn't know of the name change.

[10] Increase means Monongahela.

has experienced the best effects from bleeding in the inflammatory stage of this disorder. In one instance of delirium the patient was perfectly relieved by losing a few ounces of blood.

Sunday, 10th. No preaching except the Quakers very near. Staid at home till six o'clock, then walked up to Doct. Foster's, home by Col. Sturtevant's. The Col. wishes to go to the Ohio, but is embarrassed by his father, who is afraid that he shall not get cyder enough if he goes there, and the Col. cannot go without him.

Monday, 11th. Finally concluded to alter my plan of going to the Ohio by water, and propose taking a horse from Oakham. Mr. Willis is to be at Oakham a week from next Friday or Saturday to go on with me. Set out for Oakham by way of Bridgewater. Walked the greatest part of the way to Bridgewater, at which place I arrived at 2 o'clock. Mr. Willis & his Lady accompanied me on their way to Boston. Mr. Willis was so kind as to walk, and let me ride his horse a considerable part of the way. Tarried at Mr. Martin Howard's.

Tuesday June 12th. Went to Mr. Packard's with Mr. Howard in a chaise. Returned with him and tarried over night at Mr. Jon. Howard's.

Wednesday morning, 13th. Read the pamphlets on Masonry which I borrowed of Judge Howard last evening. Have not yet become a convert to Masonry. In one of them the author does not pretend to trace Masonry higher than the year A. D. 126. At two o'clock Mr. Nye arrived at Bridgewater. Informed me that Mr. Tomlinson was sick at Rochester. This disappoints me of setting out for Oakham tomorrow as I expected. Tarried at Mr. Howard's.

Thursday, 14th. Mr. Tomlinson arrived at Mr. Howard's at 3 o'clock. Has a slight Pneumonic inflammation. Complains now of soreness in his breast, and difficulty in breathing. At 5 o'clock left Mr. Howards. Put up at Clapp's at Mansfield.

Friday, 15th. Breakfasted at Mr. Everett's in Foxborough. Put up at night at Barnes' in Grafton. Travelled slowly all day on account of Mr. Tomlinson's indisposition. Expenses .63

Saturday, June 16th. Arrived at Oakham at six o'clock. Expenses $1.00.

Monday June 25th, 1798. Set out at 4 o'clock P. M. for the Ohio on horse back with Mr. Willis. Came as far as my father's in New Braintree.

Tuesday 26th. Mr. Parkman called on us at half past nine. Dinner at Bates' in Palmer. Travelled the turnpike road from Western to Palmer, 9 miles. Expenses $0.30.

Wednesday 27th. In the morning viewed the continental military stores at Springfield. Breakfasted at Capt. Ames'. Came on to Simsbury mine—17 miles. It is now called Newgate. Went into the cavern—the whole depth is 70 feet. There are 15 prisoners confined here, for different lengths of time, from 2 to six years, & two of them are sentenced to be confined during life. One prisoner in order to avoid making nails cut off three of the fingers of his left hand. Major Humphrey to punish him kept him pouring sand into a hopper. After running from the hopper into a tub he was obliged to take it in a dish & pour it again into the hopper. He was kept at work in this manner four months. He still refused to make nails, pretending that he could not learn. He was then confined in a separate part of the vault, where no one was allowed to speak to him for six weeks; after which time he became willing to make nails. Put up at Merril's in Berkhamstead[11]. From Newgate to Berkhamstead 15 miles 67. Travelled this

[11] Increase means Barkhamsted, Connecticut.

day 32m. Expenses $0.87.

Thursday, 28th. Breakfasted at Shepard's in Colebrook 8 miles from Merril's. Took a view at Forbes' Ironworks in Canaan. Here is a forge where large quantities of iron are made from ore dug in Salisbury. The ore affords 1/4 part of its weight of pure iron of the best quality. Their [sic] is also a large building where the iron is manufactured into anchors, sawmill-cranks, large screws for various purposes &c &c. Put up at Farnum's in Salisbury 97 Travelled this day 30 m. Expenses .66

Friday 29th. Came on to Stephen's in Armenia[12] [sic], the first town in New York to breakfast 14 miles. Dined at _____ 13 miles. Put Tomkins in Hopewell 14 miles. Travelled through the oblong this day. The land between the mountains is excellent for grain & grass. Many fields are sown down with clover and manured with plaster of Paris. These fields, by the use of this, produce large quantities of grass & hay. 138. Travelled 41 miles Expenses $1.10

Saturday, 30th. Arrived at Fishkill Ferry, 11 m, at 8 o'clock. Breakfasted at Newburgh, 2. Stopped at Blooms grove[13] Ruder, 12. Put up at Drake's, Chester, 7 miles. In Blooms Grove passed by a Liberty or rather faction pole. On a board affixed to the pole was Liberty or Death—no stamp act. Our landlord is a singular character, rough & grumbling, swears at every breath. 170. Travel 32 Expenses $1.15.

Sunday July 1, 1798. Stopped at Pasts Warwick 9 miles. Cole Vernon the first Town in New Jersey. Put up at Dariah's [?] Hamburgh[14] 7 miles, 194, Travel 24.

Monday 2nd. Breakfasted at Sussex Courthouse [?] 14. Sussex is

---

12 Increase means Amenia, New York.
13 Increase means Blooming Grove.
14 Increase means Hamburg.

60 miles from New York & 97 from Philadelphia. One building serves for a Courthouse & Gaol. Turned out at noon at a private house in Hardwick. Put up at Amy's in the old Moravian Town. Immediately on our arrival at the inn we were enquired of with respect to our political sentiments. On finding that we were federalists we were welcomed as friends & brothers. Soon after we were invited to drink with our new friends. A fracas happened between the landlord & his guests, occasioned by their dancing in his house. With some difficulty we go clear of the affair and left the landlord to settle the matter. The persons we met with were a Genl. _____, _____ & _____[15] 224 Travel 30 miles.

Tuesday, 3rd. Breakfasted at Fair's Johnsburgh[16] 17 miles from Hope or old Moravian town 5 miles from the ferry across the Delaware which divides N. Jersey from Pennsylvania. Crossed the ferry to Eastown[17], which lies on the south westerly side of the river. Put up at a Dutch tavern 6 miles from Eastown, to get some washing done. Mr. Parkman's horse got injured this afternoon, so that he will probably lose him. Our landlord is a rich farmer, owns 120 acres of excellent Land for tillage, has a good house completely finished and furnished, yet sits like a lazy drone in the house and sees his wife and daughters performing all the servile labor of the farm. The Landlady informed us that she and her daughters ploughed, hoed, reaped, worked at haying &c &c, and in return were paid with swearing and hard language. We viewed a garden which she had planted and tended with her own hands containing a fine supply of vegetables. The landlord

---

[15] I removed these surnames from the diary entry.
[16] While the diary uses Johnsburgh, Phillipsburg is located on the New Jersey side of the Delaware and is at the noted distance from Hope.
[17] Increase means Easton. He correctly uses Easton on his return trip entries.

told us that our New England women were like _____. The Landlady and her daughters listened with attention to our accounts of the manner in which our women lived, and could not conceal their uneasiness in their situation. The Landlord's name Henry _____[18]. 252 Travel 28

Wednesday 4th. Set out at 8 o'clock with Mr. Parkman's horse, which we hope will get well. Mr. Parkman set out last night for Reading with a teamster who came along. Passed through Bethlehem where the Moravians live. We had not time to view the curiosities of the place. Crossed a ferry over Lehigh in Allenstown. Put up at Kemp's, Mexatory[19] 22 miles from Bethlehem. Here we found the people collected to celebrate American independence. A true federal spirit seemed to prevail among them universally. We were treated very politely and civilly by the honest Germans. The roads have been excellent this day. The country is fine. Excellent crops of grain which they are just beginning to cut, afford to the eye a delightful prospect. The face of the country consists of gently swelling hills, which are large but not high, and beautiful plains, and meadow lots, interspersed with pleasant groves of wood. 280 Travel 28 miles

Thursday 5th. Found that the people were not so unanimous at Mexatory as I supposed last evening. Breakfasted at Barr's in Reading, 18 miles. Put up at Lebanon, 28 miles. Reading is a very handsome town on the east side of the Schuylkill, 56 miles from Philadelphia. The country from Mexatory to Lebanon is excellent. We found Mr. Parkman at Reading. Lebanon is a very pleasant town. The land something level and very fertile. 326. Travel 46.

---

[18] I removed surname from diary entry.
[19] Increase means Maxatawny.

Friday July 6th 1798. Breakfasted at Londonderry at the Irishman's tavern 10 m. Passed the Susquehannah[20] at Harrisburg which is a considerable town on the east side, 25 miles from Lebanon. Put up at Brigg's in Cumberland County, 6 miles from the river, the silver springs 357 Travel 31

Saturday 7th. Set out very early in the morning. Passed through Carlisle soon after sunrise, 10 miles. Breakfasted three miles from Carlisle at a miserable tavern, the name I have forgotten. Dined at Shippensburgh, Porters an excellent house. Put up at Davis' Strasburgh forty miles from Carlisle 397. Travel 40.

Sunday 8th. Passed over the blue Mountains. The first is called the north Mountain, is 3 miles over to Skiner's. The second is called the middle Mountain, over this to Farmingsburgh[21] 4 miles, where we breakfasted. The third mountain Tuscarora, between the two last mentioned is the path valley — Called Dansdill's at Noon — well used. Traveled over Sideling Hill, which tho' not so steep as other mountains, is very long & tedious. Put up at a tavern May's on the western side of the hill. Here found 6 families, 36 in all, moving on to the western country. 430. Travel 33 miles.

Monday 9th. Found the Juniata creek 2 miles from May's. Breakfasted at Hartley's, a good house, 8 miles from the creek. Passed thro' Bedford, 6 miles from Hartley's. This is quite a handsome Town [sic], situated between the mountains. Stopped for refreshment at Ward's tavern 4 miles from Bedford. Put up at Wright's on the top of Dryridge 10 m. 460. Travel 30 miles.

---

20 Increase means the Susquehanna.
21 Increase probably means Fannettsburg which lays at the same distance from Upper Strasburg.

Tuesday 10th. Breakfasted at Hallar's on the top of Alleghany[22] [sic], 11 miles. Stopped at Somerset a considerable town, 14 miles. Called for refreshment at Reed's, the old Irish Woman, 3 miles from Somerset. Put up at Downey's[23] 12 miles. Our inn is a log hut. We must sleep three in a bed. The landlord is a civil man and willing to do the best in his power. 500 Travel 40 miles

Wednesday 11th. Rainy in the morning. Set out at 12 o'clock. Called at Neil's for refreshment. Found civil people and excellent fare. At Stockdill's[24] 7 miles from Downings, the road divides, the right to Pittsburgh and the left to Wheeling. Neil's is 9 miles from the parting of the roads. Put up at _____[25], a private house, 7 miles from Neil's. Poor accommodations. Here we found a poor sick teamster without a friend to pity him. He was at his wagon and intended to sleep in it. I interceded with the Landlady for him, & got him into the house. The people appeared devoid of feeling for him, tho' his situation was truly pitiable. 523. Travel 23 miles.

Thursday 12th. Forded the Youghiegany[26] [sic], at Budd's, 3 1/2 miles from Robinson's. From the Youghiegany [sic] to the Monongehala[27] [sic] 8 miles. Stopped at Parkinson's 9 miles. Put up at Scott's in Washington 20 miles from the Monongehala [sic]. Here is a fine flourishing town, a Court house & Gaol. The lands from the Monongehala [sic] to this place are excellent for wheat & other grain. The face of the

---

22 Increase means Allegheny Mountains.

23 Downey's is mentioned in the 10th's entry and Downings is mentioned in the 11th's entry. Based on the location and number of miles traveled this is probably Donegal.

24 Stockdill's area where the road divides is now called New Stanton.

25 I removed the surname from the diary entry.

26 Increase means Youghiogheny River.

27 Increase means Monongahela River.

country is uneven, large hills & pretty steep. Here are few streams of water. Good wells are obtained by digging from 15 to 20 ft. The roads in wet weather are very muddy and slippery. 555. Travel 32 miles.

Friday 13th. Breakfasted 10 miles from Washington. Stopped at the head of the creek 12 miles. Down the Creek to Wheeling 8 miles. Came in view of the Ohio at 4 o'clock. Put up at Gooding's Tavern. 585. Travel 30 miles.

Saturday 14th. Turned out my horse to pasture at the Denny's. At 6 o'clock P. M. embarked for Marietta in the post boat. Very foggy the latter part of the night so that we could not proceed with expedition.

Sunday 15th. The day pleasant, but feel myself quite indisposed from loss of sleep and rest. Instead of arriving at Marietta this evening as expected we are again obliged to pass the night on the water, crowded into a little canoe.

Monday 16th. At seven in the morning arrived at Marietta. Found my brother[28] and Friends in health. Walked up to Genl. Putnam's with my brother after breakfast. Viewed the old monuments of antiquity in the afternoon ascended the big mound from whence there is a fine prospect of the town. Tarried at Genl. Putnam's over night.

---

[28] John Matthews, born 18 Dec. 1765 (vide Infra, Family Record). As John Mathews he appears on a descriptive list of men raised in Worcester County, Mass., to serve in the Continental Army, agreeable to a resolve of 2 Dec. 1780. His age is given as 16 years; stature, 5 feet, 2 inches; complexion, light; occupation, farmer. He was engaged for the town of New Braintree, Mass., 10 Mar. 1781, for a term of three years, and was in Captain Hunter's company, Colonel Keyes's regiment. (Massachusetts Soldiers and Sailors of the Revolutionary War vol 10 p. 350.) He went to the Ohio Country with the original "Forty-eight," and was on the Miami, with General Wayne's army, in 1795. He settled at Marietta and married in 1803 Sarah Woodbridge (vide Infra, Family Record). The original manuscript of a diary kept by him belongs to Marietta College. It has been published by Archer Hulbert in an appendix to a volume of the Proceedings of the Ohio Company.

Wednesday July 18th 1798. Went to Bellepre²⁹ [i.e., Belpre] with
my brother. Found our sister Stone and family in health. Capt.
Stone is in the woods surveying.³⁰

Wednesday, Aug 1st 1798. Set out from Marietta for a tour in the
woods, in company with Mr. Fearing, Skinner & Willis.
Traveled a road newly laid out by the marked trees, our course
nearly west from Marietta. About sixteen miles from Marietta
we discovered a remarkable rock which formed a shelter
sufficient to cover a Regiment of men. The under side of the
rock is but a little rising, but the ground beneath is excavated
so that the height of the roof is 12 feet. It is 7 rods long and
3 1/2 deep forming nearly a semicircle. Camped in the
woods.

Thursday 2nd. Traveled over hills & valleys. The lands good for
grain and pasturing. Our course westerly fell on a branch of
Federal Creek, followed it to the place where it unites with
Federal Creek. Pursued the course of Federal Creek to the
falls, thence to [the] Hockhocking³¹ [sic]. Traveled up the
Hockhocking [sic] on the east side. The bottoms on the river
excellent. Camped by a small run which fell into the river.

Friday 3rd. Our horses in the night had left us. In the morning

---

29 Increase means Belpre.

30 Susannah Matthews, eldest sister of Dr. Increase Matthews, was born at Brookfield,
Mass., 29 July 1756, and died in 1833. She was married in 1776 to Jonathan Stone of New
Braintree, Mass., who was an officer in the Revolution and died in 1801. They moved to
the Ohio Country in 1789, and were at Belpre as early as 1797. Both are buried at Belpre.
Jonathan Stone was a sergeant in Capt. John Grainger's company, Col. Ebenezer
Learned's regiment, in 1775, and was afterwards (1777-1781) paymaster in Col. Rufus
Putnam's regiment of the Continental Army, holding in succession the grades of
lieutenant, captain lieutenant, and captain. (Cf. Family Record, Infra, Vital Records of
Brookfield, and Massachusetts Soldiers and Sailors of the Revolutionary War, vol. 15, pp.
106, 107-108.)

31 The name was later changed from Hockhocking to Hocking. The original name derived
from the Indian "hokhokken" which meant bottle-shaped and referred to the shape of
the river's headwaters.

we found them at a distance of three miles. Traveled up the river a few miles and turned off to the blaze road. Followed the blaze road towards Marietta several miles, then turned to the left and fell upon Plumb Run, a branch of Wolf Creek. Here we encamped. This day rainy in the afternoon, which made the bushes very wet, & traveling disagreeable.

Saturday 4th Aug. 1798. Followed Plumb Run down to Ford's. The country full of underbrush. The day rainy so that we were completely soaked. Add to this we being not acquainted with the country were often forced to ascend and descend precipices & to cross the creek to get along. Arrived at Ford's at 4 P.M. Thence to Major White's by the road 4 miles where we put up. Slept on the floor.

Sunday 5th. Traveled down Wolf Creek to [the] Muskingum. Thence down Muskingum to Capt. Devol's where we took dinner. Came on to Genl. Putnam's. Rained very hard all the way from Devol's to Marietta.

Monday 6th. Returned to Capt. Stone's in Bellepres' [sic].

Monday 13th. At 1 o'clock P. M. went aboard the packet boat and intend going down the river to Galipolis[32] [sic]. Mr. Edward Tupper is with me. We called at Mr. Blennerhassett's on the island, by whom and his lady we were politely rec'd. Miss Sally London is at the island on a visit. She is on the whole an amiable girl and possessed of many of those qualities which make a good companion. She is kind, obliging, ever in good spirits and free from affectation. We called at Belleville on the Virginia shore just at night. Here is a flourishing little settlement. While we stopped to drink tea the packet went on to _____ and we followed in a canoe. A rain coming on we tarried till after midnight in a cabin. The people hospitable

---

[32] Increase means Gallipolis.

and gave us blankets, but the fleas were so troublesome we could not sleep.

Tuesday 14th. After the rain went aboard the packet at half past 12 at night, made but slow progress till daylight. We have a fine day for being on the water. The sun is hidden behind the clouds the greatest part of the time. Passed over the La Tart Falls between 12 & 1. The fall is considerable and the passing bad when the water is low. La Tart Falls are 65 miles below Marietta. Night came on when we were within about 18 miles of Gallipolis. The boatman rowed on till 9 o'clock, at which time we were about ten miles from our place of destination. Here we concluded all to lie down to rest, & float down with the current.

Wednesday Aug 15th 1798. At break of day we found that we had floated within about 3 miles of Gallipolis, at which place we arrived a little after sunrise. Took breakfast at Mr. Safford's who keeps Capt. Stone's stores. Engaged a Mr. Bufford to pilot me out to Capt. Stone in the woods. Set out from Gallipolis at 7 o'clock, and arrived at his camp on Racoon[33] Creek at 5, just at dusk. Capt. Stone came in but did not know me at first sight.

Thursday 16th. Left camp at 9 A. M. & came on after Capt. Stone. West at the first mile post found directions to [sic] packer to pitch camp on the first water he should find south from said post. West on S. about 60 rods and found a branch of Racoon Creek call'd Sandy Creek[34]. Here I waited about two hours expecting the packer along, but he not coming I returned to the mile post and waited there 3 or 4 hours. At length Mr. Carr, the hunter, came up and told me the packer had missed

---

[33] Increase means Raccoon Creek.
[34] From the directions, this is probably known today as Bullskin Creek instead of Sandy Creek.

the post & the directions at it & had gone a mile farther west & was returning to the camping ground. By the packer's mistake I had a long and lonesome time waiting for him. Capt. Stone returned from surveying before sunset. Our hunter killed a fine deer and a turkey today and we have an excellent supper. The land here is very broken and not very rich. The timber oak, beech, sugar tree & some hickory. Our camp is 3 miles west from the Ohio, & 6 miles, S. S. W. of Gallipolis.

Friday 17th. Concluded to tarry in camp today. Dug a quantity of Virginia snake root (Serpentaria Virginiana) of which there is a plenty in the woods. At noon Capt. Stone returned to camp, being unable to work by reason of an indisposition with which he was seized after having run one mile.

Saturday 18th Aug. 1798. Retained in camp with Capt. Stone all day. He was unable to work, tho' much better than he was yesterday. Find myself a little unwell in consequence of my change of diet and lying on the ground. Rainy in the afternoon & evening. It is diverting to see how our pack horse contrives to escape the flies. The woods in this country are infected with large flies that are very troublesome to horses & cattle and other animals. Our pack horse to avoid them keeps at the camp over the fire & smoke. He will almost get into it, & under the tent. He feeds but little in the daytime. He sometimes goes out a few minutes when hunger impels him, but returns with great haste to the camp. As soon as daylight is gone he goes out & continues to feed till morning. As soon as the flies begin to stir he comes back and continues with us till night.

Sunday Aug 19th 1798. At noon removed our camp 1 mile west & 1 mile south. Quite unwell today. Our hunter brought in a deer, in the afternoon of which I ate a small piece broiled on a stick, which tasted very good.

Monday 20th. Mr. Carr brought in a deer after having been out about an hour and a half. Removed our camp one mile south before noon. Find myself much better today than yesterday and the day before.

Tuesday 21st. After breakfast took leave of Capt. Stone and set out for Gallipolis with his packer, the distance 10 miles nearly S. W.[35] Arrived at Gallipolis at 12 o'clock, put up at Esqr. Safford's. Bought some peaches of an old Frenchman, which were very refreshing after having lived sometime in the woods without any kind of acid.

Wednesday 22nd. Left Gallipolis at 9 o'clock in the morning in the packet boat for Bellepree [sic]. Put up at a dutchman's on the Virginia side. Slept on a bed for the first time since I left Bellepree [sic]. Found civil hospitable people.

Thursday 23rd August, 1798. Took breakfast at the Dutchman's (Rowse's). Came on to Pond Creek where I was bitten by the fleas when going down. Slept in the boat rather than trust myself to their mercy again. Came 40 miles today.

Friday 24th. Passed Belleville 2 miles above where I tarried overnight, early in the morning. Saw a large boat here, from Illinois laden with skins & furs bound to Pittsburg. Saw the same boat when going down the river at Sandy Riffle. They make but slow progress by reason of the river's being very low. Called at Newburg at Mr. Guthrie's & got some refreshment. Arrived at Capt. Stone's in Bellepree [sic] at 2 P.M. after a fatiguing Tour.

Monday 27th. Went to Marietta in the forenoon. Called at Esqr. Fearing's & ate some excellent peaches. Crossed the Muskingum and went to Genl. Putnam's. In the evening went

---

[35] Return should be to the northeast, not southwest.

to Mr. Devol's and feasted on watermelons.

Tuesday 28th August, 1798. Accompanied Mr. William Putnam to Rainbow Creek to his farm & Mills.

Wednesday 29th. Returned to Capt. Stone's in Bellepree [sic].

Friday 31st. In the evening attended a ball at Col. Putnam's in Bellepree [sic]. We had a large collection of Ladies, some from Marietta & the island, who made a very brilliant appearance. Spent the evening very agreeably.

Sunday, Sept. 2nd 1798. At 2 o'clock, P. M. took leave of my sister Stone & family, & set out for New England. Put up for the night at Mr. Burlingame's, one mile below Muskingum.

Monday 3rd. Left Mr. Burlingame's early in the morning. Forded Muskingum. Went to Genl. Putnam's & took breakfast, detained by rain till afternoon. The weather becoming fair came on to Duck Creek, was obliged to go almost across the Ohio to get round the mouth of the creek, which is very deep and muddy. Tore off one of my horses shoes in the mud. Seem to be unfortunate at first setting out, but hope for better success. Got my horse's shoe replaced & crossed little Muskingum in a flat. Put up at Courtney's 13 miles from Marietta.

Tuesday Sept. 4th. Started from Courtney's early in the morning. Stopped a few minutes at L. Denny's, 4 miles. Stopped at Sheets 7 miles and got some milk of the old Dutch woman & some corn stalks & ears for my horse. The old Dutchman advises me to cross the river 2 miles above his house Crossed the river at the place recommended by the old man. Found excellent fording, the water not more than knee deep to a horse. Find the road cut out & very good on the Virginia side. Overtaken by a violent storm of wind & rain. Fortunately find shelter for myself and horse in an old deserted cabin where I write this. Put up at Peden's 18 miles. My landlord a

Quaker, a civil humourous man. Tells comical stories, & with his wife rails against Government because it lays a duty on whiskey &c.

Wednesday, Sept 5th, 1798. Took breakfast in the morning with the Quaker. Crossed Fishing Creek in a flat 5 miles from ye Quakers. Stopped at noon for refreshment at a house on the bank. Found a fellow there with his head filled with whiskey, who was very troublesome. At length I got clear from him & came on. The woods here abound with blade and grey squirrels. I counted 32 this afternoon a[s] I traveled along. It has been a drizzling rainy day & the path very muddy and slippery. Put up at Henry Bakers 4 miles below grave creek a civil obliging man.

Thursday 6th. My landlord came on with me to Wheeling 18 miles. Refreshed myself & horse at Neilson's. Came on 8 miles to James Craige's. The old man very sociable, invited me to buy land of him. Put up at Knox's 12 miles from Wheeling. Rainy all day by showers. Roads very muddy & slippery.

Friday Sept 7th 1798. Breakfasted at Mr. Cracken's, stopped at Washington. Put up at Parkinson's 11 miles from Washington. Rained by showers, got very wet.

Saturday 8th. Forded Monongehala [sic] & Youghiegany [sic] rivers this day. Put up at John Neil's the good Irishman. Very well used by the honest landlord & his family. A little polish to their manners, would make them a polite family. I endeavored to persuade them that they put too much hardship on their women. In excuse they plead, that their business at certain seasons of the year, particularly in harvest is very urgent. This is truly the case, but is not in my mind a sufficient excuse. The landlord has two Daughters, one of whom in particular appears to be an amiable girl. They had both been employed all day in spreading flax, which is very hard work.

Sunday Sept. 9th 1798. Left Mr. Neil's early in the morning. Passed over Chestnut ridge. Came down to Downey's on Laurel Hill intending to get breakfast but found nobody at home, so that I was obliged to come on 4 miles farther to the widow Lockwood's before I could get refreshment. Put up at Bamer's in the Glades 5 miles from Somerset.

Monday 10th. Very cool this morning in the Glades. What goes by the name of the Glades is a range of land 10 or 12 miles wide, somewhat level lying between Laurel Hill and Alleghany [sic]: the former on the west and the latter on the east. The land is cold and rather poor, but produces small grain tolerably well. Ice formed here the 14th of July as thick as window glass. Set out early in the morning, passed over Alleghany [sic]. Breakfasted at Stotler's at the foot of Dry Ridge. Dry Ridge is 10 miles in length & the road runs on the top of it that distance. Put up at Hartley's. Travel this day 40 miles.

Tuesday Sept 11th 1798. Crossed Juniata Creek in the morning. Traveled over Sideling Hill. Put up at—name I don't know & think it hardly worthwhile to enquire. Travel 36 miles

Wednesday 12th. 9 o'clock A. M. on the summit of Middle Mountain I write. Some flat stones, which some person has laid up, afford me a seat. I have passed over Tuscarora this morning. After I descend this I must cross the North Mountain which brings me to Strasburgh & a good road. He must have been a bold man who first ventured over this mountain & thought of making it passable with horses and wagons. The surface is almost entirely covered with stones, some of them large but mostly small, so that the few trees that grow on it seem to spring from a bed of rock.

Breakfasted at Skinner's between Middle & North Mountains. Stopped at Strasburgh to get my horses shoes removed. Feel very happy that I have got over the mountains. Put up at Eaken's, 7 miles from Carlisle on the new road. The landlord, his wife, & only daughter very civil people. Travel 33 miles.

Thursday Sept 13th. Passed through Carlisle in the morning. Breakfasted at Bell's, 5 miles from Carlisle. Forded the Susquehanna at Harrisburgh where it is nearly a mile wide. Came on to Hummelstown & put up my horse, thinking it too far to ride to Dearmon's, my good Irish Landlord, where I breakfasted when traveling out. Determined on changing my lodging & going to another tavern close by, and ordered my horse up for the purpose. Mr. Dearmon came up at this time & I concluded to come with him to his house 6 miles farther Travel 40 miles.

Friday 14th. Took breakfast with my Irish landlord. Put up at Reading. Travel 38 miles.

Saturday 15th. Left Reading in the morning. Breakfasted at a Dutch tavern 14 miles from Reading. Could eat but little tho' very hungry. Put up at Bethlehem the Moravian town. Travel 41 miles.

Sunday 16th Sept. 1798. Went to Church in the forenoon at the Moravian meeting. The services began with singing in German accompanied with an organ. Next a prayer & a short sermon in German. Then a short address in English & a hymn in the same language closed the services. The young ladies under 18 wear caps tied with a deep red ribband. The unmarried women above 18 tie with pale red. The married women with blue, & the widows with white. At half past two left Bethlehem and came on to Fair's, 5 miles from Easton, towards Sussex. Travel 17 miles.

Monday 17th. Breakfasted at the widow _____ 12 miles from Fair's. Stopped at the Log Gaol 6 miles from Hope. Four companies of Cavalry were collected here: robust strong men, and well mounted. Passed through Sussex. Put up at Basley's 10 miles from Sussex. Travel 43 miles.

Tuesday Sept 18 1798. Put up at Harrison's 5 miles from New Windsor toward Sussex. Met Capt. Denny from Leicester & Mr. Martin Henry from Brimfield going on to the Ohio. Mem. inform Calvin H. of his pen letter. Travel 39 miles

Wednesday 19th. Breakfasted at New Windsor 5 miles. Crossed the ferry to Fishkill side 2 miles. Put up at the Widow Vandenburgh's. Good entertainment & civil people. My horse a little lame this afternoon. Travel including the ferry 27 miles.

Thursday 20th. Breakfasted at Reasner's, stopped for refreshment at a private house. My horse had a plenty of grass & oats, and I had cider and apples all for sixpence. My horse still lame so that I was obliged to walk a great part of the way & come on slowly. Put up at a private house for want of a tavern. Travel 26 miles.

Friday 21st. Almost devoured by fleas last night. Got up in the night & lit a candle. After killing a number of fleas tried to get a little repose, after the fatigue of traveling on foot over mountains & hills and horrid roads. But little rest could I get and it was more wearisome to lie in bed than travel over mountains & hills. Left my fleas and dirty bed as soon as daylight appeared. Breakfasted at Capt. Bradley's in Litchfield. Passed through Litchfleld Street. The town handsome & flourishing, situated on high land. Put up at Hull's tavern in Farmington. My horse still lame. Various opinions with respect to the cause of it. Last evening a man overtook me who professed much skill in the farrier's art, &

assured me his lameness was caused by a sprain of the back tendon. Capt. Bradley assured me this morning that the shoe was in fault; accordingly I had it taken off and replaced. But this did not cure the lameness. At Harwinton a man who also professed skill was very confident that the lameness was in the gambrel joint. Travel 31 miles.

Saturday Sept 22nd. Came over to Hartford 10 miles. Breakfasted at Bull's. At two o'clock left Hartford and came on to Ellington to Mr. Holton's 16 miles. Travel 26 miles.

Sunday Sept 23rd. Went to meeting at Ellington to hear a Methodist preacher. Two of them attended. A Mr. Thompson preached in the forenoon. At noon a funeral was attended by the clergymen and the corpse brought into the Meeting house. Mr. Rogers preached in the afternoon, but his performance was greatly inferior to that of Mr. Thompson. After sermon the corpse was carried to the burrying ground & inter'd & the church service read by Mr. Thompson in a very solemn manner.

Monday 24th. Set out early in the morning from Mr. Holton's. Breakfasted at Sike's at Wilbraham. Arrived at the west parish in Brookfield a little before sunset. Found the regiment of infantry & company of lighthorse collected on the plain of the meeting house. Found my brother Elisha & many more of my friends & acquaintance here. Arrived at my father's at 8 o'clock in the evening.

BIBLIOGRAPHY

John Alden, *A Season in Federal Street, J. B. Williamson and the Boston Theatre 1796-1797,* Proceedings of the American Antiquarian Society 65 (1): 9–74. 1955. PDF accessed on August 17, 2020: https://www.americanantiquarian.org/proceedings/44539525.pdf

George Henry Allen, Joseph Edward Harry, Robert Thomas Belote, *The Scioto Speculation and the French Settlement at Gallipolis: A Study in Ohio Valley History, Volume 3.* Cincinnati, Ohio: University of Cincinnati Press, 1907.

Willis Adams Bailey, A.B., *Diary of a Journey from Massachusetts to the Ohio Country, 1798, By Dr. Increase Matthews with a Matthews Family Record Communicated by Willis Adams Bailey, A.B. Reprinted From The New England Historical and Genealogical Register for January, 1932 Boston.* Zanesville, Ohio: George Lilienthal & Son, 1932.

John Warner Barber, *Historical Collections, Being a General Collection of Interesting Facts, Traditions, Biographical Sketches, Anecdotes, &c., Relating to the History and Antiquities of Every Town in Massachusetts, with Geographical Descriptions.* Worcester, Massachusetts: Warren Lazell, 1884.

Charles F. Brooks, *New England Snowfall,* Geographical Review, 1917-03-01, Page 224.

Salmon P. Chase, ed., *The Statues of Ohio and of the Northwestern Territory, Adopted or Enacted from 1788 to 1833 Inclusive: Together with The Ordinance of 1787; The Constitutions of Ohio and the United States; and Various Public*

Instruments and Acts of Congress: Illustrated by A Preliminary Sketch of the History of Ohio; Numerous References and Notes, and Copious Indexes. Volume 2. Cincinnati, Ohio: Corey & Fairbank, 1834.

Mary Cone, *Life of Rufus Putnam With Extracts from His Journal and an Account of the First Settlement in Ohio.* Cleveland, Ohio: William W. Williams, 1886.

C. E. Dickinson, D.D., *A History of Belpre, Washington County, Ohio.* Parkersburg, West Virginia: Globe Printing & Binding Company, 1920.

Samuel A. Eliot, *Heralds of a Liberal Faith, Volume II.* Boston, Massachusetts: American Unitarian Association, 1910.

J. F. Everhart., *1794. History of Muskingum County, Ohio, with Illustrations and Biographical Sketches of Prominent Men and Pioneers*, Columbus, Ohio: J. F. Everhart & Co., 1882.

The Goodspeed Publishing Co., *Biographical and Historical Memoirs of Muskingum County, Ohio,* Chicago: 1892.

S. P. Hildreth, M.D., *Biographical and Historical Memoirs of the Early Pioneer Settlers of Ohio with Narratives of Incidents and Occurrences in 1775.* Cincinnati, Ohio: H. W. Derby & Co., 1852.

S. P. Hildreth, *Pioneer History: Being an Account of the First Examinations of the Ohio Valley, and the Early Settlement of the Northwest Territory.* Cincinnati, Ohio: H. W. Derby & Co., 1848.

The Historical Society of Geauga County, *1798. Pioneer and General History of Geauga County, with Sketches of Some of the Pioneers and Prominent Men,* Burton, Ohio: 1880.

Henry Howe, LL. D., *Historical Collections of Ohio in Two Volumes: Volume II.* Cincinnati, Ohio: State of Ohio, 1907.

Archer Butler Hulbert, *The Methods and Operations of the Scioto Group of Speculators.* Oxford University Press on behalf of Organization of

American Historians. PDF accessed on November 14, 2016:
http://www.jstor.org/stable/1886952

D. Hamilton Hurd, *History of Worcester County, Massachusetts, with Illustrations and Biographical Sketches of Many of Its Pioneers and Prominent Men, Volumes I and II.* Philadelphia, Pennsylvania: J. W. Lewis & Co., 1889.

Dr. Irene Neu Jones, *Guide to the John Mathews Collection.* PDF accessed on October 12, 2016:
http://library.marietta.edu/spc/FindingAids/Mathews%20-%20John%20Mathews%20Collection.pdf.

William Lincoln, *History of Worcester County, Massachusetts, from Its Earliest Settlement to September 1836: with Various Notices Relating to the History of Worcester County.* Worcester, Massachusetts: Charles Hersey, 1862.

Rev. John H. Lockwood, DD, Ernest Newton Bagg, Walter S. Carson, Herbert E. Riley, Edward Boltwood, Will L. Clark, *Western Massachusetts A History 1636-1925.* New York and Chicago: Lewis Historical Publishing, Inc., 1926.

David M. Ludlum, *Early American Winters 1604-1820*, Boston: American Meteorological Society, 1966.

George Richards Minot, AM, *The History of the Insurrections, in Massachusetts, in the Year MDCCLXXXVI, and the Rebellion Consequent Thereon.* Worcester, Massachusetts: Isaiah Thomas, 1788.

Nahum Mitchell, *History of the Early Settlement of Bridgewater in Plymouth County, Massachusetts Including an Extensive Family Register.* Boston, Massachusetts: Kidder & Wright, 1840. Page 350, Nos. 32, 37 and 38.

Samuel L. Mitchill, M.D., et al. *The Medical Repository* Vol. III. New York, New York: T. & J. Swords, 1800.

Samuel L. Mitchill, M.D., et al. *The Medical Repository* Vol. V. New York, New York: T. & J. Swords, 1802.

New Braintree, Mass. [from old catalog]. *Vital Records of New Braintree, Massachusetts, to the Year 1850*. Boston, Massachusetts: The New-England Historic Genealogical Society, 1904.

John Noble, *A few Notes on the Shays Rebellion*. American Antiquarian Society October 1902 page 216. PDF accessed on March 13, 2018: http://www.americanantiquarian.org/proceedings/44806459.pdf.

Ohio Archaeological and Historical Society, *Ohio Archaeological and Historical Publications Volume 5*. Columbus, Ohio: Fred J. Heer, 1897

Lucuis R. Paige, *History of Hardwick, Massachusetts with a Genealogical Register*. Boston, Massachusetts: Houghton, Mifflin and Company, 1883.

Mrs. Laura Curtis Preston. *History and Some Anecdotes of the Settlement of Newbury Washington County Ohio*. Marietta, Ohio: Marietta Journal Print, 1909.

Rufus Putnam, *The Memoirs of Rufus Putnam and Certain Official Papers and Correspondence*. Boston, Massachusetts: Houghton, Mifflin and Company, 1903.

Emily Ellsworth Ford Skeel, *Notes on the Life of Noah Webster, Volume 1*, Private Printing, 1912: Page 488.

George K. Tufts, *Account of the Observance of the One Hundred and Fiftieth Anniversary of the Incorporation of the Town of New Braintree, Mass., June 19, 1901 / Containing the Historical Address by George K. Tufts, M.A. and Other Speeches and Exercises of the Occasion. 1751-1901*. Worcester, Mass.: Charles Hamilton, 1902.

Sylvanus Urban, *The Gentleman's Magazine and Historical Chronicle*, Volume 58, For the Year 1788, Part 2. London, England, 1788.

C. Albert White, *A History of the Rectangular Survey System*. U.S. Department of the Interior Bureau of Land Management. PDF accessed on September 2, 2107: https://www.blm.gov/cadastral/Manual/pdffiles/histrect.pdf.

Kurt L. White, "Dr. Increase Mathews and His Family: The Massachusetts Years", *Muskingum Journal Volume 12 No. 1*. Zanesville, Ohio: Pioneer and Historical Society of Muskingum County, 2005.

Made in the USA
Las Vegas, NV
25 January 2024

84581733R00144